THE NAMING GAME

THE NAMING GAME

THE COMPANY FILES: 2

GABRIEL VALJAN

Praise for The Naming Game

"Brilliantly written, Gabriel Valjan's *The Naming Game* whisks the reader back in time to postwar Los Angeles. Spies, Communism, and Hollywood converge in a first-rate thriller."—Bruce Robert Coffin, Agatha Award-nominated author of *Beyond the Truth,* A Detective Byron Mystery

"With crackling dialogue and a page turning plot shot-through with authentic period detail, Gabriel Valjan pulls the reader into the hidden world of the 1950's Hollywood studio scene, involving murder, McCarthyism and mayhem."—James L'Etoile, author of *At What Cost* and *Bury the Past*

"Terrific historical noir as Gabriel Valjan takes us on a trip through postwar Hollywood involving scandal, McCarthyism, blacklisting, J. Edgar Hoover and, of course, murder. Compelling story, compelling characters."—R.G. Belsky, author of the Clare Carlson Mystery Series

"Gabriel Valjan's *The Naming Game* is an engrossing read, especially for fans of classic Hollywood and tightly plotted detective stories. A fascinating mystery involving blacklisted screenwriters featuring a colorful cast of characters kept me turning the pages through the many twists and turns all the way to the end, that I didn't see coming. Don't miss this wonderful book!"—Shawn Reilly Simmons, author of The Red Carpet Catering Mystery Series

Characters

- **Jack Marshall**: Company man
- **William Parker**: Police chief of the Los Angeles Police Department
- **Charles Loew**: Deceased screenwriter
- **John Hamilton**: Former associate of Jack Marshall and Hollywood actor
- **Betty Marshall**: Jack Marshall's wife
- **Walker**: Company operative. Alias: Walter Thompson
- **Jack Warner**: Studio mogul
- **Miss Elkins**: Warner Brothers secretary
- **Phillip Ernest**: Therapist
- **Leslie**: Company operative. Alias: Miss Margaret Gardner
- **Terry Doyle**: Writers' Room shop steward and Walker's mentor
- **Irving Hackett**: Writer
- **George Edwards**: Elevator operator
- **Vera Williams**: Former actress and current patient of Dr. Ernest
- **Joe Teague**: Hollywood power broker
- **Johnny Stompanato**: Associate of Mickey Cohen
- **Leonard Moore**: Clearance man
- **Jack Marshall Junior**: Son of Jack and Betty Marshall
- **Elizabeth Marshall**: Daughter of Jack and Betty Marshall
- **Sheldon**: Company ally
- **Roy Cohn**: Chief counsel to Senator Joseph McCarthy
- **J. Edgar Hoover**: Director of the Federal Bureau of Investigation
- **Walter Bedell "Beetle" Smith**: Former Army colleague and Jack's boss

Chapter One

At seven minutes past the hour, while reviewing the classified documents at his desk, one of the two colored phones, the beige one, rang. He placed the receiver next to his ear, closed the folder, and waited for the caller's voice to speak first.

"Is this Jack Marshall?"

"It is."

"This is William Parker. Is the line secure?"

"It is," Jack replied, his hand opening a desk cabinet and flipping the ON switch to start recording the conversation.

"I don't know you, Mr. Marshall, and I presume you don't know me."

A pause.

"I know of you, Chief Parker."

"Were you expecting my call?"

"No, and it doesn't matter." Jack lied.

"Fact of the matter, Mr. Marshall, is an individual, whom I need not name, has suggested I contact you about a sensitive matter. He said matter of security, so I listened."

"Of course. I'm listening."

"I was instructed to give you an address and have my man at the scene allow you to do whatever it is that you need to do when you arrive there."

"Pencil and paper are ready. The address, please."

Jack wrote out the address; it was in town, low-rent section with the usual rooming houses, cheap bars, about a fifteen-minute drive on Highway 1 without traffic.

"Ask for Detective Brown. You won't miss him. Don't like it that someone steps in and tells me how to mind my own city, but I have no choice in the matter."

Jack ignored the man's defensive tone. He knew Detective Brown was a dummy name, like Jones or Smith on a hotel ledger. Plain, unimaginative, but it would do. Most policemen, he conceded, were neither bright nor fully screwed into the socket. A chief was no different, except he had more current in him. The chief of police who ruled Los Angeles by day with his cop syndicate the way Mickey Cohen owned the night must've swallowed his pride when he dropped that nickel to make this call.

"Thank you, Chief Parker."

Jack hung up and flipped the switch to OFF.

Whatever it was at the scene waiting for Jack was sufficient cause to pull back a man like Bill Parker and his boys for twelve hours. Whoever gave this order had enough juice to rein in the LAPD.

Jack took the folder he was reviewing and walked it across the room. He opened the folder once more and reread the phrases 'malicious international spy' and, in Ronald Reagan's own choice of words, 'Asia's Mata Hari', before closing the cover and placing it inside the safe. His review will have to wait. He put on his holster and grabbed a jacket.

Betty came out on the porch as he was putting the key into the car door.

"I won't be long. Please kiss the children good night for me."

"Can't this wait, Jack? The children were expecting you to read to them tonight. Jack Junior set aside the book, and you know Elizabeth will be crushed."

"It can't wait. I'm sorry. Tell them I'll make it up to them."

"You need to look them in the face when you tell them sorry."

He opened the door as his decision. She understood and dealt him the low card. "Want something for the road?"

"No thanks. I'll see you soon."

He closed the door with finesse. He couldn't help it if the children heard the car. He checked the mirror and saw her on the porch, still standing there, still disappointed and patient, as he drove off.

Detective Brown, sole man on the scene, walked him over to the body without introducing himself. Jack didn't give his name.

At six-fifteen, the vet renting a room down the hall discovered the body. Detective Brown said the veteran was probably a hired hound doing a bag job—break-ins, surveillance, and the like. Recent veterans made the best candidates for that kind of work for Hoover, Jack thought. Worked cheap, and they went the extra mile without Hoover's agents having to worry about technicalities like a citizen's rights going to law.

"What makes you think he was hired out?" Jack asked.

Brown, a man of few words, handed Jack his notebook, flipped over to the open page he marked Witness Statement, and said politely, "Please read it. Words and writing are from the witness himself."

"'The man was a no good *commonist*.'"

"Nice spelling. A suspect?"

"No, sir. The coroner places the death around early afternoon, about 2ish. Our patriot was across the street drinking his lunch. I verified it."

Jack viewed the body. The man was fully dressed, wearing a light weave gabardine suit costing at least twenty-five. The hardly scuffed oxfords had to cost as much as the suit, and the shirt and tie, both silk, put the entire ensemble near a hundred. Hardly class consciousness for an alleged Communist, Jack thought.

The corpse lying on his side reminded Jack of the children sleeping, minus the red pool seeping into the rug under the right ear. The dead man wore a small sapphire ring on his small finger, left hand. No wedding band. Nice watch on the wrist, face turned in. An odd way to read time. Breast pocket contained a cigarette case with expensive cigarettes, Egyptian. Jack recognized the brand from his work in the Far East. Ten cents a cigarette is nice discretionary income. Wallet in other breast pocket held fifty dollars, various denominations. Ruled out robbery or staging it. Identification card said Charles Loew, Warner Brothers. Another card: Screen Writers Guild, signed by Mary McCall, Jr. President. Back of card presented a pencil scrawl.

"Find a lighter or book of matches?"

Detective Brown shook his head. Jack patted the breast pockets again and the man's jacket's side pockets. Some loose change, but nothing else. The man was unarmed, except for a nice pen. Much as he disliked the idea, Jack put his hands into the man's front pockets. Nothing. He found a book of matches in the left rear pocket, black with gold telltale lettering, Trocadero on Sunset. Jack flipped the matchbook open and, as he suspected, found a telephone number written in silver ink, different ink than in the man's own pen. Other back pocket contained a handkerchief square Jack found interesting, as did Detective Brown.

"What's that?" he asked, head peering over for a better look.

"Not sure," answered Jack, unfolding the several-times folded piece of paper hidden inside the hanky. The unfolded paper revealed a bunch of typewritten names that had bled out onto other parts of the paper. It must have been folded while the ink was still wet. It didn't help someone spilt something on the paper. Smelled faintly of recent whiskey. Jack reviewed what he thought were names when he realized the letters were nonsense words.

"Might be a Commie membership list. Looks like code." But Brown zipped it when Jack folded the paper back up and put it into his pocket.

"The paper and the matches stay with me. We clear?"

"Uh, yes, sir. The Chief told me himself to do whatever you said and not ask questions."

"Good. Other than the coroner—who else was here? Photographers, fingerprints?"

"Nobody else. Medical pronounced him dead, but nothing more. Chief had them called off to another scene—a multiple homicide, few blocks away. We're short-staffed tonight. The Chief said he'd send Homicide after you leave. They'll process the scene however you leave it. They won't know about the matches or the paper. Chief's orders."

Jack checked his watch. Man down, found at six-fifteen. Chief called a little after seven. He arrived not much later than seven forty. The busybodies would get the stiff by eight or eight thirty, the latest. Perfectly reasonable, Jack thought. He squatted down to see the man's watch, noticing light bruising on the wrist and the throw rug bunched into a small hill near the man's time hand. Intriguing.

"Thank you, Detective. I'll be going now. If I speak to the chief, I'll let him know you've done your job to the letter."

"You're welcome. Night."

Jack knew he and the chief would be speaking again.

Outside on the street, Jack pulled out his handkerchief and wiped both hands for any traces of dead man as he headed for the parked car. Compulsive habit. He pulled up the collar on his jacket. It was cold for late May.

The street sign said he was not far from Broadway. In this part of town, thousands lived crowded in on themselves as lodgers in dilapidated Gothic mansions or residence hotels, working the downtown stores, factories, and offices, riding public transit and the other funicular railway in the area, Court Flight, a two-track railway climb towards Hill Street.

Los Angeles changed with the world. The war was over and there was a new war, possibly domestic, definitely foreign. Court Flight is gone, ceased operations. Its owner and his faithful cat had passed on. His good widow tried. In '43 a careless brush fire destroyed the tracks, and the Board of Public Utilities signed the death warrant; and now Jack was hearing whispers Mayor Bowron planned to revitalize the area International Style, which meant dotting the desert city with skyscrapers.

Jack opened the door and sat behind the wheel a moment. He took the family once to nearby Angels Flight. Junior wondered why there was no apostrophe on the sign. Betty tolerated the excursion, indifferent to Los Angeles because she preferred their home in DC. He released the clutch. Betty disliked LA because it changed too much without reason. She might have had a point. He shifted gears. Pueblo city would level whole blocks of thriving masses just to create a parking lot. He pulled the car from the curb.

Chapter Two

Malibu was several miles north, on Highway 1, if Jack decided to return to the argument with Betty. Jack chose another course: west to Edition Pier, and then northwest, back home to Walker's house, but not before he had a talk with the actor, John Hamilton. A conversation with John, like any of his movies, guaranteed entertainment.

Riding the open highway reminded Jack of riding horseback in the Montana of his youth. The scenery was different and lifetimes apart. Here, there was smooth pavement with curves, similar foothills up to mountains, and lots of fog. The difference was the ocean as a silent friend, and fellow travelers in cars in their flight away from one hard city until the next one appeared in front of them. The shacks and prettied-up bungalows littered the highway's ridge before the bluff dropped off to sand and ocean. In Montana, a ride was slow, a steep ascent or a cautious descent, but always under an unending open sky. Here the air reeked of salt and kelp; white gulls were dark images of outstretched wings holding still for the long glide over tireless waves. He cut the engine after he parked.

Jack was an Army man with little use for the ocean. Land you can trust, confirm with your feet, he'd tell you, and it's easier to die on, too. Not the sea. The ocean was smooth, like a bed sheet one minute and a broken bag of marbles the next. Bleeding to death on land lets you know God's plan as you fade out, until your body is boxed up for burial in consecrated ground back home, or there in some hallowed place of stone crosses and tiny flags. Not so with the sea. Out there in those godless waves there was no memorial. A man bobbed and floated in torment, holding onto what was left of his ship, while sharks waited and watched.

There was just enough light left in the sky for his feet. Typical of Hamilton. He had moored his schooner at the end of the pier, as if to spite Jack to take the long walk seaward. The black wood of the pier glistened, smelling of pitch and tar. The two-by-fours to Jack's left were on the shallow side of the water. A fall off the pier's right side would've broken the body against pilings and rocks. Jack read the name. Hamilton's boat. The vessel at the end of the line bobbed, seemed to snore in the rhythmic swish and slap of the waves.

"Hamilton," Jack yelled out, hands cupped.

A solitary light below deck turned on.

"Who's out there?" a voice shot back.

"Marshall."

"Jack? Is that you? Show yourself, you old dog."

John Hamilton appeared on deck, lantern in hand. A lean six-five, in casual pants, no shoes, and an open shirt, hair tangled and a good start of a beard off his chin. Hamilton moved as his boat undulated, his thinking and his feet in natural compliance with the ocean.

Jack stepped up. "Request permission to come on board."

"Permission granted," the skipper replied, offering Jack an assist. "It's been what, five or six years?"

"Sounds about right. Can we go below deck to talk?"

* * *

The captain's quarters were tight but comfortable. Hamilton pointed to a table and one of two wooden chairs with burgundy leather seats. Jack saw the whiskey bottle a third full and the glass, an ashtray, and a crumpled pack of cigarettes in the dark. No surprise Hamilton was drinking in the dark. Hamilton could pour a finger of the most expensive whiskey in a storm without spilling a drop. The man possessed the steadiest of nerves in combat, but in other matters, he wavered, back and forth, like the ocean.

* * *

"What brings you my way, old friend?" Hamilton asked, as he retrieved a glass for his guest and directed him to the seat on the other side of the table.

"Found out you lived in the neighborhood and thought I'd have a look-see for myself."

"You mean you read a fact sheet thrown across your desk. No need to bull shit me, Jack."

Hamilton said bullshit in a way that made it clear he spelled it with two words. He scratched out a light to flame his cigarette. One eye watched Jack as he squinted the other and inhaled. Hamilton stretched out his long legs, never taking his eye off Jack, before he swept in the hand for another short drag off the cigarette. Jack's seen this movie a thousand times.

"I'd rather hear the news instead of reading a report. Between jobs at the studio?" Jack asked.

"Oh, the hell with those bastards. Who needs them?"

Hamilton's smoking hand waved off an invisible nuisance. When Hamilton was comfortable, done with preliminaries, he'd pour their drinks.

"Don't know," Jack said. "Maybe you need them. A man needs money now and then. Heard you're married."

"How about you? You married? Is there a Mrs. Marshall in your picture frame?"

"I am, and there is."

"A good marriage, I hope? A man can die prematurely from a bad one."

Hamilton knocked back the unfinished drink he had on the table before Jack arrived. Hamilton poured them both shots. Jack held off on his until he asked his questions.

"How about you, John? You dying on me?"

"I have my troubles, and that's why I'm here doing my thinking."

"Seems like the bottle's been doing most of your thinking. What's bothering you this time?"

"You didn't come all the way out here to play innocent with me, Jack. I have one of those analysts mine my thoughts now. Twenty-five an hour, five hundred a month, I pay the good doctor to be second mate on the grandest voyage of them all." Hamilton's finger tapped the side of his head. "The voyage into the mind, my own."

"And how's that going for you?"

"About as eventful as unfolding a deck chair."

The two men laughed as Hamilton poured himself another shot and tipped the bottle Jack's way after he downed his mouthful of firewater. Jacked pulled his short glass closer to him. "I'm good, Captain. Need to pace it since I'm driving."

"You can stay overnight if you like. Feel free to stow aboard."

"I'll think about it. Talk to me, John. Five years is a long time."

"Don't know what to tell you. Head is a mess, but you always knew that about me. Less than thrilled about seeing an analyst, but it came recommended to me, although there are happier ways I could be spending money flat on my back instead of talking to some overeducated idiot. I should be out there sailing instead, but I signed on for the family subscription, and I have bills to pay." Hamilton raised his glass to toast either the sea, Jack, or the psychiatrist taking his money. "I'm convinced the doc is doing crosswords or balancing his checkbook while I chew away the hour."

"Hate to say it, but sounds like you've gotten yourself into this mess, John. You chose to get married. For whatever reasons, you picked this doctor. Head messed up from the war?"

"Nope."

"There a reason for seeing this shrink?"

"Ah, yes. The reason, or as the egghead calls it, the dramatic event. It wasn't a mother or some bedwetting incident in childhood. They all seem to think that way. This doctor doesn't quite till that tired soil. Truth is, it's a crisis of confidence."

"That again? I've heard it all before, John. Acting is the bunk; you're making money doing nothing. You're the only man I know who feels guilty for making money when it isn't breaking his back."

"Well, I do. C'mon, it's an obscene amount of cash, and for what? Standing there and sounding off lines?"

"You're an actor. That's what actors do. You just happen to be damn good at it."

"Aw, hell, Jack. You don't get it."

Jack pushed his glass forward for the refill. Hamilton, his host, complied. Jack figured the camaraderie of drink would soften the criticism he had for his friend.

"What's there to get? Do you doubt you're a good actor? No. We've been over this once before. You blubbered about how these other actors took lessons, had more experience on the stage, but there you were doing it as good as them, if not better. Doubt your vocation in life, is that it? You shouldn't. You're the only man I know with an acting gig before the war, enlisted in the Marine Corps, used a fake name, denied his prior life when someone recognized him from the screen, and then…and then managed to become an officer, worked his way up the chain of command at the OSS to become Bill Donovan's right-hand man before Donovan realized John Hamilton was an alias. There's acting for you. There's impressive bullshit."

"You don't get it, Jack." The tall man sloshed another big splash into his small glass.

"Right. I forgot to mention you earned the Silver Star, and I forgot all those missions."

"Oh, put that away, Jack. You received the Bronze Star. Twice. You were also given the Silver Star. We both did what we had to at the time."

"My point exactly, Captain Hamilton. You deliver when it matters. So, what's with the crisis of confidence? Is it that acting is too easy, or not exciting enough for you?"

"I did, didn't I?"

Jack could tell from the distant stare in Hamilton's eyes he was looking back into time when he had shot his way out of an ambush, when he ferried a small boat through dense fog twice, once in Italy and another time off the Dalmatian cost, retrieving refugees out of the cold water. The brass had left them to drown, but not John Hamilton.

"I lived life in those mountains above Belgrade, Jack. Then I came home."

"You did your job, and you did it well. You infiltrated the Communist

Party for us then. I've read the recent brief. I know what people are saying about your politics. So, what, somebody thinks you're a Communist? Let them think you've made a mistake. Nobody gives a damn."

Hamilton was wagging his finger and there was heat to his voice, and not from the whiskey. "That's where you're wrong, Jack. Somebody gives a damn."

"Are you a Communist?"

"No. I mean, well, I had been briefly, technically." Hamilton scratched the back of his unkempt head. "I went to some meetings stateside. For the Company, you know that. Damn, Jack. I may sound like a kid here, but I liked some of those people, admired them, and I can tell you they were curious, like most folks with a half brain in their head." Hamilton used his fingers to scrub his eyes. "What's your point, Jack?"

"You experimented. You didn't take a pledge. You didn't pay dues. A meeting of Communists in this town is what…a cocktail party at some mansion in the hills? LA is where some shutterbug snaps a picture of you next to a young lady, and the next day, you read you're Chaplin, and she's having your child."

"There's more to it, Jack, and you know it. These skunks—and I mean McCarthy and Hoover—they want to destroy people. They want to destroy my livelihood and me. Insinuation and innuendo is their game. Don't underestimate them."

"I'm not, especially Hoover. The man hated Bill Donovan. He probably hates you because you were standing next to Bill. Hoover was the rat who leaked it to Truman about Bill's extramarital affair. Which finished Bill off in the Company. Hoover envied the OSS. He wants his FBI to have the entire parking lot—cars, keys, fence, and padlock. He wants it all."

Hamilton turned a knob, and the bulb in the lamp overhead brightened, while Jack nursed whiskey. Hamilton reached into a drawer. A crumpled-up letter appeared on the table in front of Jack, dated May 23, and addressed to Martin Gang.

"Gang is your lawyer?"

"Just read the letter, Jack."

Jack's eyes scanned down the letter, saw it was signed J. Edgar Hoover, informing the actor there was no formal process by which a former member of the Communist Party could be 'cleared.' Jack pushed the paper across the table to his friend.

"It's after I testified in April," Hamilton said, tired.

"I read about that."

"Some acting role, eh? I play fink, Grand Stoolie, and King of the Rodents, and now they want more. It's all in the letter there."

"Self-hatred goes a long way in this town."

"I need to make it right."

Jack's face tightened in confusion. "Make it right, how? By following up the performance with a request for clearance? What'd you expect? Expect Hoover to put on the black robe, bless you, and send you off to do Our Fathers and Hail Marys? Nuts to that. You'll play right into his hands, John. Can't you see that? He'll end the next letter telling you to come forward again, and he'll take you for all you've got."

"What do I do?"

"Can you give the man anything?"

Jack let the question sink in. Hamilton shook his head.

"I didn't think so," Jack said. "It's the principle, I know. Nobody likes an informant, but we have a country of blind mice. Most of the names people are tossing at Hoover and McCarthy are either ones the FBI already have, or they're FBI informants."

"Gang said the same thing."

"For J. Edgar, it's God, Country, and Hoover, the new Holy Trinity."

"They're chumming the water, Jack."

"I know they are, John. They're playing on everyone's fear. Not fear of Communists but simple, human fear of rejection and alienation."

"Funny coming from you, Jack, since you spent your days hunting Communists and Nazis."

"No. There's a distinction, John. Walker and I were sorting them out for what they knew about the Soviets, their rocket technology, and, of course, atomic plans. We were dealing with engineers, scientists, and agents in the field. That's a different breed of animal than what McCarthy and Hoover are after these days. Hoover and McCarthy are victimizing citizens, scared people."

Hamilton fired up another cigarette. Jack lost count of how many his friend chain-smoked.

"What can I do for you, Jack? You came for something."

"I did. You know a writer named Loew?"

"Yeah, sure I do. Vaguely. Why?"

"What can you tell me about him?"

"Not much to tell. Middle-aged guy. Flashy dresser. He's a script fixer-upper. Officially, he's with Warner, but he floats between the studios when they're in a pinch."

"How do you mean?"

"Loew was one of Thalberg's prized protégés—a real brain behind the pen and a genius script doctor." A long exhalation of smoke followed. "Like Thalberg, Loew works on a lot of projects but doesn't take the credit."

"Why not take the credit? Is the man a saint, or is he asking for a percentage at the box office?" Jack asked.

Hamilton tilted his head back and laughed until his eyes watered.

"Did I say something funny?"

"You seriously think studio heads give a percent of the profit? You really don't know this town, Jack. Loew works in hard cash, upfront, and a lot of it. He knows he's worth it."

Hamilton's drink disappeared. "Loew landed a regular gig at Warner after he left MGM, but he makes his bread and butter rewriting scripts on the sly. Loew is your man, especially when the unions threaten to strike."

"Projects run on budgets and schedules. Unions strife would jam up the works."

"Bingo," Hamilton said and pointed with his finger. "Loew delivers scripts on time, and ready to roll into production."

"Sounds like a lot of work for one man."

"He'll hire out writers who need the money but don't want their studio knowing they're making scratch on the side. Don't kid yourself, everyone knows, including the studio heads, and they all look the other way. Why are you asking?"

"He's dead."

"How? When?"

"Shot. This afternoon, in a dive in Bunker Hill."

"You don't say. What on earth was he slumming there for?" Hamilton asked.

"Asked myself the same question. He dressed well, like you said. Looked like two men did him. Likely he went to meet someone, things turned ugly, or it was a planned job to kill him. One of them grabbed him, twisted him down to the floor, and the other one shot him."

"Two sounds excessive. Loew was a lightweight. Not the physical type. Sure it was two men?"

"Certain." Jack recalled observations. "The watch he had on faced inward. I know some people wear it that way, but when I checked his wrist, there was an abrasion. Someone twisted the man's wrist, turning the face around."

"Okay, that takes him to the ground for the number two man to pop him. Anything else?"

Hamilton sat back and closed his eyes, smoking a cigarette now, not because he was tired, but rather to screen the action behind his eyes. He listened while Jack talked.

"The rug was bunched up near him, which means someone crouched down. The shot was direct from the back and not at an angle. Two different people."

Jack explained the vet finding the body, what he read in the detective's notebook, the strange piece of paper in the back pocket, and the matchbook from the nightclub.

"You said Loew made big money, was flashy. Did he frequent the Trocadero?"

Hamilton laughed. "Who doesn't?"

"Where does a man like Loew go for fun? What do writers with money do?"

Hamilton held his cigarette and grinned. "A writer with money? Like I said, you don't know this town. The Troc is show-and-tell for the stars. They go there to see and be seen. Writers hang out at jazz clubs or more low-key places with their own kind, like Schwab's on Sunset. I don't get it, Jack. Who put you up to this? Thought DC was more your pond."

"It is. The wife and I are house-sitting for Walker while he's on vacation."

"Walker is your fair-haired boy. Speaking of you two in Vienna—wasn't there another operative?"

"Stop pretending you don't remember her name. You mean Leslie."

"Yeah, Leslie. I remember her. She's quite the dish."

"I should get going. It's getting late. Oh, by the way, the name of that shrink?"

"Don't tell me you need help with the attic?"

Hamilton rose, stretched out his legs, and yawned. He hunched over a small table and opened a drawer. "Name is Phillip Ernest. Here's his card."

Chapter Three

Betty let the curtain fall back to cover the window.

Halfway up the grade, he turned right from the smooth road and slowed the car into biting gravel. The sound would give him away. He turned again when he saw the post. Another quick turn, and he entered the driveway. He knew she would wait up for him. She always did. The radio was playing the old Mills Brothers' song *Till Then*, which didn't soften the irony for Jack when he switched the lights off and closed the door with a gentle push. All the crickets hushed silent. On the porch, his foot caught the soft spot, and the wood creaked. It was too much betrayal. He closed the door behind him and saw her.

Betty took a deep inhalation from her Julep cigarette, held it while she eyed him, and exhaled the mentholated smoke he hated. She smoked only when she was angry or nervous. Wearing her best nightdress to the fight, she followed him into the kitchen, where he sat down as she opened the cupboard for a dish. The pull of a china plate made a nasty sound. She placed it on the table on a mat between the knife and fork. Next, it was her visit to the Elmira refrigerator, some white light, and yet another dish. Leftover meatloaf, repurposed as a sandwich, was placed in front of him. Jack heard the rattle of ice into cut glass, then water from a pitcher. Ice cracked. She sat, the ashtray in front of her on the table. Another white cloud blew past him.

"I never ask about your work, but we meant to get away. Us, the children, for a vacation."

"Something came up."

"Something always comes up. When does it end? Where does it ever end,

Jack?"

"It never ends. It'll never end."

"What about the children? Aren't they allowed a father?"

Her eyes continued to stare. Her face, made up for appearances, maintained its mask of subdued rage. Only eyes and her mouth revived this annual conversation.

"Something important did come up, Betty, and I'm sorry."

"And there'll be a next time. I'll understand again, but will they? There'll come a time when children won't accept excuses, Jack, because they'll hear and understand daddy is a meaningless word for a father. You might as well be a ghost, Jack Marshall."

"I'll make it up to them."

"Lost time isn't a bill you can pay, Jack."

"I know."

"Do you?"

Cool as frost, the menthol in her cigarettes might as well have been an anesthetic for the contempt she had for him. With each breath, each white ghost, everything, including history, turned to dust and ashes.

"I wish you wouldn't smoke. It's unhealthy."

More smoke wafted across the table in a slow, deliberate cloud.

"So, Walker comes home tomorrow, and we go back to DC?"

"Yes, to both questions."

"This affair—pardon my choice of words—comes home with you?"

"No. This situation goes to Walker, but I may be involved to some degree when I return home. I may provide…consultation."

"Of course. I understand. I always do."

Her lips nursed the cigarette. She inhaled. Her cheeks caved in. She exhaled.

"It must be a terrible thing not to be able to talk about your work," she said in a tone neither ironic nor New Testament compassion. Either way, she spoke the truth. He couldn't talk about the job, the specifics, and he couldn't answer her. He wouldn't.

"It's best we don't talk about it," he said.

"Finish your meatloaf and come up to bed."

She twisted the cigarette into the ashtray, and walked around the table, kissed him on the cheek before she left the kitchen.

* * *

At twenty past too early an hour the next morning, Jack watched Betty outside with the children near the hired car to Burbank. The children were cranky earlier at the table, then sleepy and moody. Betty served breakfast. She disappeared after she cleared the table to put on her face and emerged in a daffodil dress, white silk gloves, and a canary yellow handbag on her wrist. Hair and makeup, picture-perfect.

He spoke with the children, explained to them he had unexpected work, while she was dressing, but now he remembered Betty's words as he watched from behind glass, how she moved in dutiful silence. He wondered if they'd remember what he had said to them; they'd listened to him with blank and obedient faces.

He observed the family portrait through the window. Children inside the car, Betty glanced up and blew him a kiss, then looked up again from the open window of the car before she settled in for the drive to Burbank. In ten hours or so, after being aboard a Lockheed Connie, they'd be on a train from New York to DC. Soon enough, Betty would be home, happy, enjoying her new car, a Nash Rambler, minding house, taking the children to the park and other places. The hired car pulled away, a signature of dirt and dust in its wake.

Walker arrived in the afternoon. Jack saw the hardtop sedan, a Kaiser Virginian, as it wobbled on the road in the distance. When the sun struck the Pasadena Yellow paint and the extra-wide white walls, the car prowled like a fierce predator through the uncivilized grass. Walker stepped out of the car in a breezy Mohawk shirt, white with mesh weave, League pants, and a straw Trilby on his head. In one hand, a suitcase big enough for two changes of clothes.

"Good to see you, Walker. Vacation good?"

"Big Island was spectacular. You should take the family there."

Nobody in any of the windows, and no rambunctious stampede of children to the door, Walker didn't wait long to ask, "Betty and the kids?"

"Sent them home. Something came up. We should talk in the study."

"I need a cold drink first."

A tanned Walker, still in the festive afterglow of his vacation, wandered into his kitchen. In the refrigerator, Betty had left him a week's worth of food and a note about the steak marinating on the bottom tier. His dinner. He bypassed the bottles of Bull Dog she stowed on the top shelf and took the pitcher of lemonade out instead. Jack said he'd meet him downstairs.

The study hosted two luxurious leather chairs, a large area rug, and a silent fireplace. Near the wall, Walker placed an early Stickley desk with a leather top, four drawers on each side, single drawer in the middle, and simple black pull handles. Two telephones in two different colors, black and beige, sat on top of the desk.

"I have an assignment for you, Walker. Have a seat."

"Not even in my own house an hour. You don't waste time, do you?"

"This is urgent." Jack handed an envelope to Walker. "Take a look at this."

Walker set down his lemonade. He undid the clasp. He thumbed through the pages. Jack allowed Walker a few minutes to peruse the contents.

"Assignment is the crème de la cringe," Walker said as he held up the small stack of papers. "Crime scene report, forensics, and a preliminary from the Coroner's Office. I can read these later. This is fast work for a recent homicide. Tell me what's not in ink here."

"Our contact within the LAPD expedited what you have in your hands. Toxicology will take a few weeks. No laboratory can work that fast, and if there's something important in the Tox Report, I'll contact you."

Walker placed the paperwork on the coffee table in front of him. He sat back with his glass of lemonade.

"Let's assume the bullet to the head killed our man. Boozed or loaded up with drugs was a means to incapacitate the victim. Says here, name is Charles Loew, studio writer at Warner Brothers and a member of the Screen Writers Guild. In good standing." Walker fanned the stack to the appropriate page. "No priors. No indication of a robbery. Minimal struggle, possibly two perps, but no fingerprints. Shoe sizes found in the place don't tell us much when half of LA walks through Bunker Hill. A .22-caliber was used. Close-range. Nice and sweet and smells professional to me."

"There's more," Jack said.

Jack relayed what was written in Detective Brown's notebook. He conveyed the 'what's not in ink': the Trocadero matchbook, the phone number in silver ink, and the mystery on the folded-up piece of paper inside the man's back pocket. Jack handed Walker the items not in the crime scene report: the matchbook and the code sheet. Walker considered the jumble of nonsense letters and the bleeding ink. "The veteran who discovered the body?" Walker asked.

"Alibi checked out, but I confirmed he's worked for Hoover in the past. Snoop jobs, some intimidation, but nothing heavier."

"He wrote down *commonist*. Nice. So, what's the assignment, Jack? Just because I live in this city doesn't mean I know a thing about the film industry. Those people might as well be characters in a fairy tale."

"They die just the same," Jack said as he pushed himself back in his chair. "I'm afraid we might be in the cactus patch with Hoover here." Jack sighed. "Remember John Hamilton?"

"Boy, you change gears fast. Sure, I remember him. Good actor. Better soldier. Angst before the war, angst after the war." Jack endured Walker's character assessment. "What about him?" Walker asked.

"Paid him a visit to hear his thoughts on Loew."

"And?"

Jack explained Hamilton's exposition of Loew's career as a script doctor, his freelance work, and how his operation helped the studios work around union troubles for a hefty bag of money, except there was no recent scuttlebutt about labor problems in any of the studios, particularly Warner Brothers.

"Loew doesn't sound like no Communist to me?" Walker said.

"Thought the same thing, but somebody wanted to plant the idea he was one."

Walker shrugged and enjoyed lemonade. "Could be a business rival, or professional jealousy. Writers are known for their egos. Chest thumping doesn't pay the bills, but this Loew could've shorted someone out of money or a writing gig."

"Doesn't explain his secretive piece of paper," Jack said. "Which reminds me: I'll relay the results once the boys back home study it."

Jack hadn't taken his eyes off the stack of papers near Walker.

"And the number on the back of the Writers Guild card?" Walker asked. "A woman, or an associate?"

"Musso and Frank on Hollywood Boulevard. The bar has a back room for writers, a watering hole that's included Chandler, Fitzgerald, and Nathanael West."

"Makes every barfly a suspect," Walker said, lemonade set aside; he sat back, comfortable since he waited for the payload. "Think the LAPD will solve this murder?"

"The question is whether they'll solve it or the FBI shows up. We can assume our patriotic vet has reported Loew's death to Hoover somehow. Your thoughts on what you've seen and heard?"

Walker pawed through the stack of paper, silent, and sat back in his chair.

"The killers didn't know about the piece of paper in the back pocket. Report said the man was killed around two in the afternoon; body wasn't discovered until later. Plenty of time to turn the place upside down."

"Plenty of time to search the body, too, and they didn't." Jack leaned forward, hands churched. "For all appearances, this was a contract killing. If Loew wronged a colleague or a rival, or possessed valuable information, you'd think they'd rough him up some before killing him."

Walker noticed Jack checked his watch. He had seen the suitcases near the door. He was tired from the flight from Hawaii and playing Watson to his Holmes. Their relationship was such that he could be curt without offending his friend or boss. "What do you want me to do for you?" he asked.

"Become a script writer at Warner Brothers. You did a little bit of writing after the war."

"You know, I did a few weeks in a workshop in Cedar Rapids, but that doesn't qualify me as a screenwriter."

"Have a little confidence in yourself, Walker. I'll have a script someone I know wrote sent to you; use it to refresh your memory while I find you an agency that farms out temporary help to plant you inside Warner Brothers. You can take it from there to find out what you can about Loew."

Just like him, Walker thought as he listened. Jack's mind was an escalator. His plan had moving parts or even when it stood still, there were steps, a staircase, and it was up to him to find the destination and exit. "Why not use Hamilton?" he asked. "He's an actor, a known entity. You said you spoke to him."

"We both know John is volatile. He has his own troubles, but that's not to say he won't be helpful. John did give me another idea." Jack checked his wrist. "Look at the time. The car to Burbank will arrive soon."

Jack was up from his chair, on the move, while Walker checked his watch. "Care to tell me Hamilton's idea?"

"In due time," Jack said, already up the stairs and his voice, distant.

Chapter Four

The employment agency told Walker to report to a Miss So-and-So for a two-week assignment at Warner Brothers in Burbank. The directions from the upbeat voice on the phone said the studio was at the intersection of Olive and Pass Avenues and Barham Boulevard. Starting rate of a dollar fifty an hour, which moved to a dollar seventy-five should the client renew the contract. Good money.

Traffic through Walker's part of Los Angeles to Burbank was a stop-and-go affair of impatient car horns, the sit-and-wait of passengers on buses and trolleys. Cars waited to move, drivers strummed the wheel with fingers while eyes sampled the human menagerie of the ignorant, the idiotic, and the hard-working illiterates, their shadows cast against numerous walls and on graying sidewalks. When everyone moved forward, the freeway fed them into brown hills, green fields, and orange groves. Automobile exhaust drifted up with the desert's dust behind them.

The young lady giving Walker the tour pointed out the supply cabinet for pens, pencils, and paper. Her feminine sensibility dictated the use of the word lavatory, not toilet. "That's down the hall and to the right," she told him. Time cards were to be time-punched at start and end of day with thirty minutes for lunch. Personal phone calls to parties outside the studio were frowned upon, she said, but a wink implied what everyone knew about rules in LA.

Miss So-and-So was an attractive brunette with marvelous skin in a Bergdorf Goodman knit suit from the Broadway-Hale Stores. She said between stops that she accepted a desk job after a screen test. The test went well until she was told, 'Too bad nobody produces silent films anymore.' When he heard her, Walker understood: She spoke in a voice strained through unfortunate adenoids.

The itinerary would've continued if not for a crowd gathered outside an office, making it impossible to move around or through it. Two screaming voices—one in the hall into the office and the other in the office out into the hall—attracted bystanders waiting for blood to spill on the buffed floors. Walker recognized the hall voice as belonging to a famous actor.

"You've typecast me as a girl-hitting mick. I do five pictures a year for you when my contract calls for four—you ungrateful son of a bitch."

"Yeah, and two years ago, you ran your own production company. See how that gave you a world of success," screamed the voice inside the room.

"Why, you little Jew bastard—you would bring that up, wouldn't you?" the actor said before he rattled off Yiddish obscenities.

The voice inside the office started laughing, which initiated a stalemate, a gunfighter's quiet in the hall. A hand appeared through the open door for the handshake of peace. As the crowd parted, Walker saw two diminutive men. Cagney and Warner.

"What you gawking at, kid?" Cagney said.

"Didn't mean to, sir. It's been a long time since I've heard Yiddish."

Warner, with his hand on Cagney's shoulder, said, "He grew up in Hell's Kitchen. How about you…" and then Warner said something to Walker in Yiddish. Walker responded in kind.

"Where'd you learn Yiddish, kid? Over at Fairfax?" Cagney asked Walker.

"No. In the Army. I was part of the company that liberated Dachau."

Warner paled, and Cagney straightened up. Cagney and Warner dusted each other off, and Cagney left Walker with Miss So-and-So and Jack Warner in the hallway. Miss So-and-So, seeing Warner stare at her, took it as her cue to leave.

"Dachau, you said."

"Yes, sir."

Warner gave Walker the once over. "Haven't seen you around here before."

"I'm an agency man. First day here, sir, and assigned to the Writers' Pool.

Name is Thompson, sir. Walter Thompson."

"Write much? You must, otherwise the agency wouldn't have sent you. Work hard, be conscientious, and you'll do fine. I'm a difficult man and an opinionated one, as you no doubt saw in this recent tawdry episode, but Mr. Cagney and I have a long history, so we give each other some margin."

"Thank you for the advice, Mr. Warner. I should report to the pool. You don't pay me for standing still."

"I like your ethic, Thompson. Miss Elkins tell you where the Writers' Pool is?" he asked.

"She did and gave me a tour also."

Walker started walking down the hall. He turned around at the sound of a noise. Warner's shoes squeaked on the waxed floor.

"Mr. Thompson?" the smaller, mustachioed man called out.

"Sir?"

"What is your opinion of television?"

Walker paced slowly back to where he stood before in front of Warner. He had done his research on the Warner Brothers and knew about the one brother's feelings on the subject.

"Might I be frank, sir?" Walker received a shrug. "I don't see the point. I don't see the appeal in staring at a small box, even if it is in your living room with your family around you. Convenience, no doubt, but you can just as well take the family to the theatre and see a well-made film. Television is too small a format to transport the audience into a narrative. There'd be too many interruptions with commercials, and there's that temptation to walk away. Not so in a theatre. Shall I continue?"

"Please do." Warner's face betrayed no emotion.

"I imagine from a business perspective there's the anxiety of paid advertisements, sponsors and all, and becoming beholden to stockholders. Next thing you know, you spend all your time justifying your creativity to committees. Furthermore, television isn't a forum for socially instructive work, but I think I should go now because I might've overstated my case."

Warner stood there silent, eyes narrowed in assessment.

"Mr. Thompson, I like your way of thinking, and I admire your candid nature. Just this morning I was arguing with one of my brothers over this very topic, which you summarized for me eloquently. I'm afraid my argument was far more colorful than yours. It's my nature to speak my mind. I admit I often fail at diplomacy. My brother wants to dedicate a studio lot to television shows. He's championing some old vaudeville comedian. Never mind. I think you'll find your stay here most welcoming. I want you to report to the screenplays section in the Pool and dedicate your skill there. Be patient and learn from the crew there, and don't let me hear of you wandering off to Columbia across the way—bad enough I have to share the lot with Harry Cohn."

Walker is Walter Thompson, screenwriter. He walked away to find the Writers' Pool, knowing he knew about as much about writing as Cagney did about grapefruit.

Chapter Five

Hamilton dreaded the long climb up the stairs to Ernest's office. The drive over was bad enough; finding parking was worse. Then Hamilton jammed his six-five frame onto a small island of office leather for an hour, from which he peeled himself off after Phillip Ernest raked his psyche with accusations and insinuations like a gardener. Ernest was no medical doctor but one of those intellectuals with a doctorate. A psychoanalyst. Hamilton thought it best to select someone without the power of prescribing medication.

Phillip Ernest, Ph.D. Licensed Therapist was stenciled in black on the pebbled glass of his office. The rest of the door was professional for a psychological undertaker. Ernest ran daily sessions and collected a handsome fee by the hour for himself.

Hamilton had told Jack he started session work after appearing before HUAC, the House Un-American Activities Committee, in April, but that wasn't the complete truth. He told Jack twenty-five an hour, five hundred a month, and that part was true. It wasn't that he lied to Jack, rather he bent the truth because the details of a man's marriage were a private matter.

In front of the door now, the sight of the gray shadow behind the pockmarked glass and the inevitable session ahead of him, Hamilton wished he could carry a fifty-pound sandbag up twelve flights of stairs instead. He told himself to take the elevator but never did.

The unlocked door opened into an anteroom, where there was a lonely desk for a future secretary. Hamilton saw a well-polished Oxford shoe and dark sock calf in front of him. Hamilton contemplated a quick swig from the flask in his coat pocket, a dying man's courage. Hamilton could hear Ernest had no patience with him; the tap-tap of the foot stopped when Hamilton closed the door behind him with a deliberate click.

"Just in time. Please come in and make yourself comfortable."

Like a well-rehearsed scene, without floor marks, they took their positions. They followed the script. Hamilton will take off his suit jacket and hat first. Ernest will sit in the chair behind the sofa. Hamilton will air out the leather Chesterfield. Today, the window, cracked open, permitted a breeze between priest and penitent.

The doctor wore a three-button grey flannel suit in May. His jacket hung on the hook, and the rest of him was bland as a schoolboy in a blue Arrow dress shirt and nondescript tie. The priciest item on his person was the ballpoint pen he used—a Reynolds Rocket from Gimbels. Ernest prided himself as a collector of fine writing instruments. He mentioned on more than one occasion he used to own an Argentinean Birome pen, but somebody absconded with it while he was at a party.

"Shall we begin, Mr. Hamilton? We last discussed your feelings of remorse about naming colleagues."

"I don't like the idea I'm a stoolie."

"When we assign labels to ourselves, we create stories we believe to be true about ourselves, the world, and how we function in it. Instead of seeing yourself as a stoolie, as you call it, I'd prefer you view it as performing your civic, if not a patriotic duty. Your so-called colleagues can fend for themselves."

"You must've had a hard life on the playground as a kid, didn't you? You don't rat out acquaintances or friends. It's that simple, Doc. You don't do it with your brother or sister, friends, coworkers, or even your enemy. You settle your differences in private."

The 'I see' was due next, and Hamilton loathed it.

"I see, Mr. Hamilton. Your mother and father taught you moral relativism."

"Leave my mother and father out of it. They were good, decent people. Salt of the earth types, so no Oedipus, no Electra, or any other mumbo-jumbo mythology. Hear me? And yeah, they taught me to tell the truth, but it wasn't no chopping down a cherry tree either. Life is complicated. If you took your head out of a book, you'd know that."

"Please remain calm, Mr. Hamilton. Life is complicated, but some values should be indisputable." He paused. "Like honor and duty."

Hamilton turned himself to a seated position. "I do my job," he said. "I pay my bills. I may not like my job, but who am I to fink on the man next to me? This is a free country. We were founded on certain freedoms. This country exists because our forefathers… aw hell, I don't know why I bother." His hands pushed the air away as if it stank. He wondered why he came to these sessions. Intellectual bull shit, he thought.

"Let's explore freedom." Ernest tapped his notepad. "There's the First Amendment. Your colleagues have the right to invoke the Fifth Amendment. Free speech and the right to avoid self-incrimination are their legal prerogatives. Their rights have not been abridged."

"You haven't been kissed before, have you, Doc? What good are those rights? Bogart and the Hollywood Ten formed the Committee for the First Amendment and see where that got them."

"Mr. Bogart is a fine actor, an intelligent man, but he himself said he was duped when it was pointed out to him some members of the Hollywood Ten were Communists."

"Bogie backed himself into a tight corner, Doc, but the principle was right. The First Amendment shouldn't be empty words on a page, and big government should have limits."

"The Fifth Amendment affords the accused the right not to belabor their situation. Isn't there the moral right to self-defense? Communism has declared Capitalism its enemy. Therefore, as a capitalist society, we are every Communist's enemy. With atomic technology, they—"

"Yeah, yeah, Doc. I've heard that record until it wore out. Isn't that just a song we sing to ourselves? We used A-bombs first. Indisputable fact. As for me, I was a Party Member. Emphasis on *was*. I'm a man with children, staring at a divorce, and there are judges in this town who'd prevent a man like me from seeing his kids because of his pinko past. Moral turpitude is what they'll call it. Play the canary, and I also lose my livelihood. Some mineshaft I've fallen into."

"Are you angry with me because I counseled you to testify?"

The bobbing foot stopped.

"No. I made that choice. You're no lawyer. What I didn't expect in court was that it was all rigged. The script and the parts were already written out long before I walked into that room. A staged inquisition, it was, and I played my part. A chump I was then, and I hate myself every minute for it now."

"You did your civic duty, Mr. Hamilton."

"Knock it off, Doc. Sure, I wasn't cited for contempt like the others, or listed, but the phone isn't exactly ringing off the hook with roles for me, is it now? My wife's lawyers bill me overtime and create every possible excuse for why I can't see my kids."

The doctor flipped a page in his little notebook. "A holding pattern. You will weather it."

"See how you feel about that pattern when I can't pay you."

Hamilton squirmed on the leather. He craved a cigarette, reached for his chest, and sighed, frustrated. His smokes were inside his jacket outside.

"You mentioned last time Mr. Hoover requested you visit one of his offices."

"That's what the letter said." Hamilton would've said more, but he noticed a shadow behind the closed door. A female of the species. Even the cerebral Ernest perceived it.

"Ah, that must be the girl from the agency," Ernest's voice rose a few notes in the octave. "Do you mind if we end our session early, Mr. Hamilton? I'll tack the time onto our next session." The doctor lifted himself up from his chair. Hamilton called it the throne of judgment.

"What happened to your receptionist?"

"Her husband didn't want her working. He received a raise, so that was the end of her. Rather an unfortunate situation for me, but the agency was prompt to find me a replacement. Can we continue our session another time?"

"Sure. Sure, Doc. It's not like I'm not seeing you soon."

"Thank you for being so understanding."

Ernest eased the door open to let Hamilton out first. The young woman in the elegant polka-dot dress smiled but Dr. Ernest wasn't the one to see her, Hamilton was; he also saw the reaction on her face before it turned serious for Dr. Ernest.

She introduced herself as Miss Margaret Gardner.

Ernest shook hands. He smiled. Hamilton also shook hands and smiled because sometimes the best acting was done without lines.

It was Leslie.

Chapter Six

The Writers' Pool was the pinnacle, the latest in office design. The desks were arranged according to the status. Junior writers worked on black Remington's Noiseless Model Sevens in the back of the room. Proofreaders used large desks for the continuous slush pile of scripts. The better writers with the best desks used Army-green Remington Super-Riters with Tempo Touch.

Warner encouraged a mill mentality, the churn of continuous production, for writing and revision. He didn't care for a writer's idiosyncrasies because he paid for tight writing, from script to screen to pocket. His pocket. A Warner spy walked the narrow alleyways between desks to verify only scripts were on the rollers and under key. No literary novels on his clock.

Every writer received a blotter, an ashtray, a cup for his pens and pencils, and one replacement ribbon for their typewriter. Inkwells were rationed. The new-fangled ballpoint pen was expressly verboten—the only German word permitted on the Warner premises.

There were strict rules around lunch. There was to be no commingling of the sexes. Women writers had their own room, as Warner's concession to Virginia Woolf. He gave the women smaller desks a smaller room, and fewer supplies. Women, he said, knew how to do more with less.

Two weeks into the assignment, out of place and cursing two Jacks, Walker received his dollar seventy-five an hour and a desk in the last row. He spent most of the working hours last week and this one reading screenplays to learn the Warner Way to Studio Style.

He learned who the office characters were. Arthur, the writer's writer, worked in every genre the studio put to screen. It was rumored he'd fled to Hollywood after committing a crime. When pressed about what he had done, he replied, "I stole a typewriter." Henry was the sad fellow with the cheating wife and kids of questionable paternity. He excelled at comedy. Louie, a former door-to-door vacuum salesman, was the Concept Man. His specialty was dialogue. Mean Bernie, up front at the largest desk, was both copy editor, line editor, and alleged Warner mole. Walker saw a lone desk, materials on it, but no man in the chair. Then there was Terry: the office know-it-all, shop steward, union agitator, and peacekeeper. Walker heard all the stories.

Warner and Terry had it out once in front of everyone in the Writers' Pool. Warner insisted all employees take a Loyalty Oath to 'the Government of the United States of America… and to the State of California.' Terry, the provocateur, questioned its constitutionality. Warner lashed back with, "What the hell is your problem, Doyle? Are you not a loyal employee and American citizen?"

"I am, Mr. Warner."

"Take the damn oath then."

"Why should I? Words and a signature are supposed to prove my loyalty? What about hard work, and good conscience?"

Even Warner's balding head turned red. "Let me tell you something. I've had my share of loyal employees. Remember Rin Tin Tin?

"The German shepherd?"

"Insolent mutt mongrel is what he was, our hero on the screen, our biggest draw at the time. Spent a lot of money on that four-legged bastard. You know what happened when I took the son of a bitch out on a publicity tour?"

"No idea, sir."

"Bit me on the ass, and I promised myself I will never get bitten again. I fired him."

"You fired a dog?"

"I did. Fired and escorted off the lot. Nobody will ever bite Jack Warner again. Not Flynn. Not Cagney," he screamed, "or Davis and certainly not that runt of humanity, Raft. No actor, ever. Period. And I'll be damned, if I'll allow any writer to do the same. You take that Loyalty Oath, Doyle, and sign it. All of you."

Warner stomped back to his office, and such was the legend of Warner v. Doyle.

This day, though, one screenplay occupied Walker's blotter. One hundred and twenty pages, about two hours of melodrama bound with trade string and prefaced with a memorandum, stared back at him. His instructions were to have it edited and ready by early afternoon. The title sheet said *She Went Too Far.*

With his jacket on the back of his chair, his beaten and scuffed leather Platt briefcase stowed next to his feet, Walker selected a blue pencil from his cup and returned to the first page. He read it, oblivious to the conversations around him. Writers in his neighborhood smoked and drank and talked or did all three at their desks while they worked. Walker could find nothing to cut. Walker's concentration broke when he heard chewing gum snap and crackle next to him.

"A real dog, ain't she?" the gum-chewer said.

"Come again."

"*She Went Too Far*. The script there in your hands is a dog."

"I wouldn't know. I'm trying to read it."

"Don't think we've met. Name is Terry Doyle."

"Walter Thompson."

Terry kept talking through the handshake and name exchange. He turned his chair around and straddled it. "Not from around here, are you? I mean, you're not a born-and-bred Californian."

"No, guess not. Sorry to disappoint you, Mr. Doyle."

"No need to apologize. Nearly everyone here is from someplace else."

"Is it that obvious?" Walker said with a mischievous smirk.

"What's obvious is the large basset eyes and your long face. Don't worry, all the new guys around here look like that until their probationary period is over, and that's when you should worry." He cracked gum again. "Allow me to mangle the metaphor further. The honeymoon nears its end in two weeks when it's time to move from the bedroom to the kitchen and see what you can cook. How am I doing so far?"

"Overcooked the metaphor, Mr. Doyle. Stick to similes; they're easier."

"What's with the Mr. Doyle? No need for formality, Walter. Can I call you Walter?" Terry didn't wait for a response. "You're probably wondering what you have to do next to get the brass nameplate on your desk."

"It has crossed my mind."

Terry snapped his gum again. And again. Those sharp sounds didn't distract any of the other writers. "Let me make it easy for you, kid," Terry said. "Open up to the first page."

"She Went Too Far?"

"What else could I be talking about? The title is a clue." He motioned to the bound screenplay with his pointer finger. "Read the first few lines, and you tell me what you think." The man craned his head to read the page with Walker. "How does it begin?"

"With a voice-over."

"Blue-line it. Kill it. X the whole block of text. Trust your new friend, Terry."

Walker marked the text with a big blue X. He wondered why Terry was palling with him.

"There you go. A nice fat X. Terry's first rule: trim the fat."

"Why?"

Terry chose not to answer. He asked for and received the screenplay from Walker, spread the bound pages against his chair, and continued chewing while he slashed text with a blue pencil from behind his ear. Terry's eyes did typewriter's carriage returns while his mouth issued noise. After a few minutes at the purge, he said, "The reason to nix the voice-over is because they're passé; they tell the audience how evil and corrupt the city is. Doesn't work. Clichéd and irrelevant, if the director has a good cameraman. We should start the story another way."

"What do you suggest?" Walker asked.

"Always read your story from front to back before you do any edits. The voice-over here is nonsense; the city isn't a character. Moviegoers live in the real world; they already know how cruel and indifferent city streets are, so let the opening camera shot set the mood. Audiences are interested in people, in relationships. This story is about a gorgeous girl gone wrong for the right reasons, right?"

"Right," Walker said.

"Find her character arc first. A story can work in the first few pages and fall apart at the end. Open with action that reveals her character, so the audience sympathizes with her from the get-go. No wasting time with set-up and..."

"You've read this script?"

"We've all read the script, Walter. *She Went Too Far* is an inside joke around here. They use it here as your final exam." Terry displayed the front page to Walker for him to read the title again. "This screenplay is nothing more than a skills test, my friend. This film will never get made. Here, I penciled in all the changes and you can write in some suggestions. Study what I did, and you'll pass."

Walker fanned the pages and saw blue slashes and a word here and there scattered throughout the text, while Terry continued chewing gum. Edits reduced the text to ninety pages, about ninety minutes of story.

"Some editing," Walker said. "Thought my job was to write?"

"Studio writing is formula, or variations on themes. This drama, for distance, is about a tough girl; she's either bad or she hides her heart of gold. No ambiguity. If the protagonist is male then the female is his downfall. Let's see...variation on a theme is good girl falls from grace...hard luck story, or she has a nervous breakdown, drinks too much, murders someone, or becomes too indiscriminate with her affections, despite the interventions of friends, family, and the sap who's been in love with her since childhood. Classic Awards material. Never fails. Your job is to make the studio money. Half the time, the director and the actors have their own ideas. Those edits there," he pointed to the booklet, "show the studio you have an eye for economy with words and Warner's wallet."

Terry turned his chair around and sat in it proper. Walker saw no need to work Doyle. He learned in the field, in Vienna, the talker-types did all the work for him.

"Keep *She Went Too Far* as the title?" Walker asked.

"Sure. Warner wants his films to have morals. Our girl here went too far, so the title is a warning. She's feminine in love, but masculine when she wants revenge. Too far is when she tells the audience, 'You had your chance. I'm taking what's mine now.' Can't have that; Warner won't have it. A woman can't say, 'The hell with your rules.' You're a big boy, Walter. You know why."

Walker nodded slowly. "Because in the real world and in make-believe, a woman who violates the rules pays the price," he said, thinking of Leslie in Vienna.

"Bingo." Terry snapped and cracked his gum.

"Anyway, thanks for this," Walker said. "Economy aside, I'm still worried there's no writing. I was hired to write."

"Don't write; think of it as you make suggestions," Terry said. "Look around you," he said, moving his hand like an emperor with his kingdom before him. "You're in a room of writers. Think there's any originality in this beehive? Before they ask you to create material, you have to learn the rules." Terry winked. "Thing is, we don't discuss them here because it's like actors discussing *Macbeth*. It's bad luck. Read, edit, and suggest. I use the acronym RES, also Latin for matter, as real as concrete and not the abstract. Give yourself time, but learn the rules fast."

Terry pointed to the screenplay on Walker's desk. "Hand that in, and you'll have your nameplate next week. Like I said, Warner will never make *She Went Too Far* in a million years. Besides, he's too busy experimenting with other ideas."

"Experimenting...what ideas?"

"Warner is paranoid about television. He's exploring some screen gimmick called 3D. Camera tricks. The man will do anything to herd eyeballs away from television. It's not the first time he's been obsessed with a trend. Last time, he sold off cartoons."

"What did Harry Warner have to say about the sell-off?"

"Him and Harry are at each other's throats night and day, like Cain and Abel, except there's no God for a referee."

"When three brothers start a picture studio, you'd expect family drama,"

Walker said for levity. Terry's face turned sober as one of the stone faces on Easter Island.

"The Warner Brothers aren't family," he answered in a low voice. "More like gangsters fighting over turf. I'm going outside for a smoke. Join me?"

"Don't smoke, but I'll keep you company. You seem to know a lot about this studio."

"Stick with me, Walter, and I'll show you the way around here."

"Like a protégé, or something? Teach me all the rules."

"Yeah, I'll teach you the rules."

Outside the white building, Terry struck a match and lit his cigarette. Near their feet was a sand bucket. Walker saw the nosedives of other cigarettes wedged into the gritty surface, but some hadn't made it. Their owners simply snubbed them and left tarry streaks on the white pavement. Walker recalled a similar signature left behind by a flamethrower. While Terry smoked, Walker enjoyed the sway of the palm trees in the breeze. A man across the way waved at Terry, and he waved back.

"That's the Columbia lot, and he's a writer I know," Terry said.

"Thought Columbia was the enemy."

"We're only enemies if we believe Warner and the moguls. Writers are like stocks; they're traded between studios, Walter. Quicker you learn that the longer you'll survive this racket. It's no secret writers go back and forth between the studios when needed, but nobody talks about it. It's an unspoken rule in the rulebook—the Writer's Rulebook and not the Studio one. You are an asset, my man, so do your best to manage your fate and value."

Terry's long drag on the cigarette, the way he savored the inhalation, didn't make Walker crave smoke. He lost the habit in Vienna when thugs tied him to a chair and interrogated him under a pendant light. Another assignment, another mess he's fallen into for Jack.

"Can you give me an example from the Studio Rulebook?" he said to Terry.

"October of 1945, the Battle of Burbank." Terry's eyes narrowed as he exhaled. "Set decorators and union members declared a strike, which turned into a riot. Fights and blood, a real nasty mess. Lesson from the rulebook? Never complain about the job. Ever hear about the strike?"

"I was overseas at the time."

"Right. The war and then Dachau. I heard."

"How did you…never mind."

"I hear things, like Warner has you earmarked for a pet project. I don't know the exact details, but the grapevine says it's a war picture."

"You really do have your ear to the ground, don't you?"

Terry's smile denoted pride. "Maybe you and Dachau inspired him, though I don't see a film on Dachau happening." Terry neared the end of his cigarette. "Not the right time for allegory. You do that film decades after the fact when everyone feels safe." Terry jutted his chin. "You see that lot over there?"

"Columbia?" Walker answered. He didn't have to look; he studied everything Jack had sent him. He'd let Terry narrate this tour, repeat the contents of the dossier Jack had sent to him, like an eager docent at the art museum.

"Columbia belongs to Harry Cohn, a meaner son of a bitch than Jack Warner. The one thing Jack and Harry have in common is they're Jews and hide it. Some say the moguls went along with the Nazis when they came to power because they were worried about losing the German market. Business is business, right? The moguls put religion in the bottom drawer. Cohn over there has two pictures in his office to prove how all-American he is. One picture is him with J. Edgar Hoover, and the other one? With Cardinal Spellman."

"And what did Warner do to show he was patriotic?"

Terry kicked a pebble out of the way and flicked his cigarette towards the sand bucket. He hit the rim but missed nonetheless. Terry rested against the wall behind him.

"Hoover talked Warner into producing *Confessions of a Nazi Spy*. Film cost and lost Warner a fortune, but he recouped it with *Sergeant York*, but then came along *Mission to Moscow*, and Warner exacted his revenge."

"Against Hoover?"

"That, and for doing *Moscow* at FDR's request, which put him in the hot seat with his Republican friends, who accused him of being soft, pro-Communist, and pro-FDR. Talk about double negatives. Warner's own brother Harry took a swing at him over that picture. But Jack Warner kept score; he remembered the unions, remembered all the grief they caused him, remembered the backlash on *Confessions,* so when HUAC called him up, he spouted off twelve names as payback, which is why I can see he thinks he can get away with doing a Nazi film. With McCarthy's Commie hunt, Warner is dead wrong. Don't see it happening."

"Warner named names to HUAC?"

"Named four of the Hollywood Ten, and he saved his sharpest arrow in the quiver for Howard Koch."

Terry let the name sink in. Walker recognized the name as the writer for *Sergeant York,* but he picked another film. "*Casablanca*'s Koch?"

"One and the same, and the man Warner blamed for the Burbank Strike. Anyway, the studio went on to produce a few anti-war projects after Warner's HUAC Award performance for 1947. More writers were called up as a result of his little speech, and some were threatened; a few lost their jobs. But you know what? Films still got written and done."

"Writers write," Walker answered him.

Terry nudged his arm. "Writers write. I like that; if only it were so simple. Hey, I meant to ask, where do you live?"

Walker lied. "Downtown LA. Renting until I find something local."

"I know some digs. Simple living. There are some cheap bungalows south of Mariposa and Magnolia. I know the landlord of some apartments near Alameda if you're interested. Let me know."

Walker said nothing. He nodded to indicate thanks. An apartment would free up time and keep him close to the assignment. Walker rolled around the words 'digs' and 'simple living' in his head, and the postcard his imagination delivered was a stucco walkway as faux marble to a bland exterior, or what Californians called adobe, fronted by faded grass and weeds.

Walker noticed a man across the way. Decent suit, though a bit big on him, which no amount of tailor's magic could fix, and he walked fast, nervous fast, and with determination etched into his face. "Columbia man?" Walker asked Terry.

"No, he's one of us."

"Haven't seen him before."

"Lucky you," Terry said with a sigh. "See that empty desk this morning?" Walker nodded. "Thought you would. You're an observant man, Walter, and that'll take you far as a writer. Anyway, the desk is his. My advice is that you stay far away from him, unless you own a good life insurance policy. His name is Irving Hackett."

"Is he trouble?"

"Did Truman drop the bomb?" Terry said. "Just remember his name for now, so you can forget it later. Let's call it an unofficial amendment in the rulebook."

"I'd like to learn more about the rulebook."

"The one for us writers or the studio version?"

"I'll need both, won't I?"

"Smart man. I'll meet you inside."

Walker, as Walter Thompson, the writer, scanned the sky and saw the mild haze had burned off, and he could see the Verdugo Hills. Everything was blue and sunny, bright and clear again. It didn't matter whether you called them hills or mountains because everyone here was writing the music close to the fault line.

Chapter Seven

"Is Dr. Ernest in yet?"

"Not yet, Miss Gardner.

"Thank you, Mr. Edwards. The usual stop, please."

Leslie disliked calling Phillip Ernest 'doctor' because it was unethical and misleading. Mr. Edwards, the Otis elevator operator, raised his cap when he answered her. Edwards was an elderly man, congenial to his passengers. He opened and closed wire-mesh panels and then the regular doors with a distinctive professionalism. He controlled the motor with a deft wrist and could tell you the feet-per-minute speed, if asked. He delivered his passengers with such precision the elevator's floor was always smooth and continuous with its destination. The courteous Mr. Edwards offered his assistance with any packages, and provided suggestions, when asked, about the best and affordable places for lunch or a decent cup of coffee.

Leslie found him pleasant and, in a queer way, endearing. On occasion, she'd bring him coffee or, for a special surprise, a doughnut from Kindle's on Normandie. Warmed to her, the ride up to the top floor to Ernest's office would begin in silence, then he would whistle a tune, which always made her smile.

"Hasn't Dr. Ernest given you a key yet, Miss Gardner?"

"No, he hasn't because I'm temporary help. Maybe he'll give me one when my trial period is over."

"I sure hope so, miss, and a raise accompanies it. Twelfth floor is your stop. Have yourself a good day." The man lifted his cap again before he closed the doors to his contraption.

She was early. Punctuality was part of the cover. Establish a routine, show up on time, and behave like a reliable employee. Appear like a normal girl Friday, and please the mark. Fit into the office as Miss Margaret Gardner.

Phillip Ernest, for his part, responded in typical masculine fashion. The Ph.D. did not set him apart from the male herd. The degree conferred on him a more expansive vocabulary, but he remained true to his half of the species. Miss Gardner soon slipped to Margaret and then Maggie. Formality, on his part, degenerated faster than Rome. Within two weeks, she was running his errands to the bank, dropping them off, and collecting his dry cleaning. All part of the plan, she repeated to herself.

The keys to the office and cabinets. They were next on her list. She didn't have them and she needed them. Ernest kept three filing cabinets in his office. Locked the entire day. Leslie remembered what she had read and typewritten from the doctor's handwritten notes, but any other proof was inside those green cabinets. Two tasks Ernest performed himself; he destroyed his handwritten notes, and he filed the client folders she typed at the end of the day.

Minutes later, she heard the elevator door open behind her, the sounds of Mr. Edwards and Ernest's voices. She heard the soft shuffle of his Oxfords next. He said hello without looking at her. Head down, his hand searched his pocket for the door key. She stepped aside for him to put the key in.

The metallic clatter against the doorframe told her he had more than one key, although she'd never seen the keyring. Ernest was not casual about his personal items, whether it was the key, his notes, or one of his prized pens. He marked the number of pages he gave her for typewriting and numbered the final copy. He habitually checked his jacket pocket for his pen. Ernest was all methodical coldness, she concluded, like water ready to freeze in January, except this was LA, and summer was coming. There was one other thing about him once he was inside his office.

"You look especially nice today, Maggie."

There it was, she told herself. Standard male. She hadn't even made it to her desk before he made a comment about her appearance. First thing in the morning, too. A compliment was a compliment but Ernest delivered it like an awkward student, more familiar with books and his own hands. It could've been amusing, but it wasn't.

"Vera Williams should arrive soon. Nine a.m. appointment. I'll take my coffee in my office."

"Yes, Dr. Ernest."

Miss Vera Williams was a star. Past tense. They called her the Platinum V, and she loved every insinuation in the name. As a child, she emulated her mother, a failed actress turned successful writer who worked with Lois Weber and Frances Marion, two pioneers among the forgotten women directors in early Hollywood. A few scandalous love affairs, one divorce, and approaching an unsubstantiated age in her fourth decade, Vera discovered the roles went to newer flesh and traveled curves.

Leslie recognized the name from the progress notes she typed. Vera had been relegated to the has-been pile, a musty fume like those mimeographed sheets the schoolmarms handed their students. When the tabloids and society pages lacked material, they would ring out her name in a salacious register. Now and then, the public wanted her, and the studios would offer her a role. Nothing ever panned out. Her career in rigor mortis, Vera suffered from depression.

Vera arrived and entered the office, minutes before nine for her hourly session. For a woman of glamour, she played against type, in Happy Jill dungarees and a buttoned-up plaid shirt. The ensemble suggested housework, but Leslie found it honest and unpretentious. For all the cynical stories about Hollywood, Vera hung her purse on the coat-rack hook, innocent and trusting.

An hour later.

Vera emerged transformed into an effusive and happy woman. Ernest, hands in his pockets, appeared content with his masterpiece. Leslie waited at her desk to collect payment after the doctor closed his door. Vera peeled off two twenty-dollar bills, waiting for change. Fifteen dollars.

"Say, your name is Margaret, right?" Leslie handed over a ten and a five, after she returned the lockbox to her second desk drawer and sat down to listen to Vera say, "I don't mean to sound forward, dear, but there's a nice quality to your voice. Distinctive and charming."

"It's called an accent."

"I'm sorry, but I intended it as a compliment."

"I know you did, Miss Williams. Thank you."

"Where are you from?"

"England."

"I was there once, in another life. Must've been difficult for you during the war years. All those horrible bombs and air-raid sirens."

Leslie feigned a smile to suggest British politeness, as if to say unpleasant topics were not discussed. She hadn't spent the war making tea or hiding in the Underground during The Blitz. Vera prolonged her stare. The woman's eyes, nice as they were, unsettled Leslie.

"Is there something else I can do for you, Miss Williams?"

"Vera, please. Could you stand up for me, please?"

Leslie found herself complying. "I don't quite understand Miss… Vera."

"Turn around. Yes, that's it. Anyone ever tell you that you have a lovely figure, Maggie?" That name again, Leslie thought. He had her doing it, too. "Peach pencil skirt, spring blouse, nice bosom, subtle makeup, nice bone structure."

Leslie sat down, uncomfortable from the physical evaluation. Vera reached for a piece of paper from her desk without asking and scribbled something.

"Here is my phone number. Do call me. I'd like to take you out to dinner."

Leslie examined the writing, read the exchange. Lincoln Heights. Money.

Vera caught the appraisal in her eyes. "My apartment in town. My home is in the hills, on Mulholland."

"Vera, I can't. Work, you understand. You're asking me out for a dinner date."

"A date that happens to include dinner, yes. I'd like to help you."

"Help me? With what?" Leslie said, intrigued and surprisingly, flattered.

Vera leaned over and whispered. "I think the doctor is planning to ask you out. I know just the dress for you."

Leslie surprised herself, finding herself whispering back, "Really?"

"I know my men." Vera winked, pointed to the piece of paper, and walked out.

After the next patient and the ritual of payment and departure repeated itself, the doctor's door opened. Ernest came out, and Leslie handed him the typewritten pages from Vera's session inside one of his patient folders. He thanked her, holding the folder in front of his chest.

"Maggie…I was wondering whether you are free Friday night or not?"

"Free for what?" she answered, wanting him to suffer like a schoolboy. "What did you have in mind?"

"Dinner at six. I'll pick the club."

Interesting. He doesn't say when or where to meet him before dinner. He might add those details after her acceptance. He didn't. Ernest turned to his office. "Wait," he stopped to say, "How about you impress me in something slinky and black for our night on the town? I'll make it worth your while, I promise."

Deflated. Disgusted. She smiled nonetheless. "I'll see what I can do."

"Great. Thanks."

All that education, and he's an amateur, she thought as the door closed. She recalled the last man who custom-ordered the fashion, the evening, and other details. He liked Rita Hayworth. Leslie dyed her hair red for him. He liked nylons with a certain pattern. She wore them. He wanted to tango. They did. Part of another plan, too. She needed information from him.

Difference between then and now is he was an SS officer and Ernest, an LA psychotherapist. The man she remembered spoke German with the Führer and Himmler. Phillip Ernest, Ph.D., had Hollywood's ear and used Freud's German in translation. That's all right, she told herself. Ernest didn't need to know his secretary, his girl Friday was fluent in Czech, German, French, and knew a smattering of Russian.

There was another difference, too.

Leslie played secretary before. Hours before another high-ranking SS officer was scheduled to interrogate a Resistance member at a secluded location, she arrived and convinced the guards she was a secretary authorized to record the prisoner's preliminary testimony. When the SS officer arrived, he found two dead guards and an empty room.

Leslie read Vera's number again. It might be fun to pick out a dress and even more fun to discover what else Vera knew about the charming doctor.

47

Chapter Eight

"There he is," Terry whispered. Walker leaned in for a look, but Terry stopped him. "Don't be so obvious."

"Relax," Walker replied, knowing the man across the restaurant had seen them. Terry walked alongside Walker, moved through the crowd with him toward Joe Teague's table.

Boy's night out at Slapsy Maxie's, now called Billy Gray's Band Box, on Wilshire, was Terry's idea. Terry said people in town had to see the new writer, Walter Thompson. Terry remarked the club's original name was the marriage of a character from Damon Runyon with a washed-up boxer and "Whatever you do, Walter, don't try to flatter him. Joe dislikes insincerity."

They approached the table and Terry introduced him. Joe Teague remained sitting. Terry and Walker apparently didn't merit handshakes. Teague, however, indicated with his cigarette they could sit opposite him. Terry excused himself to use the restroom.

"Terry says you're the new addition at Warner."

Walker sized up Teague. Sitting down, the man in the white dinner jacket was at least six-foot standing. Smoked left-handed. Starched shirt. Shirt studs matched the black cufflinks. Bowtie butterflied. Elegant. Irish last name matched the dark wiry eyebrows above gray eyes, and below the nest of styled hair, the starving immigrant's face had vanished a generation ago. Two drinks waited in front of Teague. Black coffee, the aroma so strong Walker's heart quivered. The other drink was a snifter of brandy, large enough to hold a goldfish inside it, and the vintage probably cost a week's pay. Teague blew a silver veil of smoke across the table into Walker's face and said, "Done typing the exposition inside your head?"

"Not sure what you mean."

"Sure, you do," Teague's finger tapped ashes into an ashtray. "The best eyes in this town have marked me up. Some guys are so good at it they can guess my weight down to the ounce." He pointed at Walker with his lit cigarette, "Your eyes tell me you're no cop, but you're a man of some experience."

"Could be I'm just a writer, keen on observation."

"I'm a writer too. As for observation, you prefer being seen with Warner's mole?"

"Doyle seems all right."

Walker noticed Terry in the mirrors behind Teague, making his way back to the table. Teague didn't smile when their eyes met. "You notice everything," Teague said. "Here's some unsolicited advice from one writer to another, by way of two stories."

The man used his cigarette like a prop to indicate Billy Gray's, "There are two tales about this club and its former owner, the boxer Max Rosenbloom. Story one says George Raft discovered Max one day in a street fight in East Harlem. Story two says Mickey Cohen discovered Max. Which one do you think is the truth?"

"I'll go with Cohen. Always go with money. This club looks like a place Mickey would enjoy. Enough glitz and glamour to hide dirt."

Teague's smile ended when Terry sat down. A waiter appeared, and Terry ordered a drink for himself, and Walker added his own to the bill. Teague passed on refreshing or replacing his drinks.

"Walter here is new to the Pool," Terry said. "On the regular payroll next week."

"Congratulations." Teague stubbed out his cigarette.

"You said you were a writer," Walker said to Teague. "You're not a regular at the Pool, so I assume you're for special projects."

"You're direct," Teague said. "A quality I admire." Teague scripted another smile, stopping to light another cigarette with a handsome lighter from his breast pocket. "Do me a favor, Terry. Get me a pack of smokes from one of the concession girls."

"Yeah, sure, Joe," Terry said, his glance at Walker ambiguous, either annoyed that Teague dismissed him as an errand boy, or impressed Teague wanted alone time with the new writer. Teague waited until Terry was several feet away.

"Let me tell you another story, Walter. This one involves a famous screenwriter, Mickey Cohen, and our recurring boxer, Slapsy Rosenbloom. All three men held a fundraiser last year for the state of Israel, not unlike the one Slapsy did before with a promoter named Sam Rosoff before the Stock Market Crash." Teague exhaled smoke away from Walker this time. "Come 1950, same fundraiser, different Public Relations man. Two hundred grand filled the coffers. None of it ever made it to Israel. Mickey claimed the ship was torpedoed. Imagine that."

"Imagine that. I don't know much about Israel or politics, Joe." Walker detected no twitch in Teague's eyebrows when he used the man's first name. "All I know about Mickey Cohen is he's having legal problems now, from the Kefauver Commission to tax evasion with the IRS and other headaches. I doubt Cohen still has a hand in PR. Legally, that is."

"I mentioned Raft and Cohen earlier."

"In your earlier parable about Slapsy, yes, and your point is?"

"In this town, you can believe either the Hollywood version or the other one. From my experience, the Hollywood cut is always easier to believe. Now, about your friend, Terry."

"The alleged mole?"

"Personally, Walter, I have no problem with Terry. Likeable guy and smart, too. The thing about a mole, though, is it likes dark places, it's blind, but a mole possesses a remarkable sense of smell. Terry is good at smelling opportunities, at fronts, and some of them should be left alone. My advice to you is be careful of the dark places. Have a look at your friend Terry."

Walker glanced up and checked the mirrored reflection. Terry had stopped to talk with a heavyset man dressed in a dark double-breasted suit. The shirt was white. The cufflinks sparkled when the light caught them right. His ensemble appeared dapper and debonair, except for the dead fish of a tie on his belly. He had knotted it too early, so it fell short of both belly button and belt buckle.

"The gentleman Terry is talking to," Teague said, "is a generous donor. A Republican."

"A man's brand of politics is no crime," Walker said.

"Man is with the local Loyalty Board, a member of the Legion, and his wife heads the local chapter of the Minute Women of the USA to support Senator McCarthy."

"I'm sorry if I don't grasp your point, Joe."

"Terry, the consummate diplomat, seems to have an eclectic and convenient group of friends, wouldn't you say?"

With perfect timing, Terry appeared with a fresh pack of cigarettes. "I was talking to the cigarette girl," he said, "and she told me Lou Costello discovered Dean Martin and Jerry Lewis in this club."

"I heard different," Teague said. Another soft exhalation. "I heard Frank Sinatra discovered them one night here with Mickey Cohen."

Teague stood up. "I'd best leave now, gentlemen. And Walter…remember what I said. He took bills from his billfold and placed them on the table. He raised his hand for the waiter to see him. "The next round is on me, boys, since Terry went for cigarettes. Night."

Terry waited before he asked, "What happened between you two?"

* * *

At Vera's place, Leslie entered a vestibule the size of her apartment. Dark marble flooring glistened with specks of white where she expected the blood of a Roman senator, and against the far wall was a little boy in ceramic with his not-so-innocent part passing water into a pool at his feet. A stark whiteness shone down from the overhead light, bright enough a suspect would confess to the crime.

Leslie saw the doorknob turn. The door opened.

In a silver dress, Vera could still turn heads. Office Vera was plain and modest, but Party Vera was sin. Small silver scallops ran, not stumbled, from about the knee, over a flat stomach, hugged her hips, and ended with two straps over nice shoulders above a contained bosom. A pendant, the stone as blue as the Atlantic Ocean inside a filigreed grasp, hung from a silver chain around her neck. Vera's platinum hair was parted to one side, swept back, her lips done in a light shade of pink, and her eyebrows teased and thinly touched with mascara. Seduction was one part Cleopatra and two parts Salomé.

A tall glass of iced water in her hand, she beckoned Leslie inside without saying a word. Actors didn't need them most of the time. Vera stepped aside, leaving Leslie a last moment of free will.

"So glad you called, dear."

"I wanted to take you up on your offer of finding the right dress."

Vera took another delicate sip. The ice tinkled.

"Don't tell me a girl like you needs an old horse like me to take down a man." The glass obscured Vera's mouth again. Leslie let the comment go into the air and complimented Vera on her décor.

There was a library of leather-bound books in several languages. Leslie hadn't expected that. Most actors, she assumed, didn't read anything more cerebral than a script and a signed check. Leslie felt ashamed because Vera's eyes told her she knew what she was thinking. "Beautiful, aren't they? You didn't expect them, did you?"

Leslie figured it best to admit it. No downcast eyes here. "I'm sorry."

"Don't be. In the old days, the studios gave an actor a real education. We were taught how to talk, how to walk, how to dance, and how to deliver our lines with conviction. We might've been property, but we were trained professionals held to high standards. Acting, we were instructed, was more than mouthing lines on a page. Today, I suppose they call it Method Acting. Don't kid yourself; we knew who Stanislavski was back in the Thirties. These new upstarts today think they're inventing the wheel. Revolutionaries, the critics call them. My eye, I say. It's all been done before. Go back to Sophocles, and I'm sure he had a Stanislavski in his group."

"Your library is impressive."

"Some French, some Italian titles because my ex-husband was a fan of opera, and I have some German for the opera and other dramatic works.

I forgot—some Spanish, too. How anyone can live in this state without learning some Spanish is pure ignorance. Care for a drink?"

"Water, please."

Vera held out her glass. "You didn't think this was gin or vodka, did you? One thing I learned was not to drink. Keeps your head clear and your legs closed. Too many women in this town use drink as an excuse for poor judgment. A few decades of that indulgence and your face goes, your figure goes with it. By that, I mean too much drinking, not too much sex. Don't smoke, either. It ruins the skin. My vice, if you must know, was sex."

"Past tense?" Leslie said. Deadpan as Eve Arden. "You said something to me at the doctor's office, something to the effect of, you know, your men."

"I did, and I do."

"Were you implying the doctor was interested in me?"

"He asked you out for an evening, didn't he?"

Leslie stalled. "Yes."

"Then I am vindicated, and it's safe to say he's interested in you."

"But why?"

Vera put the edge of the glass to her lips. "You're awfully coy, aren't you?" The glass came off those pink lips but left no hint of lipstick. "We should go. I've made a reservation for us at Windsor."

"The French restaurant on West 7th Street?"

The Windsor was French elegance of dark wood and red leather booths. Ben Dimsdale ran the establishment, designed the menu, and collected the hefty price for the privilege of dining there. Forty-two dollars for filet de boeuf forestiere or, in English for the masses, larded tenderloin sauced in olive oil and served with a garnish of bacon and diced potatoes.

"Yes. You know it?" Vera asked.

"I know of it, but Vera, I'm embarrassed to say I can't afford it."

"I asked you out, Maggie. Both are my treat: late lunch and the dress. I insist."

Leslie didn't mind the doctor's contagious habit of calling her Maggie this time.

"Thank you."

"I know this is imprudent of me and a symptom of my being out of touch with so-called reality, but what does a secretary make these days?"

"Dollar twelve an hour," Leslie answered.

Leslie expected a dramatic wet mess, the glass and the ice falling to the floor. It would have taken Maggie nine months of office work to pay for her part of the meal at Windsor and more for the dress. Vera regained her composure. Her years of training in the studio came back to her like a reflex.

Chapter Nine

Walker clocked in early. The machine mounted on the wall thumped his time card. He had saved himself commuting time with a furnished bungalow near Verdugo Park. Terry's lead panned out well. The weekends were for Malibu.

Having arrived early enough, Walker made his own coffee. He started the office pot for the other writers. Caffeine was a personal matter after Vienna. Walker disliked office coffee, the mass-produced swill, the pot of water with a brown crayon dropped in. Coffee should be blacker than hell and memorable as love. He had purchased a Chemex flask, some square filters, a bag of coffee, dollar a pound from a specialty shop in Little Italy in Lincoln Heights, for his choice brew. He thought of Vienna cafés while the water trickled down. He thought of Sheldon, the man who hunted Nazis.

At his desk Walker read Louella Parsons's article first, and then a scandal sheet he picked up on the way into the studio. The cover showed a risqué photograph of some unknown starlet from behind, bent over to do her eyelashes in a mirror. The stockings were mid-thigh, garters with the clips beneath a girdle that shimmered something metallic under the photographer's explosive bulb. The photo seemed staged. Some poor actress needed the job and the cash. He thumbed through some pages. The garish cover scheme, the colors of blue, red, and yellow begged for a reaction.

Terry walked in, saw the magazine, and the pretend photograph of the girl caught immodest and suppressed his commentary. Too early to make a statement before he had his coffee.

Office coffee mug in hand, Terry said, "I see you've discovered the highpoint of journalism. For twenty-cents at the newsstand you can enjoy the girl next door while you fake your interest in *Life* or *Time*. Makes a statement for our intellectual quiescence, eh?"

Walker took a sip. "It's early for five-dollar words, Terry."

"And yet you're here early."

"I have a tree of paperwork to prune." Walker didn't lean his head to the stack of bound paperwork on his desk. Every writer had their share of real estate. Terry raised his cup to toast Walter Thompson, the newest talent at the Pool.

"Ah, the wonderful world of editing, and you're in early to build the beaver lodge by yourself. Admirable, Walter, but at the end of the day, they'll drop another stack on your desk. Ever hear of Tantalus?"

"Wasn't he the guy who tried to drink, but every time he bent down for a sip, the water escaped him?"

"He's you, but with coffee instead. Moral of the story: pace the work, and don't get attached to it. You'll get depressed if the story you love isn't made."

"Any other advice?"

"More of a warning than wisdom: Warner's security man is making the rounds. Warner is back on the wagon with Loyalty Oaths."

"Thought you put that to bed with the Battle of the Long Hallway."

"You heard about that?" Terry sat upright in his chair. "Never mind." His face was paler than his white shirt, and his black tie hung loosely knotted under his collar. Walker was ready to ask when Terry said, "You have nothing to hide, Walter, whereas I've made enemies."

"What enemies? Warner fired a dog but kept you on. As for the Pool, every office has its jealous types. You have solid skills and performance, Terry. You've got nothing to worry about."

"I have enemies," Terry repeated himself, this time with the seriousness of a Greek chorus.

"Who?"

"Joe Teague, for one. Bernie, Warner's mole, told me about Warner's clearance man."

"Funny you mention Joe, because he said you were the mole."

"Teague said that?"

"He did, and he mentioned something about fronts, but I never got around to asking you what that meant because I figured you were sore about fetching him cigarettes."

"Joe really thinks I'm a mole?"

There was silence and a soft "Joe said that, huh?" Terry's blue eyes widened like clear seas, and the weather on his face changed from pink to red. Walker thought of another rule from a rulebook, one that sailors used: 'Red sky at night, sailor's delight. Red sky in morning, sailor's warning.' Walker waited for the calm before he pressed again. "Tell me what Joe meant by fronts."

"I've meant to discuss them with you, honest, but I thought you needed more time to get yourself acclimated here. Geez, you just earned your nameplate, Walt, and here you are asking me about fronts. Talk about pacing yourself."

"Acclimated? A lifetime in this place wouldn't be enough time, Terry. All the personalities, these never-ending scripts, the bad writing, and Warner…"

"I'm no mole, and I'm no rat. Honest."

"Why would Joe Teague say it then?"

Walker tapped his pencil. He stopped when the eraser touched the blotter the twentieth time. Terry leaned forward, and Walker joined him in a conspiratorial huddle, the two of them, piles of scripts like sandbags, and the lingering smell of black coffee around them.

"The guys who get listed, the ones HUAC sends to purgatory…they can't work, you see, or at least at face value, they can't walk into the Pool, like us, sit down and write. For most of these guys, writing is their whole life; it's all they've ever known. They lose their job, and what do they do?"

"I don't know. What do they do?"

"Like you said once, and I quote, 'writers write.' These guys write using a pseudonym. The new name is their front."

"Pseudonym, as in alias?"

Walker liked the word alias better because it implied danger and secrecy. Pseudonym sounded genteel, pretentious, even aristocratic, as in Baroness Orczy. Nom de plume reeked of someone with silk stockings and powdered wig, and in need of a hobby. Alias implied you had to hide.

"Yeah, alias works, too. But here's the thing about fronts, Walter. Everyone in the studios knows it. Good writers leave their signature."

"You mean style."

"More than that," and this time, Walker noticed a brightness to Terry's eyes, as he explained himself. "The great ones, you know, because you can turn to any page, run your finger down to a line of dialogue, read it, and you know exactly which character spoke the line. That's a great writer. Once you fall into the story, today or tomorrow, or years from now, you pick a page and a line, and you can name the character without reading another word or refreshing the context; everything comes back to you: story and all. Those are the writers I'm talking about."

"You're saying they just use another name and continue writing, and everyone looks the other way?"

"Sure, and why not? A blacklisted writer has three choices." Terry counted finger one. "Write for television, and you know how Jack Warner feels about that." Finger number two. "He can go to Europe or back east and write for theatre. Broadway. Third choice is move to Mexico or some jerkwater town and keep his expenses low, be invisible, and write from behind a front."

It made sense.

Terry wasn't finished. "Use a front or do jail time or name names. Sing and fat chance, you're rehabilitated like the Russians call it, because it's suicide, a bullet in the head. You're on the hook as a HUAC rat. Remember when I mentioned Burbank '45?"

Walker thought back to his first few days in the Pool, to their first conversation and the final exam of the script. "Yeah, you told me about bad blood and riots and—"

"I told you scripts still got written and delivered on time. When the labor issues settled down, the Production Department rolled forward like nothing ever happened."

"Strike or not, fronts wrote scripts," Walker said, adding, "and Jack Warner knew it. He'd win either way."

"Not just Warner but all the moguls. It's all about money, like I said when you asked about writing, Walter."

"Cynical but effective. Still, why would Joe say you're a mole?"

"Because he has it all wrong. Bernie is the mole, Bernie is Jack Warner's ear to the ground and walls around here for Reds, or union problems."

"But, Terry, the way Joe talked, he implied you were something, if not a mole, or a rat. Something."

"I'm something," Terry pushed in closer and rubbed his fingers together. Universal sign for money. "I'm one of the guys between the studio and the fronts. Call me the ambassador."

"One of the guys? Are there others?"

"Charlie Loew. A go-between, like me, except he was also a script doctor, a great writer."

"Name sounds familiar," Walker said. "Loew?" He released the lure, feigned amnesia, and then snapped his fingers. "The guy found dead downtown? Papers said he was a Commie."

"Charlie was no Communist. He was the second son of Capitalism, after Edison. If Charlie could've patented the recipe for ice cubes, we'd all be paying him a nickel. Charlie was the front of the train, the cowcatcher, to and from fronts for Warner."

"Think another front killed him, or someone in the studios wanted a script bad enough to off him?"

"I doubt it," Terry said, bending the tip of his nose with his finger. "Charlie had friends. Call it insurance. He knew Cohen before Mickey came out West to keep an eye on Bugsy Siegel for the Syndicate. Charlie from Chicago was no dummy. He paid up on insurance after Burbank '45, after he saw how the moguls squashed the strike."

Walker played another idea. "Perhaps Loew was greedy, or he ran afoul of Mickey Cohen, and one of Cohen's boys pulled the trigger?"

"Mickey is too busy juggling a hornet's nest with the government problems on his hands. His number-two, Johnny Stomps, is illiterate. You couldn't interest him in a script unless it had legs and a rack. The less the script talked, the more two-syllable words it used, the more Johnny might understand it, but he knows numbers. Why bump Charlie? He was a bank, a gold mine on two legs, and Charlie had no beef with Warner, Cohen, or anybody else, so long as his part of the lawn was watered and kept green. Your guess is as good as mine as to why someone killed him."

"Not a Communist, not Cohen, then a desperate writer?" Walker said.

"It's possible, but why kill your paycheck? I'm no detective, and neither are you, Walter, so leave the case to the private dicks and the homicide detectives. You're out of our element."

"How 'bout I meet some of these fronts? It's inevitable, right?"

"Let me think about it, Walter. Timing is a bit queer now. I could introduce you to a few, but you best focus on this clearance man Warner hired first."

"Aw, c'mon Terry. This is exciting stuff. I could learn a few things. It'd be nice to know the name behind the name."

"Suppose it couldn't hurt. Here," Terry said, writing out an address with a pen from his breast pocket.

"Nice pen there, Terry. Ballpoint?"

"Yeah, beautiful, isn't she? Argentinean. I don't care for the ink, though. Silver isn't my color."

Terry clicked his expensive pen. Other writers milled in from their commute and began their hunt for coffee and desk.

"Nice," Walker said. "Where did you get it?"

"Hate to admit it, but I stole it from a shrink."

"You see a shrink, Terry? I would've never guessed."

"Everyone needs someone."

"Does it help with your problems? Talking to someone."

"Problem? Only problem I have is a mild case of kleptomania."

Terry pocketed his expensive pen, quiet as a banker who foreclosed on a property.

Chapter Ten

He suggested drinks Friday night at the Cocoanut Grove, with dinner afterwards. The weekend wasn't quite on the horizon but the doctor's voice insinuated he had intentions.

The Cocoanut Grove club was part of the Ambassador, and like most places in Los Angeles, it took forever to get from the curb to the front door of the hotel. Then there was the nightclub. The hotel, like a Henry James preamble, sat at the far end of a very long cultivated sentence of twenty-four acres off Wilshire Boulevard. The logic was deceptive but calculated, its geometric lawns and trained trees were way out in front like a mirage of color schemes, the designs descended from gardeners who created the Hanging Gardens of Babylon. It was here Bacchantes of another day and age descended from the Hollywood Hills or from elsewhere in the desert to have their Award ceremonies, sexed-up affairs on hearths of Italian stone, their celebrity tantrums, complete with champagne glasses dashed against tiled floors while the fountain's water out front pulsed the rhythm of time's cruel cadence.

The Cocoanut Grove was dedicated to nocturnal decadence. Palm trees were imported inside, stuffed monkeys sat on top of them, their choreographed arms groping the leafy foliage and their glass eyes forever gazing at a ceiling painted midnight blue with unmoving stars. Here, the desert people came to dance, forget their troubles, and mingle with matinée royalty. Here they dined and here they listened to music beneath Moorish arches and tried to forget the Crusades and the inconvenience of Christ on the cross. On a grand night they might see ghosts or the gauzy image of Pola

Negri walking her pet cheetah on a long leash through the garden.

Seven p.m. and early, Leslie saw Ernest at the bar in tailored silk pants and a patterned jacket, white shirt, and no tie. She might've walked fast across the floor to surprise him, but she enjoyed every set of male eyes (and some female ones, too) on her in a strapless cocktail dress made of plush black velvet and layers of cream tulle. Leslie didn't believe in makeup. Simple pink lipstick sufficed. In her small purse she carried cash and a .22 caliber pistol, a gift with a red Croix de Lorraine on the white grip enamel. Neither the gun nor the caliber punched like a .45 automatic, but at close range the .22 was feminine and lethal.

"You're early, Dr. Ernest."

"Please call me Phillip, or Phil. A drink?"

"What are you having?"

"Stinger."

Brandy and crème de menthe. Upper-crust choice of either flyboys or college men. She motioned the bartender over with her gloved hand. He ambled over, a big man in a tuxedo. He offered his clientele cool stoicism while he made their drinks or dried glassware. He listened, or pretended to. His hand on the counter and the forward tilt at the shoulders signaled he was eager to take her order.

"An Old Fashioned, please."

The barkeep smiled when he set down her short tumbler not far from her date's Stinger. He put in the sugar cube and doused it with Angostura bitters, added water halfway up the sugar cube before he dropped ice cubes and added a shot and half of rye whiskey. He hitched a maraschino cherry on the back of an orange wedge.

The jazz musicians in the background burned through a slow number of horns and muted drums. He moved near her, and she smiled. She could smell his cologne. Not bad. Not overpowering. She wore no perfume. Leslie learned perfume always lingered in the air or on fabric. It left a trace, a damning signature. Phillip pushed the cocktail to her on a napkin.

"Quite the drink you have there."

"I can handle it." Let him think I'm easy prey. "So, Phillip, what do you suggest for dinner?"

"Place up in the Hills, exotic and with a spectacular view of the city if you don't mind Asian food."

"I'll give it a go. That's what the weekend is for."

"You're full of surprises, Maggie. Didn't figure you for the living type."

He realized his awkward turn of phrase. She saved him from embarrassment. "As opposed to the alternative?" she asked. "Don't worry, I know what you meant. You don't do so bad yourself." Awe and flattery always chipped a man down. "It can't be easy listening to people's problems all week. Shows character."

"Nothing too challenging or anything I can't handle."

"You're saying you don't feel challenged?" she asked.

"Not at all. My patients are motivated, which is crucial to the therapeutic process, and I enjoy guiding them to recovery so they can live meaningful, productive lives."

"Say, ever had a client you couldn't help? Someone you couldn't fix."

"I've had my share of difficult cases, but I try to persuade them to see the destructive consequences of their choices," he said between sips of his minty drink.

Leslie drank a small sip of hers. "I never hear frustration in your notes. You're always clinical, very professional. I daresay you sound confident. Self-assured."

"You haven't seen all my cases, Maggie."

"Really?" she asked, letting him see her take a hefty gulp drink from her glass, turned so he saw more flesh. He responded with another sip of his toothpaste drink.

"I've had two, maybe three intractable cases. All men. One with inordinate guilt, the other one, a thief, and the last one was a deviant. The thief and deviant I thought I could cure, but not the guilty one. All three men kept company with people who exacerbated their conditions."

The doctor explained all of this as he paced his drinking until he emptied his glass. Leslie left a wee bit of drink in her glass. There was an uptick in the drums and the soft shudder of cymbals. A piano added light sprays of laughter from the high keys. Smoke floated over the crowd.

"I'm no clinician, Phillip, but I'm clueless as to what constitutes deviant behavior. As for criminal urges, I'd suggest an avoidance strategy. Not much I can say about regret. I've always thought guilt was a useless emotion."

"I wish it were so simple, Maggie."

"It is. The human mind confuses childhood with the responsibilities of adulthood."

The perplexed expression on his face arrived on time. "That sounds familiar," he said.

"It should, Phillip. I quoted you."

Quoting him had worked. He smiled, his shoulders rounded, and he leaned forward, and intent, relaxed. She savored that small victory more than the cherry clinging to the orange wedge on her glass.

"Shall we go eat?" she asked and deliberately misplaced her foot as she stepped off the metal chair. He caught her arm in time. She released that little laugh all women practiced for embarrassing moments. He left a generous bill to cover the drinks as the drum kicked the air with a one-two beat and a crash of cymbals.

Ernest drove the roads above Hollywood Boulevard to the restaurant. High up in the hills and under a half moon, The Mountain Palace rested on a hilltop like a shogun's castle carved out of teak and cedar. There was a pagoda, too. An architect plotted, a landscaper tilled the California hill into an enigmatic kōan with trees, shrubs, numerous gardens, and waterfalls. Koi fish meandered through ponds. The only thing missing was the plucking sound of the koto asking for rain.

Ernest recited his name and the time of his reservation to a tuxedo at a podium. The man snapped his fingers, and a waiter appeared and paraded them through a series of rooms with different-colored silks and tapestries, rooms of lacquer wood, rooms with kiri dragons under cloisonné chandeliers, and low tables and comfort cushions. Leslie heard the chirping sound of the nightingale floors as they walked the wood to their seats. The pleasant sounds underfoot were intended to warn the shogun of assassins in his home. Their table was in an enclosed patio with a view. Her chair pulled out and pushed in, menu received, the waiter departed. She found herself facing Phillip Ernest again. "I'm impressed," she said.

"My plan is at work."

She joined him in reading the half-mix of English with foreign words on the menu.

"Maggie, I want you," he said, but stopped to correct himself, "What I mean is I want you to come on board. Work for me full-time. Permanent. No agency."

"And I thought you were shy. Thank you for the offer, but is that all you want? You could've asked me at the office without going through all this trouble. I'm a simple girl."

The doctor gulped cold water, his face pink with embarrassment. "I wanted to make a good impression, and you're not simple. You're sophisticated. The British accent, and all."

She lowered her menu. "I'll depend on your expertise with the menu. I'm famished and haven't a clue of what's good to eat." Deference, in her experience, made men feel secure with their prey.

"An expert with patients, yes, but with a lady, I can't make the same claim."

"You're doing just fine." She offered a smile. "The night is still young. The rest remains to be seen, Phillip."

Intentional use of his first name. Intimate.

"To be seen?" he said as he smiled at his menu. "About my offer, will you take the position?"

He realized his choice of words and turned crimson. A waiter arrived in time, his notepad ready. Ernest ordered with a combination of exotic pronunciations and the occasional pointing at the menu for those words he couldn't sound out. Leslie begrudged admiration at the man's effort at seduction. The waiter left.

"Yes, I accept your offer." She turned her head to take in the view below. "Charming house over there." She didn't point west of them, down a distance where there was an extravagant cluster of buildings. He'd know it, she was confident of it because the restaurant, the table were a practiced routine and setting for Dr. Phillip Ernest.

"That's the Chateau Marmont," he said, "a famous refuge for movie stars and celebrities. It's a hotel with several bungalows."

Their drinks arrived—two sparkling champagnes to cleanse and prepare their palates. That or he knew carbonation expressed alcohol faster into the bloodstream.

"I've treated a patient or two there," he said.

"You made a house call. Were you impressed?"

"With the patient or the facility?"

"Either. Doesn't it tickle you sometimes when you're talking to a movie star? I can't imagine the glamor. You must've talked to at least one you admired on the screen before you became a doctor?"

She subscribed to flattery, still believing that to call him Doctor was a form of malpractice. Their first course arrived, announced as salmon carpaccio.

"Celebrities are still people. Albeit made extraordinary by a combination of fate, fame, and money—they still have problems, like you and I."

He ruled out talent, she thought.

"True, and money does solve problems. In England, no matter how much money you have, people will always know your station. Artifice accomplishes nothing. Why did you think I left?" she said.

"This is America. Here, you can reinvent yourself." He cut up a small piece of the thinly sliced fish on his plate.

"You make it sound so easy. Didn't you just say success was a combination of fate, fame, and money?"

"Excellent recall. I did. I should elaborate." He said it with a grin and that smug, intellectual tone. She had baited his pride, the bookworm coiled inside him. "Therapy is a complicated matter, Maggie. Ordinary clients come to me for help, often with common problems. Actors are different because they are so poorly defined psychologically, often before the distractions of fame and money visit them. I think of them as the characters they've studied in scripts, to the point they can't separate the role from reality. That's one type of famous patient."

"Is there a second?"

"There is." She noticed he had rested knife and fork on his plate in the

European style. "Actors are trained in deception," he said. "Everything around them perpetuates illusion until that is, the money stops, the roles dry up, and they're discarded, forced by circumstances to define themselves."

"Like Vera Williams?"

"Exactly. Vera is a casualty of the Hollywood machine. Think of her as the unfortunate character in *The Pit and the Pendulum*, strapped to the table with the ax swinging overhead, ready to destroy her. The blade of time vanquishes youth and beauty."

She swallowed the terrible allusion, along with the last of her champagne. Worse yet, he had misinterpreted Poe. "I recall the unfortunate character survived, thanks to rats chewing through the restraints," she said to him.

His mouth hung open. A waiter swept in and removed the plates while a second waiter replaced them with their second course, duck with rice in an oolong reduction for her, and chicken tossed out of a wok with angry spices for him. Wine was poured.

"Because I mentioned beauty and youth, you must think all men are dogs," he said.

"Men run Hollywood, Phillip. Male actors become distinguished and accomplished, while actresses such as Vera are relegated to the roles of matron or spinster," she said.

Ernest showed no reaction as he worked his chicken with a knife and fork. She decided on chopsticks, set on the table for the adventurous.

"Some men are like dogs chasing cars. I've always wondered what a dog does when he catches the car. How about we change the topic of conversation for a moment? You said you had one incurable. The guilty patient."

"Ah, yes. Him. He named names to the Committee. Communists. How is your duck?"

"Crisp. I like that the breast isn't greasy."

"The bird is picked before it gets too fat."

"I see. How do you try to treat guilt?" She watched him turn over his vegetables.

"Guilt is ultimately a form of murder. Like the son who has killed his father," he said while eating. "The conflict is manifest in the testifying before

HUAC. If he doesn't give up names, then the father might die. Communism is the enemy of the father and family. You can see my analogy, don't you? The father is society, the ultimate parental authority and provider. He gives up names, and he'll save Father from his enemies, and if he doesn't, there is guilt."

"Freud is everything to you."

He lifted his napkin to cover his mouth. That condescending male laughter she detested. "You've read Freud?"

"I have," she set down her wineglass. "Analysis as process is 'from unmanageable unhappiness to manageable unhappiness.' *Civilization and its Discontents*. Ironic quote, isn't it?"

"That's what I like about you, Maggie. There's more to you than meets the eye. You have opinions. I don't have to agree with you, but I respect that you do your job well."

Most women had opinions; she was thinking before she decided on her closing.

"Thank you, but I have conditions if you want me to stay on. First: a raise of seventy-five cents an hour. Second: keys to the office, both doors, and the filing cabinets. I'm tired of having to wait for you in the morning before I can start my work. I also don't like having folders pile up on my desk because you're slow to file them. I type them up promptly, don't I?"

"You do. I do my own filing. Thought I'd save you the work."

"I like my desk clear. Do we have a deal?"

"You'll have your raise. As for the keys to the front door, I'll think about it. You'll have to persuade me about access to the filing cabinets."

She saw the dessert menu coming and lifted the last of the wine to her lips. She let the rim linger against her lips long enough for him to notice it.

"Any other terms?" he asked.

"We have the rest of the night for you to find out how persuasive I can be."

Chapter Eleven

The urgent air of the Friday deadline pervaded the Writers' Pool. Tense faces glanced up at the wall; the small needle ticked away the last seconds on the clock. Writers yanked sheets off rollers, collated, covered, and bound their pages before the big hand touched twelve and the bell sounded. Fresh air through the windows should have reminded the captives in the room a world outside awaited them, but they were too tired, too exhausted, and too unaware of the sunshine outside. Walker had witnessed this before, in prisoners behind wired fences.

He had graduated from Editing to Writing. The week wasn't easy, and neither was this writing that wasn't writing; the only thing Aristotelian about the beginning, middle, and end around the drama here was that every writer wrote each day, every day, in one room.

Terry clacked away at the keys for hours, and Bernie chewed the same stogie all day long. Walker's last page on the Remington curled halfway between Implausible and the wastebasket. Terry recognized a desperate man when he saw one, placed his editing pencil behind an ear, and walked over. "I know the look," he said.

"That obvious?"

"Cut yourself some slack about meeting a deadline, Walter. People know you've just moved from editing schlock to the keys. You'll be burning through reams of paper in no time. Trust me."

"Appreciate the booster, Terry, but I'm not convinced." Walker pointed to the lifeless sheet of paper. "This scene has me pretzeled. No matter what I write, it doesn't work. They want a flashback within a flashback."

Terry sat on the edge of the desk after he set aside Walker's brass nameplate and whistled. "No easy task there, brother, but you know what? Take it as a compliment somebody in Production thinks you're the man for the job." Thumb in the direction of Bernie, "They asked you and not him. You can't cash the ticket yet, but your stock is on the rise. What are you doing this weekend?"

"Thought I'd relax, go to the beach, and check out a jazz club near Hermosa Beach." Walker lied because he wanted to drive up to his house, enjoy Malibu, the seclusion.

"Interested in a party instead? Simple mixer with writers."

"I don't know, Terry. Writers? Not exactly scintillating."

"Scintillating? You sound like a thesaurus. Sure, some of our guys will be there, so will other scribes from other studios." Terry leaned down over and whispered into Walker's ear. "Remember pseudonyms? An alias is up from Mexico, and another is in from Greece. What do you say now?"

"And does Bernie over there know?"

"He knows everything. He'll be there. Some in this party set are old chums and worked in this room with him. Relax, and don't worry about him."

"But he tells Warner everything,"

"As does God. I'll pick you up tomorrow night."

Terry specified the time and walked away.

* * *

Terry kept his eyes on the serpentine road. "Party is on Mulholland," he said. "House belongs to Vera Williams. She hasn't been in anything recently, but she knows how to throw a party. You won't be disappointed."

"She knows blacklisted writers?"

"Knows them…are you kidding? The gal knows everyone there is to know, since she was knee-high to a garter belt. Vera has partied with the best of them. Her mother was a protégé of one of Hollywood's first women. Can't remember her name for the life of me, but those two were ahead of their time and before the moguls. Her mother helped some of these writers get their start. As for Vera…did you know she found Thelma Todd's body? Papers said it was the maid, but that was to protect Vera. Know Thelma Todd?"

Walker didn't respond. He knew the name of the blonde actress from the Marx Brothers, a glamor girl with gangster boyfriends, and the owner of the Sidewalk Café in Pacific Palisades. Her café made him think of Malibu.

"You listening to me, Walter?"

"Yeah…I am, Terry. Thelma Todd. Suicide, found behind the wheel of her car. Death from carbon monoxide poisoning."

"And some car she died in, a Lincoln Phaeton. Suicide is what the what the cops called it, but nobody could explain how she broke her nose. Vera always said Thelma could hold her liquor and walk straighter than an Irish priest, and I'd take her word for it. Sounds like murder to me."

"And here's the guy who told me to pack it in when we discussed Charlie's death. You've been reading too many scripts, Terry."

Terry eased the car into a driveway minutes later. Vera's house, like anything off Mulholland, sat off the curve of the road. The man who planned houses on Mulholland loved his geometry teacher, because everything involved bends and dangerous tangents. There it was in front of him: a swanky house with a view of Century City, Beverly Hills, and, in the distance, Catalina and San Fernando Valley. From the outside, Walker saw attached bungalows, for those overnight guests too hung-over for the winding drive home, or for friends who needed a place for their liaisons.

Terry and Walker walked into the noise in the living room. Terry surveyed the room for familiar faces while Walker played the awkward partner in tow. Terry pulled Walker in close and whispered, "They're here."

"Writers from work?"

"No, Reagan and Holden."

"The actors?"

"Who else?" Terry turned his back to the two men to fill Walker in on another slice of hidden history. "Ronald can be a real pain in the you-know-what. In '46, after the Burbank strike, he crossed the picket line into Warner Studios. Him and Robert Montgomery. Reagan was president of the Screen Actors Guild by special election. Rigged voting, if you ask me. How convenient is it that he's the sitting president on all the labor disputes? Funny seeing him here since Reagan insists there is no such thing as a blacklist. Ronnie is virulently anti-Communist, and he's given names to the FBI."

"And Holden?"

"Good friend, I suppose. Bill is apolitical. Not a bad guy, though. He gets feisty with a couple of drinks in him." Terry turned around, waved to someone. "Like I told you, everyone knows each other. Work together, sleep together, but politics is the corpse in the closet." Terry pinched Walker's arm. "Here comes Vera with her girlfriend. What a doll, she is. Act casual."

Vera walked through the room, turned here and there in a black-beaded sequin dress with a gold pattern in the shape of a monarch butterfly across her shoulders. In her one hand, a fluted glass of effervescent champagne, and in her other hand, around the waist, her worldly prize, a leggy brunette, also in black, wearing a diamond choker that could've been lifted from the Victoria and Albert Museum.

"Vera, darling, you look stunning," Terry said when she approached.

"You always say the sweetest things to a girl, Terrence. Ah, I see you've brought a friend." She extended her hand to Walker during the introduction. "Pleased to meet you, Mr. Thompson. New writers are always welcome. May I introduce the two of you to my friend? Here is Margaret Gardner. She works for Dr. Phillip Ernest."

"Pleased to meet you," Terry said with a handshake. Walker did the same.

"Do pardon me," Vera said, "I must say hello to Ronald before he starts a grudge for feeling slighted. I'll leave Maggie with you gents, for just a moment."

Vera pulled Leslie closer, and Leslie, thinking Vera was going to say something, turned her head. Vera placed a delicate kiss not on her cheek, but softly on her lips and followed it with a sip of champagne.

"I'll join you," Terry said and took Vera's arm.

Walker and Leslie waited until the hostess and escort were out of earshot.

"You look like you can use a drink," Leslie said first.

"I'm good. Vera said you work for a doctor."

"A psychotherapist and you're straight to the point, aren't you?"

"Someone once told me it's best to remain professional, objective, so nobody gets hurt."

Leslie's lips parted to respond, but just then, a man stood up on a table and tapped his champagne glass with a small spoon. He pocketed the utensil after heads turned his way.

"Ladies and gentlemen, may I have your attention," he announced in a baritone voice. The crowd shifted into a low chatter. "First, I'd like to thank our gracious hostess, the gorgeous Vera Williams, for having us here tonight in the comfort of her own home." His hand was outstretched to indicate Vera, standing next to Terry and Reagan. There was polite applause. "We are privileged to have some extraordinary talent in this room, ladies and gentlemen. With us on a quick visit from Mexico is Mr. Dalton Trumbo. How he managed to get himself past Border Patrol is a mystery that we hope is never solved. Dalton, we welcome you." More applause. Trumbo didn't bother to get up from the sofa. "With us is our friend from Greece, or is it France? Ladies and gentlemen, Jules Dassin." Small applause again. "Though nobody can pronounce his last name, the Europeans think he's European, and let's hope the folks in Customs continue to remember that he's one of us…an American citizen. Bienvenue, Monsieur. Welcome home." Dassin raised his glass; his forced smile suggested he was uncomfortable with the attention. Walker noticed Irving Hackett sitting quiet and alone behind the two expatriates.

The emcee continued. "Since we are bound together in this craft called moviemaking, I thought we might enjoy a film together this evening." On cue, two men made their way into the room to set up a screen and projector. "This film we are about to see experienced its share of difficulties. No less than eight writers participated in writing the screenplay. Without further delay, I hope you enjoy *Riso Amaro* or, in our language, *Bitter Rice*. Gentlemen, please tell us when to kill the lights."

Walker watched. Reagan, like an eagle, moved his head slowly, right to left, as if he were cataloguing the attendees in the room. Terry, mesmerized, nursed a champagne flute. Trumbo sank deep into whispers with a man to his left. Dassin, the world-weary Odysseus, eased back into the cushions and tried to think up his next trick. Irving Hackett sat in the corner of the room, comfortable, it seemed, in the darkness.

Aware of Leslie next to him, he sensed she was observing him. Three years later, after their brief romance in Vienna, he's in a dark room listening to the onscreen voice-over narration while living the flashback within a flashback he couldn't write at the office.

Chapter Twelve

Terry and Walker escaped to the enormous patio outside under a clear night sky. Vera's idea of a courtyard was the size of a tennis court without the net. Writers were on the one side, actors on the other, and nobody stopped the two men walking toward them.

They weren't cops. In good suits, the bulges under their arms said they were armed. Hired help. Vera tried as fast as the black beads of her dress would allow her to intercept them before they reached Terry and Walker.

"Come with us," one of them said.

"Which one?" Terry asked.

One of them pointed to Walker while Terry continued smoking. "Think he means you."

"Just come with us," the man said.

Walker suggested another idea. "Mother told me not to talk to strangers. Mind me asking who's calling?"

"Look, Joe," he said to his partner, "we have a comedian."

"Why don't you bugs fly off?" Terry said.

"Precious words, coming from the studio lizard. Shouldn't you be sunning yourself on a rock somewhere?"

Walker asked, "Know these guys, Terry?"

"Unfortunately. I can make a call, fellas."

"Didn't I tell you these writers read too many pulps," the tough said to his partner. "This one thinks he's Marlowe with the quick wit, while his friend Doyle here sharps every business card in the shoebox. Or is it the desk drawer?"

Terry's suck and release on the cigarette was the only sound between the four of them. Writers and actors turned spectators waiting for the next serve.

"Who's requesting my presence?" Walker asked.

The lug named Joe had Vera to his left; he let his eyes drift south to enjoy the view down her dress. "Fine," the other heavy said to Walker. "Mr. Moore, by way of Mr. Warner, requests the pleasure of your company. Satisfied?"

Terry held his cigarette out in front and said softly to Walker: "Clearance man."

"Can't this wait until Monday morning?" Walker asked.

"C'mon, Marlowe. It's been fun, but I'm not laughing anymore."

"As a writer, you're starting to hurt my feelings."

"You two are sober. Dress well, too, given the party favors in this pad," Joe's partner said. "We might have ourselves two homos here."

"Hey…" Terry said and moved, but Walker grabbed him at the elbow. "Don't Terry. They're fishing for an excuse."

Vera stepped in front of the two goons. "I have the mind to call Mr. Warner and tell him what a disgrace the two of you are."

"And you are?" the man asked, Goliath to her David.

"Vera Williams. You are on my property, uninvited."

"Never heard of you. Remind me, Joe, to ask my mother if she's ever heard of a Vera Williams. This broad is before my time."

"Enough with insulting the lady," Walker said. "Take me to Mr. Moore. We should go before sunrise, or you two might lose your way home in the daylight."

* * *

The '46 Town & Country two-door convertible with the Newport hardtop impressed Walker. The two escorts, Walker guessed, expensed travel at a dime per mile. The steel out in front could part waves, and the wood-paneled doors in mahogany plywood conveyed an antiquated touch. His escorts stopped so Walker could express his admiration.

"Nice car, you two have. 135 horsepower, Spitfire eight-cylinder, Fluid

Drive transmission, coil springs with rear rigid axle and semielliptical springs, four drum brakes."

"Get in," one of the men said and seized Walker's elbow.

The car oozed luxury and leather. Walker had forgotten about the dual downdraft carburetor as the yacht floated out of the driveway, the sound of gravel beneath it before resuming Mulholland's curves. The concrete vein of blacktop above LA was fifty-five miles of chartered loneliness and darkness. The canyons below and around offered up the menthol of eucalyptus trees and the calming drift of jasmine in warm weather. Outside his window, the desert and the scrub of hillsides sat under a sky with not enough stars to match the dreams of the poor in the valleys below.

The driver lit a cigarette with an electric lighter. His partner cracked open a window without saying a word. These two played to type, silence with menace. There was no manhandling or gut punch, like in the movies, unlike the ride Walker took with Leslie one night long ago in Vienna, an excursion that ended up with them upside down in a ditch. From chestnut tree-lined streets of old Vienna to another chauffeured ride, this time through a landscape of mission-style Spanish haciendas and raw steel and glass. The world has changed.

The Chrysler turned on a road into a grove of trees where sat a ranch-style house in serious disrepair. The car door opened, and Walker stepped out without being asked. He saw the entrance and understood what the other door meant.

He walked in. A cold, dark chair awaited him in front of a sad desk that had lived its last life at Good Will. The heaviest curtains this side of the Victorian Age covered the windows. A Peeping Tom worked hard for his reward here. Behind the desk sat a balding man with two thin strands of hair combed over. In front of him was a hefty legal pad, a scrawny pencil, and a pink eraser for him to revise answers as he saw fit. His host appeared fresh and starched for someone in the middle of the night, which implied experience in this line of work. Three men, Walker counted. He was thinking all that, and this trio had manners of either auditors or undertakers.

"Please take a seat, Mr. Thompson. I'm Mr. Moore. This shouldn't take long."

"Why couldn't this wait 'til Monday? You embarrassed me in front of friends, sending Heckle and Jeckle here."

Walker ad-libbed. A little outrage might put Moore on the defensive. Moore mimicked Keaton's Stone Face instead. He didn't blink. Not once. Walker wouldn't relent:

"Doesn't Mr. Warner have better ways to spend his money than on these two magpies?" Walker understood his two chaperones were his only means of getting home. Mr. Moore motioned for the duet to leave. "I won't take too much of your time," the balding man said.

"Since it's for Mr. Warner…shoot."

"The HUAC committee is reviewing files of new employees…you do know who HUAC are…" to which Walker nodded, "Good, as I was saying, they're reviewing files, and since you are a new employee, I would like to ask you a few questions."

"You mean coach my statement."

"Mr. Warner would like to think of it as anticipating unexpected complications. He dislikes surprises, as much as I do, and he plans accordingly. Answer my questions, which are their questions, and everything remains civil. Shall we proceed?"

"Ask away, Mr. Moore."

"Excellent. How long have you been employed at Warner Brothers?"

"Approximately a month now."

"And in what capacity are you employed by Warner Brothers?"

"All-purpose writer."

"Sounds pretentious, Mr. Thompson. Best say, writer."

"But I edit, and I write in different genres."

"The answer writer will suffice, Mr. Thompson."

Moore's pencil moved to make preliminary notes. "They will ask this, and I will quote them exactly, 'Are you now or have you ever been a member of the Communist Party of the United States?'"

"No."

"Excellent," he said and ticked his pad with the pencil. "Next question to which you can invoke your Fifth Amendment right, 'Do you know past or present members of the Communist Party?'"

"No."

"Are you sure, Mr. Thompson?"

"Answer is no. Been here only a month, remember? Nobody has walked up to me and told me they were a member."

Moore's pencil scratched paper. "Do you suspect anyone at Warner Brothers of being a member of the Communist Party?"

"Is that your question or theirs?"

"Please don't parse semantics, Mr. Thompson. You will be asked these questions in one form or another."

"No."

"Really? My men collected you from a party with a rather distinguished list of known subversives in attendance."

"Wouldn't know, Mr. Moore. I didn't get a chance to mingle before I was collected, as you so put it. In fact, I spent most of the evening trying to talk to Ronald Reagan. I'm a big fan."

"And your colleague Terry Doyle?"

"What about him?"

"He's sympathetic to labor causes. In fact, it's known he has corresponded with Harry Bridges. Do you know the name? Harry Bridges is an avowed Communist and labor agitator."

Walker pulled his head back in surprise. "News to me, Mr. Moore. Like I said, I've only been on the job for a month. Sounds like what you're talking is history before my time. Terry was assigned to me at the Writers' Pool."

"You mean he is your mentor."

"You can call him that. Terry showed me the ropes around Warner's."

"In showing you the ropes, did he offer you guidance?" Moore asked.

"Now, who is parsing semantics? I just said he showed me how things are done at Warner Brothers. Like a mentor, your words. Things like how to edit, how to write better, acquainted me with the style sheet. If that's guidance, then sure he guided me."

"I see. Has Mr. Doyle tried to persuade you to entertain any political viewpoints?"

"No."

Blunt answers, Walker knew, didn't open doors, or enough room for a prying chisel.

"I will read you some names, Mr. Thompson, and I want you to tell me if you know them." Moore pulled out a loose piece of white paper from out of his canary pad and read from it. He allowed a small pause to bracket Irving Hackett when he said the name. Walker felt like the deaf. He saw only the lips move. "Know anyone I just named?"

"I think you forgot Mr. Warner."

"Why do you say that?"

"You just about named the entire staff of the Writers' Pool. Mr. Warner puts himself at the top of everything at the studio, so why not include him?"

"I don't particularly subscribe to your sense of humor, Mr. Thompson. Do you know these names or not?"

"I don't know every individual personally."

"I see. How about this name, then?"

"Dr. Phillip Ernest?"

"Heard the name but never met the man."

"Margaret Gardner?" Moore asked. He wasn't reading from his paper.

"Met her once."

"When and where?"

"This evening at the party. She was a guest of Vera Williams."

"Talk to her at all?" was the next question. The pencil did an up-and-down mark on the yellow pad, like the needle on a polygraph test.

"Small talk. Nothing more."

Moore's sudden smile broke as if he could make a change with this information. "I was told you had a good look at her. One might say you were surprised."

Walker leaned forward to the edge of the desk. "One might also say I appreciated her, Mr. Moore. Your stooges might be dead from the neck up, but I'm sure they're alive from the waist down and would agree with me that Miss Gardner is a very attractive lady. Isn't that in your notes? If it isn't, it should be."

"I see," Moore said. He flipped a page. "Let's carry on, shall we? Do you know John Hamilton?"

Walker's calf twitched. "The actor? Was he at Vera's party? Because if he was, I didn't see him there."

Neither Moore nor his pencil moved. Walker could hear himself swallow.

"I didn't ask you if you saw Mr. Hamilton at the party. I inquired whether you knew him."

"I know him."

"From the screen? Perhaps talked to him at the studio? Be specific, Mr. Thompson."

"I know him from the military."

"You served?"

"Didn't you?"

Moore put down his pencil. Walker had located the weak tendon. "You didn't serve, did you, Mr. Moore? John Hamilton did, and with distinction. Silver Star and Bronze Star for a combat jump and there's more, but I don't like discussing the war. Hamilton's service is a matter of public record."

"It's also a matter of record that Mr. Hamilton has named names. He's admitted to being a member of the Communist Party. He has since recanted; also a matter of public record," Moore said with satisfaction. "And not a minute ago, I asked you if you knew any past or present members of the Communist Party. You answered no. You can see we've arrived at a contradiction."

"What I see is a syllogism, Mr. Moore."

"A what?"

"Syllogism. If I know John Hamilton and he knows or knew members of the Communist Party, then you assume I know or knew members of the Communist Party. In logical terms, Mr. Moore, it boils down to: if A knows B and B knows C, then A must know C. Basic logic."

"HUAC might not see it that way, Mr. Thompson. How about I ask you some general questions?" Walker sat back and crossed his leg over.

Moore's pencil was poised, the point sharpened. "What was the last thing you read?"

"Don't remember. Probably a script. I read so many of them I wish I could forget most of them."

The briefest of smiles creased Moore's face, a sign that morticians possessed live humor in their veins. "A danger of your profession, I suppose. I meant, have you read any contemporary fiction? Our research shows you possess a library card."

"Research?"

"What is your answer, Mr. Thompson? Last book you read, contemporary literature, if you please."

"*Catcher in the Rye.*"

"You purchased it?"

"Believe, I did. Dawson's Book Shop on South Grand Avenue."

"HUAC might not take kindly on that. Mr. Salinger's book has over seven hundred profanities in it. You not only read the book but saw fit to own a copy. Moving on now. I have another question for you. Do you know any languages?"

"I don't understand the question."

"Simple, really. Do you know any other languages? Do you, for example, read literature in another language?" Moore twirled his pencil on its point against the pad. Walker knew they'd visited his apartment. He owned a German edition of Thomas Mann's *Doctor Faustus.*

"I don't read Russian if that's what you're implying, Mr. Moore, but I can read German."

"Speak or write the language? Consider yourself fluent?" Moore asked.

"No, Mr. Moore, I don't consider myself fluent. A person with some humility would never say they're fluent in a language, not their mother tongue. I suggest you read Mark Twain's essay on the German language for a dose of humility and humor, or does HUAC disapprove of Mr. Twain because he wrote *Huckleberry Finn*?"

"Probably not, Mr. Thompson, but they might cast suspicion on him, if he were alive today and called himself Mark Twain and not by his real name, Samuel Langhorne Clemens."

"Are we done yet?"

"Yes. You should go home and get some sleep. Heckle and Jeckle, as you called them, will drive you back to Burbank."

83

Chapter Thirteen

Joe opened the back door for Walker, said nothing, and closed it like a gentleman. His partner drove without needing directions. These two probably visited Bob's Big Boy in Burbank. One man kept his eyes on the road while Joe tipped his hat back and closed his eyes. Hired muscle, two stiffs, and from their make and model, they were a two-for-one-special in cheap suits in a shade of coal, rumpled slacks, white pocket squares, and ties as thin as their personalities; these two were as milquetoast as Mr. Jones on Main Street, Anywhere, USA. The LA variety worked nights and slept days, ate at NoHo diners, and their coffee included the grounds on the bottom of the cup.

Joe wheeled down the window some. The quiet night air rushed in, as if all the rumors in southern California settled down, after dinner had been served, televisions watched, the clock set to repeat the ritual of get up and go after idols of clay.

The Verdugo Hills hid in the Burbank darkness. The parallel lines in the parking lot flashed white under the car headlights. The car parked, nobody said anything at first. Joe opened the door. "We're done for now," he said.

Walker stepped away, with one last peek at his chauffeur and companion. Country-boys, eyes too close together, and their hair cropped close under their fedoras. Corn-fed and clean-shaven boys who knew how to kill and how to follow orders without question. These two were a pair of parentheses, so alike, without any ambiguity about the message between them.

Walker turned on the light in his place. Everything appeared kosher. Careful as a bald man with his toupee, the search team left everything tidy.

Neat and considerate of Jack Warner. Thomas Mann's *Faustus* was where Walker left it. Adrian Leverkühn was still syphilitic, and the Devil had come to town. No sign of the Apocalypse yet, though damnation stalked nearby. Walker remembered somebody saying it was rattlesnake season around Mulholland.

** * **

Sunday morning and he wanted to visit Malibu. Highway 1 changed names several times before it became Pacific Coast Highway or PCH. Whether it was Pacific Palisades Road to one person or Roosevelt Highway along the Santa Monica beachfront to another, it was familiar blacktop to Walker, familiar as boys with boards on the left side of the road and the pale girls in bikinis with kerchiefs on their heads, eyes hidden behind glamour shades on the right side of the road. Girls descended on Malibu Beach for boy-watching, to catch a surfer by nightfall, in time for bonfires in a sweater.

The ocean was his constant. Civilization appeared in Malibu in the form of a Post Office at the foot of Rambla Pacifico. The Wayne Wilcox Photography Studio and other construction projects chewed up the brush and grazing land. Walker's place was, as a lawyer would argue, technically in Calabasas, up and over Saddle Peak and down either Rambla or Las Flores, but that would change once someone built a direct connection to Malibu. There was talk of building a road called Malibu Canyon Road and installing a water line.

Walker had learned about Malibu Colony from a friend of a friend of Whittaker, an Army buddy. This friend had done a stint in the Coast Guard Beach Patrol. Walker heard about long nights of Calypso music in a jeep under romantic skies as this friend of a friend peered out to the horizon in search of Japanese subs. Girls, he was told, were as numerous as sand dollars by day and turned into mermaids at night. Pristine beach, parcels of land for plentiful seclusion. After the war, Walker went west and found a superhighway, high hills, big houses, and the distant shimmer of waves.

He settled the Kaiser Virginian into the gravel.

None of the strings he placed near points of entry had been broken. Walker traveled downstairs and collapsed into one of his leather chairs. Three hours of laid-back Pacific time separated him from Jack in DC. Walker didn't need a notebook, or time to organize his report. His mind was as clear as the glass on the coffee table in front of him. He dialed the number from memory.

"Walker here. This a good time?"

He relayed facts to Jack, information in vivid Technicolor from start to finish, from the time he stepped into the Writers' Pool to Moore's reference to Mark Twain as a nom de guerre. He left out the question Moore asked about Hamilton. Walker explained everything else, from meeting Jack Warner, Terry, the crew of writers at the Pool, and how work began in the back of the room and worked its way to the front of the house. He glossed over editing, the bits and bobs of writing snippets or marginalia around scenes. He concluded by giving Jack the run-down on meeting Teague at Billy Gray's. Everything, except one detail.

"Imagine who I ran into?" Walker heard silence. "Jack?"

"I needed her to work an angle on the Loew murder. Is this network of fronts Warner's solution around HUAC, or a solution to union beefs?"

"Both, I suppose. All the studios are involved. For years, Loew was their go-to man, although it seems he's a Warner man. Paid well for it, too."

Walker waited for Jack's carriage return on Leslie's insertion into the operation.

"What's your read of Terry? Think he'd bump Loew for top drawer?"

"Wouldn't rule it out, Jack, but here's something I don't get. Loew was the golden goose, and yet there's been no reprisal for his loss. If Terry did do it, I would think Warner would've meted out justice. Everybody is in each other's business." Walker worked his own angle now. "Like, this party I attended at Vera Williams' was a Who's Who of listed writers. A writer up from Mexico didn't seem to sweat about his visit across the border. The man didn't look over his shoulder once, as if he had safe passage and papers in order. Everyone at this shindig was relaxed enough to take in an Italian film. Loew's dead, and life carried on."

"And what's the connection to Vera Williams in all of this?"

"Hollywood royalty. She appeared taken with Leslie by the way she was sporting her on her arm."

Walker edited out the breathy kiss, and Leslie as Maggie Gardner working for a doctor. Jack had to know about the doctor and that alias.

"Did you act surprised when you saw her?" Jack asked.

"I tried not to, but apparently, I wasn't convincing because Moore brought it up in our chat. I have a question of my own, Jack, and tell me as much as I need to know."

There was no sigh, no sign of impatience. Jack knew how to listen. The telephone moved, Jack's voice adopted a more relaxed tone.

"Phillip Ernest is an analyst to the Hollywood crowd. I planted Leslie with him. Ernest's name came from Hamilton. You remember him, right?" Jack asked.

Walker pictured the scene: Hamilton walking into Ernest's office, seeing Leslie as the secretary, and swallowing his cigarette. He'd need the extra drink to wash the sight of her from his eyes.

"I remember him. Not sure of any connection between Ernest and Loew, but there's one between Terry and the doctor." Walker sighed. "Terry mentioned he had stolen an expensive Argentinean pen from a shrink's office. Silver ink, like what you found on Loew. Only thing is Terry, or the doctor could have written the number, Jack, and we don't know when. Doesn't prove either man is a murderer. Trace the number?" Walker asked.

"An office in a building with plenty of floors. No tenant and half the building belongs to an associate of Mickey Cohen. Professional types on this property. Tax accountants, doctors, and lawyers."

"Any shrinks because Terry didn't give a name?" Walker asked.

"Anything else?"

"Moore the Inquisitor." Walker preferred the title to the one Terry assigned him. Inquisitor fit the man determined to sort out heretics. "He's Warner's Clearance Man. I was poached from Vera's party on the pretense I'm the new guy and my story had to fly straight when HUAC reviews Warner's personnel files. Moore knew a lot about me. He knew where I lived, what I was reading. He knew Terry, he knew John, he knew Dr. Ernest and Margaret Gardner, and he knew blacklisted writers at the party, but of all those people in the soup, he never mentioned one name."

"What name is that?"

"Joe Teague. How should I proceed?"

No sound over the wire. No breath. Not a rasp, like when the receiver returned to the other ear. "Jack?"

"I think it's time you saw a shrink."

Chapter Fourteen

Jack had problems. Like most troubles they came in triplicate, like celebrity deaths or relatives on Thanksgiving, Christmas, and New Year's. Betty was Problem 1. Two men parked in a car across the street were Problems 2 and 3.

The odd phone calls started on a Tuesday. The first few calls were wrong numbers, silence on the line or anonymous breathing for subsequent calls during the rest of the week. Betty dialed the operator, but then she had been unable to locate the call.

On Wednesday, the mail arrived later than usual and not with their usual postman. On Thursday Betty reported the mail had been opened, and the Post Office claimed it had been an accident. On Friday, there was no mail.

Two men parked their car across the street from the house; they sat in the car all day. She noticed them on Wednesday. They would arrive soon after Jack left for work. She described them as clean-shaven men, black suits, white shirts, thin black ties, and wearing dark hats. They had no other distinguishing features, since they wore Hudson eyeglasses with black frames. When Jack asked her to write down the license plate number, next time, she broke down, and the children ran upstairs to their rooms.

Saturday at ten-thirty in the morning, Betty confronted Jack. She stood in front of him, cold and emotionless. She placed an opened oversized envelope addressed to her in front of him and waited for him to review the contents.

Item 1 was an 8x10. Location: Foggy Bottom, a drinking establishment near the D.C. waterfront. The photograph was a close-up of Jack with work colleagues. So perfect was the photographer as a sniper, Jack could read the labels on the Heurich beer and bottles of Rose's Lime Juice and Old Dad in the background. A typed message was glued to the bottom white margin: 'Working late tonight, Dear.'

Item 2 was another 8x10. Location unknown, but the image burrowed under her skin like a tick. Suit jacket off, Ray Bans on, the wind licked his tie over his shoulder, and between him and another man was a smaller man, his hands tied behind his back, terrified. Jack cracked a smile beneath the sunglasses. Two things disturbed Betty: the holstered Mauser on Jack and the typed message: Jack Marshall, agent for what and for whom?

Item 3 was the last 8x10. This photograph was of Jack with Walker and Leslie in Vienna. All three were smiling, and it reminded Jack of a rare happy moment. He wanted to smile, but didn't dare with Betty there, trying to snap a flame for her Fatima cigarettes. She'd replaced the Julep brand. He looked up when he heard her working the lighter. His eyes reconsidered the photograph.

Leslie was the centerpiece of this picture. She stood at the far end and gazed leftward, affectionate. Open to interpretation as to which man her eyes admired. Jack thought of Walker instantly, but he knew Betty's assumption. The typed caption was a quote this time, a line credited to the French writer Antoine de Saint Exupéry. Translated into English, it read: "It is as a soldier that you make love and as a lover that you make war."

Jack slid all three photographs back into the brown envelope. He confirmed what he suspected: Betty's name and their home address had been typed. Stamps cancelled locally, probably at the Postal Square Building on Mass Ave. Fingerprints would prove inconclusive since half the postal clerks in the Beaux-Arts building touched the envelope. Gloved hands probably handled the photographs inside, and the model typewriter could be narrowed down to several hundred in a twenty-mile radius. Most of them aspiring writers.

Betty exhaled. Fatima cigarettes was a woman's brand, until Jack Webb started hawking them because the maker sponsored his television show, *Dragnet.*

"Please don't smoke. It's unhealthy."

"Don't tell me what to do in my own house. I don't say a word about your drinking. What do you have to say about these pictures?"

"What do you want me to say?"

"The truth would be nice."

"These photographs are intended to provoke suspicion. There's your truth."

"Damn you, Jack. Well, it worked. I am provoked. You tell me you're working late. Well, there you are having yourself a jolly time there with the boys. Exhibit One."

"Please stop it, Betty. I get together with the boys from the office for a drink, now and then, but I wouldn't lie to you about it."

"Really? I don't recall you saying on the phone, 'Betty, I plan a quick one after work with the boys.' When have you ever said that, Jack? Because I can't remember once."

She had a point. He hadn't.

"You tell me you are with a new agency. I believed you. I asked you if it could be dangerous. You said you didn't do dangerous work anymore. I asked you if you would be armed, and you told me No, but there you are, in Exhibit Two, with a six-shooter under your arm."

He refrained from correcting her about the specifics of the weapon. The Company didn't arm men but left the decision to the agent's discretion. The Mauser had belonged to a dead Nazi. Jack waited for the full brunt of her assessment of Exhibit Three.

"And then we have Leslie in that last photograph making baby eyes at you."

Jack treaded this dilemma with care. Dismiss her as ridiculous and shrill, she'd think affair. Respond with glacial denial; she'd think he was a liar nonetheless.

"Look at the photo, Betty. She's admiring Walker, not me."

"How can you know for sure?"

"I know. I just know."

"You're so sure, aren't you?" Betty asked at close range, blowing smoke.

"Watch how Walker and Leslie interact with each other the next time you see them."

Betty did a slow intake of her cigarette. The lit end pulsed, the paper burned and shrank.

"Who would send this? And those two men parked across the street? I didn't think you believed me when I told you about them."

"I believed you."

"No, you didn't. You asked me for license plate numbers."

"I believed you."

Chapter Fifteen

Curled in comfort in the nowhere hours between Saturday evening and Sunday morning, her eyes opened when she heard the Mae West moan behind her. An arm draped over her. The hand moved, found flesh, and pulled her in for warmth. Leslie stared ahead. She reminded herself she was sober. Vera, behind her, was not. Come morning, her head had to be playing a bass section with an extra drum kit and the horns ready to scream when she saw daylight.

Leslie recollected the night. Dinner with Phillip in the Hollywood Hills. After-dinner drinks with him somewhere else. She remembered soft music, conversation, and champagne bottles with little ascots around their necks. More drinks, more music, and gaiety. Then they agreed to attend Vera's party. She changed into something black, a dress with a matching cape.

As Vera's party hit its stride, an inebriated Phillip introduced her to writers and whispered diagnoses into her ear until she stopped listening. Hypochondriacs, this or that disorder. He started to sound like the teenager trying so hard to impress her at everyone's expense.

More drinks. The room became hotter. Bump or bumped, apologies, and other excuses to break away from dying conversations. Too many voices and faces. She met Trumbo. He was pleasant but preoccupied. She met Dassin, who acted sad. Phillip was across the room watching her. She plotted an escape.

Vera saw her. Vera rescued her. Vera swept Leslie into one of her many rooms, loaned her a diamond choker. She refused at first. The sparkles and play of the light against the stones were too much. Vera insisted. Vera's hand took her elbow. "There are people you must meet," she said. There were more names, scraps of gossip, pretend laughter, and the strong undertow of socializing, which came to a halt when she encountered Walker.

Startled at first, she maintained the façade of composure. Introductions. The handshake. Vera said something, but she couldn't hear so she turned and then the kiss, soft but pressing with a suggestion. Vera's hand had pulled her in at the small of the back. Leslie felt lost in Vera's perfume next.

It was time to get up.

Leslie moved the arm. Another moan escaped from Vera's lips, and she groped the bed for a pillow to replace her. Leslie climbed out quiet as a jewel thief. She searched for her cape and her purse. She surveyed the room. Nothing. She saw a chair in the hallway.

The cape was there and the purse, a lump under it. She noticed the rest of the house was quiet. She noticed photographs on the walls. Vera captured in silver as a platinum blond with a Marcel wave, a rose under her chin, and pearls around her neck. The next photograph was Vera in a summer dress; her back turned to the camera. Then Vera's voice behind her.

"My mother's favorite. Max Autrey suggested the pose. He did a similar portrait with Myrna Loy. Know of Max Autrey?"

"I'm afraid I don't, Vera. How do you feel?"

"I feel fine. Max was Clara Bow's favorite and Chaplin's photographer on the set of *Modern Times*. Clara and my mother were good friends. Two women who didn't give a damn what men thought." Vera touched the frame. "Clara could curse. She was also the object of lurid rumors. None of them true. Then…well, then the lights started to dim for her, figuratively and literally, but I loved her just the same. She was an important part of my childhood."

"What happened to her," Leslie asked and regretted it. "I shouldn't pry."

"Mental illness. This town will make anyone crazy. I need coffee. Want some?" Vera didn't wait for an answer. "Let's go make some."

Leslie followed Vera in the long walk from the bedroom out to the kitchen. Vera was holding up well. She didn't need the walls for support. The rest of the house appeared respectable. Minimal trash, and the potted plants were unmolested. Sofa cushions could use plumping. Open the windows for a few hours to rid the place of the stale cigarette smell. Everyone had behaved and left no accidents to deal with. Vera banged out the drawer for a silver spoon. The cabinets made less noise for the cups. Vera ran the water and spooned out Chock Full O' Nuts.

"Were you playing doctor with the doctor, or did he run off to make a house call?"

"I'm not doing anything with Dr. Ernest."

"So defensive. Just making girl talk. I figured it was only a matter of time."

"There've been others?"

"Don't be so naïve, Maggie. Why do you think the man can't keep a secretary?"

'Secretary' annoyed Leslie. She played the part in Vienna and now here, too.

"Oh, don't worry," Vera said. "Phillip is like most men who can't talk about anything outside of their jobs. Let him talk his clinical mumbo-jumbo. Do your nods and have yourself a nice dinner, a night out on the town, and…"

"It hasn't come to that yet…although we did have dinner and a night on the town."

"See…you're off to a good start. Had dinner and a night out. But the way you say yet. I detect a mild rash of ethics, Maggie."

"And you said mumbo-jumbo, as if you didn't believe he did you any good as his patient."

"Correction, honey. I'm a paying client. Yeah, I go to him, and for an hour, I tell him what ails me. I pay for a confessor without the moral judgment. It's a symbiotic relationship. Rock and starfish, ship and barnacle…you get the idea."

"Clear as crystal."

"I'm not trying to down you or tell you what to do, Maggie. You're your own woman. Do what you want. You're young, and you're holding the deck of cards. Take it from me, you're holding aces."

"You're not exactly retired,"

The coffee was ready, and Vera poured.

"I might not be Miss Haversham, but I didn't marry a Thalberg to secure my future."

"You seem to do just fine."

"All I'm saying, Maggie, is use men before they use you. Men talk. Learn to listen. Phillip is a talker. He doesn't seem like it now, but he'll talk. He's just a little shy boy. Mother him a little. The problem right now is you intimidate him."

"I intimidate him?"

"Honey, you haven't seen his other secretaries."

"You think Phillip will open up more?"

"I do. Give it time. But be ready to be disappointed."

"Disappointed?"

"Yep." Vera stopped for a sip. Leslie did the same. The coffee was strong. "Phillip is like the winter weather report. You hear all the hype in the forecast. When the storm happens, all you get is a few inches that'll leave you wondering if it was worth all the publicity."

Leslie wanted to laugh. She imagined the same observation coming from Clara Bow or Carole Lombard in saltier language.

"Phillip is no lover, but I'll tell you who is, though," Vera said without giving Leslie a chance to respond. "That fellow with Terry Doyle last night. Walter something-or-other."

Leslie coughed and choked on the Columbian coffee.

"You OK? The fellow had the wolf in his eyes when he spotted you, and you didn't do so bad when you saw him. Now, there's something that can't be invented. You've either got it or you don't…and you two have it. I saw the way you two were sizing each other up."

"I should call a cab, Vera. Good thing it's Sunday, the day of rest, right?"

"I'll get you the number for a cab, or you can let me drive you. I don't mind."

Leslie checked her purse for cab fare, didn't hear Vera's offer. She had money, but she noticed her .22 caliber was missing, red Cross of Lorraine, white grip enamel, and all.

Chapter Sixteen

Between the parallel lines, he parked; he then turned off the ignition but kept his hands on the wheel. He was back in Burbank at the studio, there for the job. He was ready for the walk into Warner's on a nice sunny day with a breeze strong enough to lift a skirt and show some leg. Storm weather.

God may have made this world in six days, but Mondays were the Devil's day. And today, behind the wheel, he remembered his mother. She would sing *Missouri Waltz* before his bedtime or tell him family legends of Quantrill before she would sing a hymn she called *Burnt District*. Today the past, the air, and the sounds haunted like a postcard from the Valley of Death.

Make some coffee, he told himself. Ritual calmed him. He went inside. He found his Chemex, found himself square filters and doled out the dark stuff from his bag of coffee for his brew. This procedure, this habit, the small part of the morning he could control. He was early, but not too early for Jack Warner.

"Seems we're the only ones here in the Pool," the mogul said. Warner dressed without the flash of a gangster. He wore understatement well with a navy suit, white shirt, and a simple, dark tie.

"Morning, Mr. Warner."

"I'm here with a proposition, Mr. Thompson."

"I don't know whether to feel flattered or terrified."

"Terrified of me? I'd prefer you feel flattered. I do have a proposition for you, nonetheless. Please have a seat." Walker took to his chair, and Warner pulled up one and asked, "What are you working on now?"

"A flashback within a flashback for a woman character." Walker sneaked in one sip.

"And how's the writing going for you?"

"To be honest, difficult."

"I suggest you consider *Backfire*, a film we did in '48."

"With Virginia Mayo, right?"

Backfire wasn't an A-list film with A-list actors, but it was still one of Warner's children. Walker eyed Warner through the steam. "Miss Mayo's character provided a good example of a flashback, but I was thinking of a girl with dim prospects, like Susan Hayward in *Deadline at Dawn*, an RKO film in '46. Odets screenplay."

Warner absorbed the suggestion without betraying a response. "Don't care for the man's politics, but a hard worker and a fine writer, that Odets. Did you know he wrote *Rhapsody in Blue* for my studio?"

"Can't say that I did," Walker said, raising his coffee cup up, as if to say touché.

"Uncredited. Clifford wrote it for me and for RKO, as you have duly pointed out. He drafted *It's A Wonderful Life* for RKO. Uncredited, of course. '46 was a good year for RKO before it was beset with financial problems and difficulties with the House Un-American Activities Committee." Warner crossed a leg up and over and rubbed his hands together. "How about this for your flashback? *The Killers*. I can get you the screenplay."

"You surprise me, Mr. Warner. That's a Universal film." Another sip. Good coffee.

"I can get whatever helps you, Walter. Your knowledge of cinema is impressive, but I should remind you *The Killers* started here at Warner. The producer, Mark Hellinger, wanted one of my directors, Don Siegel, but the borrowing fee was too steep for him."

"Seems rather curious to me, Mr. Warner, that you'd loan out talent."

Warner's tone turned avuncular, permitting Walker another sip. "Where money is to be made, talent can be loaned out if permission is asked and the fee paid."

"Permission from the talent or the studio?"

Strong coffee had made him brave, maybe too bold.

"You have a sense of humor, I see. It's all part of business, Walter. As I was saying…I came here with a proposition for you. It does involve a flashback of sorts. I wish to do a film about Dachau, from a prisoner's point of view, and the storyline should include American GIs liberating the camp. Throw in a love interest for a solider, if you like but no melodrama, please. I thought you'd be an excellent resource, have some insight of your own, on the subject."

The acidity of the Italian coffee burned Walker's throat. Jack Warner was asking him to script his own flashback. He stopped drinking. His face dropped faster than a Venetian blind.

"Are you sure people are ready for it, Mr. Warner? What I mean is, are you sure the public would spend good money to have real life from not so long ago served up to them on the screen? Might make people uncomfortable. This is dark history, not some war hero on the mend from a crack-up."

"Let me worry about that," Warner said. "I'd like to see a draft. It's about time something like this is written. You know my background, Walter, so I'd think you'd understand my motive. I've always taken pride in doing socially conscious films and not just entertainments. I'd leave it to you to craft the narrative. You decide flashback or no flashback. All I want is a draft. We can shape the writing up later, but for now, just get it down on paper." Warner took to a low whisper. "I ask that you keep it to yourself, though. I don't want any of the other writers knowing. You're the man for the job for obvious reasons."

"I appreciate this vote of confidence, Mr. Warner, but just so you know, my background might be called into question."

Warner feigned ignorance like a bad actor. "You mean that unfortunate after-party experience with Mr. Moore?"

"Precisely."

"You worry too much. I'll handle it."

"And what about HUAC's review of personnel files? Moore said you hired him to do a once-over should HUAC call me up. He said you dislike unexpected surprises, or words to that effect."

Warner stood up and returned the chair back to its home. "What do you have to worry about, Walter?" The balding head and black mustache appeared severe in the lighting. The men in Walker's family kept all their hair. "Tell me right now. Are you a Communist?"

"No, I'm not a Communist, Mr. Warner, but…"

"All I need to know then. The rest will take care of itself."

Walker didn't seem relieved, and Warner noticed, saying, "You seem distressed."

"I am."

"Why don't you see someone about it? I don't want you falling to pieces on me. Ever think of talking to a professional?" Walker acted surprised. "There's no shame to it," Warner said. "I'd rather you do that than drink yourself into a stupor. I've already had myself a handful with one writer who couldn't tell the difference between a bottle of booze from his typewriter. It was one hell of a job for the director to get that film into the can. I'd rather you talk to someone and have your head on straight."

"Do you have a recommendation?" The coffee was now cold paint thinner.

"I do. He does wonders. He has an office downtown. Top floor. Warner took a blank piece of paper from one of the desks to scribble the name and placed a question mark after it.

"There you go. I don't know the address. Hence, the question mark. An operator should be able to help you with that. Tell you what…take the day off, paid, and drive down and see the man yourself. If he can take you today, then great and, if not, set up an appointment soon. Return refreshed to start the special project and give Bernie the flashback assignment."

* * *

Walker started up the car. As he pulled out Terry and the other writers were pulling in. Terry honked his horn, and Walker waited for Terry to walk over to him.

"Where you headed?" Terry asked.

"Downtown. Not sure of the address, but I can figure it out later. All I've got is a name."

"Can I see?"

Walker offered up the scribbled note. "It's Warner's writing."

Terry ignored the comment. "Oh, yeah, that's Dr. E's office; it's on the twelfth floor. There's a nice elevator man named Edwards who'll take you up."

"You know the doctor?"

"Who doesn't? I've talked to him a few times. Dr. Ernest should have an office on the premises since he treats most of Warner's staff. Don't worry, Walter. Talk is good for the beans," he said, tapping his temple.

Details converged. Walker had an address, the owner of the stolen ballpoint pen, and a doctor. A nice warm breeze washed in through the window.

He drove downtown and found the office near City Hall. Walker parked close to the building, and what he saw put his stomach through the windshield. There were starched blue shirts and rounded hats. Beat cops. Patrolmen. One man in the crowd stood out, though. Checkered shirt and solid tie marked him as lead detective on the scene. His partner had to be inside asking questions. Next, orderlies in white uniforms appeared, then a stretcher, a white blanket with straps holding the injured in. He saw Mr. Edwards taken away in an ambulance.

Just then, the LA sky started throwing down rain.

Chapter Seventeen

California rain never landed right. It didn't for Mr. Edwards that Monday morning. His rituals before work offered him no protection against the day. He enjoyed a small glass of orange juice with breakfast, said it helped his blood sugar, and then he would have his hard-boiled egg, a slice of bread toasted in the Delta toaster he and his wife received from their neighbors as an anniversary gift. The chrome-plated dropper toaster bore their initials.

Nice neighbors, though superstitious. Good people from Louisiana, he said, though they plagued him with their endless rules about avoiding bad luck. He should've listened to them. They had ideas about which door you entered and exited, notions about windows, and joked white people believed in Creole truths but didn't know it, like ears ringing meant someone was talking about them, or pinkie swears were serious oaths.

Bad luck. He guessed later he should have asked his neighbors about Mondays. He knew they believed planting a cross in the middle of the yard and sprinkling it with salt would stop the rain, but the cross reminded him of the Klan. No amount of salt would ever make that go away.

Mr. Edwards lived in a single-story Craftsman along Jefferson Boulevard. Whites moved out in '48 after the Supreme Court ruling broke covenant housing. Little New Orleans was born overnight there in LA. Those good people next door to him were hard workers and were doing their best to remodel their plot into a mini Champs-Élysées with soft bricks in a herringbone pattern. The crooked iron gate outside was an eyesore Mr. Edwards and the new Japanese couple across the street wished away.

There were no signs, no omens. Thermos in hand, Mr. Edwards went out the door that morning. His foot didn't turn left or right when he walked the sidewalk. Right would mean bad luck, and left, good luck. He left to catch one of two buses to Western Ave and his building. The two little girls next door were playing hopscotch and singing a song about the proper time of day to kill a spider.

Western and Wilshire is where his building grew up within the city's strict height limit: no building was to be taller than City Hall. He enjoyed manning the elevator up the twelve-story Art Deco masterpiece, from its ground floor all the way up the tower to Dr. Phillip Ernest's office on the top floor. The building turned eyes skyward with its blue-green color while it remained respectful of City Hall.

Too soon after he arrived, before he could get comfortable, a white man entered his elevator. Like a fork used to stir coffee, something seemed off about the man to Mr. Edwards. Fresh rain didn't even want to stay on the man's coat or hat. This man didn't small-talk about the weather, like most folks. Mr. Edwards made a light comment about the rain. His passenger said nothing until he closed the grating.

"Where to, sir?"

"Top floor."

"Right away, sir. Twelfth floor has a fine view of the city. Office of Dr. Phillip Ernest is down the hall to the right..." Mr. Edwards said, stopping when he realized his guest had no interest in pleasantries. Letting the hum of the steel sing its song, Mr. Edwards couldn't help but evaluate his new friend. The coat puckered a little, and Mr. Edwards discerned the profile of a .38 revolver under the man's armpit. The man's eyes at a slant caught his, but Mr. Edwards turned his head in time to face the doors for the Silent Express to the top floor.

The door opened with a chime, and the man exited. "Another crazy white boy," Edwards mumbled after the doors closed. He thought to himself during the descent: "Dr. Ernest ain't in, and neither is Miss Gardner. New class of clients these days, I suppose, but ain't none of my business. My job is safe passage from floor to floor," and as the elevator pulled him down,

"Leave as is, and don't be no fool now, George," he said to his reflection in the steel doors. Halfway down, however, he stopped, reversed his direction, telling his mirrored self he was no Ahab and the white man was armed. "No good will come of this, you fool, but I won't have Miss Maggie alone with a crazy first thing this morning."

The blank numbers turned white with each floor: 9..10..11..12. Ding.

The two doors opened into the cold darkness of offices and hallway, waxed floors so shiny it should be a crime to walk on them. Mr. Edwards locked the elevator so it would stay on the floor.

A loud crash and the sound of breaking glass took him from a walk to a run to Ernest's office. The door to the office was ajar, and the shards of glass were like walking on diamonds. Papers everywhere. Through the second door, Mr. Edwards saw the flash of a shadow across the room.

The intruder had his back turned at a filing cabinet, which he shook, cursed as he worked the lock with a steel shank. One of the cabinets tipped over with a thud.

That was when the white man saw Mr. Edwards.

The rest of it Mr. Edwards remembered well. The man reeked of stale tobacco. A big hand seized him at the shoulder. Shirt bulging, coat all wet, the gun holstered until they reached the elevator. He fumbled for his keychain to unlock the elevator while the man screamed at him. "Down to the bottom floor, nigger."

It was a long ride down. They each watched the countdown of numbers, from gray to white on the strip of metal overhead. Mr. Edwards glanced. The .38 wasn't in the holster. At floor three the man's jaw tightened. Floor two, he relaxed enough to say, "You didn't see a thing, understand?"

"Yassuh." He hated tomming the man, but it might mean living another day.

First floor. Ding. The butt of the .38 came down on the side of his head.

* * *

A man emerged from the elevator, hat brim tipped forward to hide his face.

He clipped Leslie before she found Mr. Edwards on the floor, trying to use the wall of his elevator the way a prizefighter uses the ropes to stand again.

"My God, what happened, Mr. Edwards?"

"Nothing, Miss Maggie. Head just hurts."

"You're bleeding."

"I'll be all right. Your office upstairs…he broke into it."

"The man who just rushed out of the elevator?

"Yes, ma'am. He was searching for something, but he didn't take a thing. He upended a filing cabinet."

"You need help, Mr. Edwards. I'll call for an ambulance."

The ambulance came, but the police arrived first. The beat cops kept a crowd from forming. Someone called detectives. A man in a checkered shirt and solid tie appeared on the scene. His partner started his questions with Mr. Edwards.

"Can't you see this man needs medical attention?" Leslie to the detective.

"They have to ask their questions, Miss Maggie," Mr. Edwards said, holding his handkerchief to his head.

"A doctor ought to see you first," she said.

Edwards answered questions. Height, build, approximate weight, the burglar's frustration with the filing cabinet, their confrontation, and the ride down in the elevator that ended with the knock to the head.

"All right," the detective said and called out to one of the patrolmen, "Call in the stretcher. He can go to the hospital now."

The stretcher came in. Mr. Edwards lay down in the gurney, and the two male orderlies strapped him in.

She heard a different detective behind her, "Hold on, Miss. We have some questions for you." Leslie knew police policy was to switch during interrogations to compare notes later.

"I want to go with Mr. Edwards. I want to make sure he's taken care of."

"You can't go with him. He's going to the hospital. Segregated, and they won't let you in. How about you answer some of our questions?"

Mr. Edwards went out into the drizzle as a specimen mounted to a stiff cot. Two white orderlies, dressed in white, carrying a live black man was not a common sight for the crowd. Edwards said nothing. He still had the drive to the hospital. A fruit seller was sweeping the wet sidewalk. Mr. Edwards started to remember some Creole superstitions about brooms. Always were bad luck.

"You get a look at the man, Miss?"

"Not really. He brushed past me so fast I hadn't a chance. I saw Mr. Edwards, and I rushed to help him."

"You mean the Negro?"

"I mean the victim," she said.

"Right. You work for Dr. Ernest on the top floor."

"I do."

"And what time does the doc come in?"

She read her watch. "In ten minutes."

"You always come in earlier than him?"

"I'm his secretary. I open the front office for him."

"How about the second office, the key to the filing cabinets?"

"No. Dr. Ernest has those keys."

"I see. Last question. The doctor—did he have any violent patients?"

"None I know of, Detective."

"That'd be all. Here's my card in case you remember anything else, and I'll need your address and a phone number."

* * *

She walked outside. The crowd was dispersing. In a car she thought she spotted Walker. To her right, about twenty feet from her on the sidewalk, she found John Hamilton standing there smoking a cigarette. He saw her and touched the brim of his hat.

She hadn't seen Edward's attacker's face. She might recognize the coat, the hat, guess the height and weight within an inch and a pound, but she was certain about one item.

The man carried a K-38 Combat Masterpiece in his hand. Five-screw revolver, Baughman ramp sight, four-inch barrel, blued metal, and a Smith

& Wesson K-frame. Respected for its balance and smooth double action, popular within the FBI.

Chapter Eighteen

Jack's turn to make the call this time. He hated it. He also disliked the three-hour time difference. Asking for a favor was always painful. A few minutes past seven, like the last time, he dialed the number and let it ring. The recipient picked up on the second ring, but Jack didn't hear a voice at first. "Chief Parker?" he asked.

"Speaking."

"Remember me?"

"How may I help you, Mr. Marshall?"

"I'm calling about a 406 the other day. Western and Wilshire."

Pause. Jack knew that Chief William Parker had inventoried all the reasons why he was receiving a call about an insignificant matter, a daily occurrence in Los Angeles.

"Breaking and Entering. I'm aware of it." The sounds of papers and typewriters in the background. Jack half-expected Parker to lean back in his chair, enjoy Fortune's reversal. Instead, he heard a deliberate silence, wide enough to swallow the music of the spheres.

"Four-o-sixes happen a lot in your city," Jack said.

The 'your city' was an intentional dollop of flattery.

"Indeed, Mr. Marshall. Since I'm the recipient this time, let me be frank with you. This matter floated to my attention because it concerns the office and property of one Dr. Phillip Ernest. Assume you know of him?"

"I do."

"Good, then you know he's connected to Jack Warner. My detectives have confirmed property was damaged but have not ascertained whether property was stolen. I need not remind you I have Warner's man buzzing my ear closer than my own barber."

A pause before Jack spoke. "The name of Warner's man?"

A chuckle from the other end before the unexpected answer. "Joe Teague."

"I see, and your detectives questioned two people."

"Let's cut to the chase, Mr. Marshall. You and I both know their names. Miss Margaret Gardner and Mr. George Edwards. Might I ask the reason behind the social call?"

"I need you to divert the investigation."

Jack heard the chair squeak. If the chair sprung forward any harder, it'd break wood.

"I see. Mr. Edwards did give us a description of his attacker. What do you propose I tell Warner's boy next time he comes around? And he will come by."

Jack disliked the idea, the words out of his mouth. "Mr. Edwards is a Negro."

"He is, and what's that got to do with anything?"

"Nobody questions routine, if your men were to, say, lean on him."

"Mr. Edwards is a law-abiding citizen. The man almost owns his own home. His employer speaks highly of him. If I believed only half of what his passengers say about the man, he ought to be canonized. And one last thing: Mr. Edwards is a veteran." Jack had not known this last fact, since the complete report on Edwards from the one of his analysts had not come back yet.

"First war. 369th Infantry," Parker said.

"Harlem Hellfighters. I tip my hat to you, Chief. Your men are thorough."

"Now, you might see the quandary ahead of me if I send my boys after Mr. Edwards. Any insinuation of an inside job, of Edwards's involvement with a 406, will have unfavorable repercussions for the man, such as jeopardizing his pension, his employment…or have you forgotten the man was the victim?"

"Wouldn't be the first time your department followed up on an investigation."

"Wouldn't it be better if we dragged our feet instead? Wouldn't be a first for my department, either."

"It's your city. Drag your feet, and what will this Joe Teague do?"

A long sigh exhaled over the phone.

"All depends what kind of man Teague is and if Warner feels exposed about whatever was in the doctor's office. Can't tell you how I appreciate the irony that a Negro might be safer in LAPD hands than with Teague."

Jack did not reply. Sometimes, the truth deserved silence.

"And if I were to take your suggestion, and lean on Mr. Edwards, as you put it, Mr. Marshall, and the Negro community gets wind Miss Gardner was treated lightly, then I have a race situation on my hands. Poor choice of words on my part here, Mr. Marshall, but I have a black eye either way."

"What can you tell me about Teague?"

"Keeps his nose clean. He likes the nightclub circuit of girls, money, and the notoriety of being seen with gangsters. He's in like Flynn with Cohen and his kind, but there's no proof he profits from the association. Beyond that, I have nothing on the man," Parker said.

"Thank you for your time, Chief," Jack said, worried, and hung up.

* * *

Moore disliked calling on Jack Warner at home.

It wasn't the drive to San Simeonette in Beverly Hills that disconcerted him. The fountain with Cupid riding a seahorse didn't bother him. The imported sycamores were nice. The baroque parquetry and all the dark wood Ann Warner loved intently were not to his liking, nor were the grounds, which included a four-hole golf course and a tennis court Florence Yoch designed for the Warners. Ostentatious, Moore thought. Everyone let Jack Warner win at tennis. And the mansion's name was Warner's awkward bow to another ego, Hearst.

Warner had phoned and asked Moore to meet him in the library. Moore knew the routine. Amidst the bound studio scripts in the room, Warner will ask him to sit in one of the George III mahogany armchairs. He would have a nice dinner first, served by Roget, the butler, in the dining room to the left

110

of the library, and then Roget, as Virgil, would escort him to the dark chair where he'd experience Warnerian wrath and judgment.

No dinner this time. Roget led the way to the hot seat.

Jack Warner, wearing a robe with the imperial JL on his breast pocket for his cigarettes, waited behind his desk in the library, a bound volume splayed in front of him when Roget announced Moore. Moore took his place in the armchair with all the reticence of a San Quentin prisoner, and Warner ordered Roget to bring them drinks. Jack Daniel's times two.

"Give me a minute, Leonard. I'm making some notes here."

"What are you working on?"

"Reviewing the script for *The Killers*. Need ideas on a flashback."

"Might try *Citizen Kane*," Moore said and regretted the suggestion when Warner's eyebrows peaked. Warner returned to his document with the vigor and intensity of a lawyer in search of a loophole for his client. Moore hoped for those drinks. His mouth felt suddenly dry. Roget returned with the drinks in cut glass. JD neat. Moore didn't care for Warner's choice of drink either. Drink on his desk, Warner was ready.

"I called you because I wanted to discuss Walter Thompson. I've read your cryptic memo. Are we prepared in case HUAC calls him up or not?"

"I wanted to talk to you about him in person."

"Aw Christ, Lenny, please don't tell me there's something incriminating on him. The earache about my employees in the last month alone is enough to make me drink strychnine. You'd think they were all rejects from reform schools."

Warner held up a sheaf of papers; the stack could've been anything from contracts to photographs, but let Jack talk, Moore told himself. Whatever it was, it'll come out. Warner peeled off one sheet and dealt it like a dealer from a Vegas card deck. The pivotal item was a photograph of a Warner heartthrob, male, caught in an incontrovertible smooch with another man inside the cab of a truck, snapped from behind.

"You believe it, Lenny? He's a fruit. Imagine what I'll have to do to keep this out of *Confidential*, or away from Louella Parsons. One of Cohen's boys sent it. I have another matinée idol in the stable, ready for the big-time, and guess? He's a fruit, too." Warner sighed for effect. "And the women aren't any better, Lenny."

"I know," Moore sighed. Agree with the emperor. Humor him.

"One broad is climbing in and out of hotel rooms, as if it were a turnstile, and another one burns through men like cigarettes. You wouldn't know they wore skirts the way they keep opening their legs."

"About Walter Thompson, Mr. Warner."

"Please don't tell me he's a fruit."

"I wouldn't know, Mr. Warner. Curious thing is I can't tell you much about Walter."

Warner sat back, adopted a patrician's New England severity, which for Moore in the Georgian chair, reminded him who had lost the Colonies. "Explain," Warner said.

"It's as if the man doesn't exist."

"What do you mean? Perhaps he changed his name? Jews have done it. The Italians sometimes simplified their last names. Some Germans and Russians are doing it, in this political environment."

"It's not that, Mr. Warner. I mean, I can't prove Walter Thompson exists. When you gave me the assignment, you said Walter told you he was a veteran."

"Army man, by the way, he spoke about Dachau. I was with Cagney in the hall the day I met Walter. That crazy mick Cagney spouted off some Yiddish, and Walter understood it."

Moore took a sip of the Daniel's and pulled out a piece of paper from inside his suit. "The 42nd and 45th Infantry Divisions liberated Dachau. I can't find a Walter Thompson among the rolls."

An expressionless Warner sipped his Daniel's. "Did you ask the man about his service when you spoke to him?"

"Briefly. My purpose that evening was to determine if he had any ties to Communists. My priority was to minimize any liability for the studio. It's all in my report."

"I read it, but there's no mention of a discrepancy with Walter's military service."

"HUAC goes after matters of public record. You register Republican, and they'll want to confirm you voted Republican. They search for inconsistencies. Consistency implies character. If you lie or waffle, they think you've got something to hide, and they'll attack and accuse you without naming their sources. You know the game, Mr. Warner. I don't have to explain it to you."

Warner closed the bound volume on his blotter. "The naming game. It's all wordplay and arm-twisting."

"Walter isn't registered as a CP member, past or present, but he was at Vera Williams' party on Mulholland. They start with his service record—a matter of public record again, and if that's vague, his credibility is shot, and then they'll use it as an opportunity to question him about Vera's party. Like who was there and…" Warner waved his hand for him to stop, but Moore didn't. "He's as good as a tarnished penny. Which means you have a problem, Mr. Warner."

"I get your point, Lenny, but I don't think Walter was lying to me."

"Why are you so convinced, Mr. Warner?"

"I've met camp survivors and others who've seen the camps. I saw it in his eyes. I know he was there, Lenny. Call me crazy, but I know what I saw in his eyes; it's not something you can fake. Is it possible Walter was there but in some other capacity for the military? He could've embellished details to impress me. After all, he needed a job, and he was meeting me."

"I did research, Mr. Warner. I can't find anything in service records. I double-checked. You know I stand by my work."

"Now, now, Lenny, I'm not questioning your research. You've always done good work. I'm suggesting a detail overlooked somewhere. I'm convinced Walter was at Dachau. Please look again. You'll find it. I have confidence in you."

"Thank you, Mr. Warner. There's another matter I need to discuss."

"There is? What now?"

"Dr. Phillip Ernest. He's on your payroll, right?"

"You know he is. Why?"

"An elevator operator told detectives a man tried breaking into Ernest's filing cabinets."

"Any files taken?"

"None that we know of, but Ernest is screaming up a storm."

"Of course, he would," Warner said.

Leonard Moore was happy to leave Warner among all his books and bookcases, as if all the answers to unanswered questions might emerge from them.

Chapter Nineteen

The air in the vestibule to the doctor's office moved with all the solemnity of a heretic's appointment with the Inquisitor. The ride up the elevator was an exercise in patience for Walker since the operator was new at working out all the subtleties of the lift. When Leslie saw him in the doorframe, she stopped typing short of the bell.

"Have a seat. Doctor Ernest will be right with you," she said.

She returned to hammering the keys.

"I appreciate your taking me on short notice," he said in a loud voice over the metallic music. "I'd tried the other day, but there was a commotion in the lobby."

He peeled off his jacket and hat and searched for the rack.

"Over there, Mr. Thompson," she said in a cold voice that could've taught Bette Davis and Joan Crawford a thing or two about frost. He thanked her and let her know his eyes appreciated her latest dress and the silver earrings with crushed sparkles. In Vienna, she had said she didn't care for earrings because they were liabilities in close combat.

The door to the second office opened and out walked John Hamilton. Walker saw Hamilton, saw her wry smile. Only thing missing was the letter opener in her hand. Hamilton played the stranger in a room of old friends. He said hello, paid, and left.

"Mr. Thompson?" Ernest motioned with the 'you first' roll of the hand, ballpoint pen in his shirt's pocket square. Walker acted nervous as a schoolboy at the principal's office.

"Inside, please," the doctor said. Sunlight streamed in through windows with an uninterrupted view of horizon and sky.

"On the leather couch?"

"Yes, please. To be clear, what we discuss here stays here. Understand?"

"I think so," Walker said with faked uncertainty in his voice.

"Before we begin, I'd like some preliminary information for my records."

Laid back against firm leather, Walker assessed the room. The office was Spartan for an interrogation. Simple chair, a leather couch on an area rug, and four walls, one of them with the doctor's credentials. The desk, newish, and two metallic filing cabinets behind it. Floors were done over, not with Murphy's Oil, but some concoction with rosemary and mint in it because the scent jangled the nerves awake. Antiseptic and inhuman.

"Name?"

"Walter."

"I mean full name, Mr. Thompson."

"Walter Thompson."

"No initials or suffixes, like junior?"

"Just Walter Thompson, one and only."

"And Thompson is spelled with a p, correct?"

"Is it spelled any other way?"

"The Scots do without the p, but Americans and the British include the p." Ernest made some fast remark about wanting his files to be accurate.

"Occupation is writer for Warner Brothers, correct?"

"How'd you know?"

"The studio called ahead about your visit. I've treated studio staff in the past."

"You must know Terry Doyle."

"I can't discuss clients, Mr. Thompson."

Interesting. Clients and not patients, Walker thought.

"Religious denomination?"

The question surprised him, made him pause. He hadn't thought about religion or church service for a very long time. The doctor drummed his pad with his pen. "Protestant or Catholic. Minister or Father. Did your parents tithe…recall them giving the church a percentage of their income?"

"The only thing my mother tithed was the family cat. She used tuna juice." Walker hoped humor helped. He enjoyed the masculine smell of leather around him.

"What are your parents like, Mr. Thompson?"

"Dead."

That should warrant Sensitive Issue in his file. Interrogators always used open-ended questions. Close-ended answers were dead-ends. Keep the interrogator moving forward like a good story, and there was no need for torture. Walker anticipated the doctor trying another avenue. "What did you do before you took your position with the studio?" Ernest asked.

"GI Bill. I studied a language. German."

"Interesting choice. Why German?"

"I wasn't very good at it during the war, and I didn't know what else to use the money for afterwards. It gave me time to figure what to do with my life."

"I see," the doctor said as if found a clue. "Did you feel you needed the time to recover from your experiences. How did you feel about the war?"

"War is hell. It's a cliché, but an honest one."

Walker heard the man's pen scratching paper. "And perhaps German was a way for you to confront your wartime experience, a way of achieving mastery over the difficulty of combat?"

"Never thought of it that way, doc. You could be right. You know I'm working on a project right now for Mr. Warner. You did say earlier that what we discuss stays in this room, right?" Walker lifted his head up for the doctor to see him.

"Yes, and we can discuss whatever you like, Walter."

He lowered his head. "I wanted to make sure. As I was saying, Mr. Warner has me on this project. It's just me and no other writers, and I don't think I can do it. Bad memories, doc, are hard to put on paper."

"Is Mr. Warner's project asking you to draw upon your war experiences?"

"It is. I suppose this is what you'd call a crisis in confidence, huh?"

"In layman's terms, yes, but there is a clinical term for it. May I ask you to name the wartime experience that troubles you most?"

Walker cupped the back of his head and let the elbows stretch out his upper back. He had found his script and was reading off the lines to Phillip Ernest, Ph.D.

"Dachau. Warner wants me to write about liberating the concentration camp."

"And you were there? You remember it well?"

"Not something you'd ever forget. Yep, like yesterday. Look, doc, the traffic is terrible this time of day, and my watch says the hour is almost up." Walker pivoted to a seated position on the leather couch.

"We can go overtime, Walter. Please lie down and continue."

"Oh, I'd rather not, Doctor Ernest. Not fair to your next patient, and I do need to get to the studio. Mr. Warner is a stickler about our hours. I wouldn't want Mr. Warner to think I'm taking advantage of him. Too bad I couldn't talk to you when I had the day off, but there were police and an ambulance downstairs."

"I can call the studio for you, Walter. I can let Mr. Warner know we need more time. He'd understand," the doctor said, standing and about ready to throw a body-block if Walker went for the door.

"You know Mr. Warner personally?"

"I can get his attention. Please don't leave."

"I really should be going, Doctor Ernest. I'll make an appointment with your secretary."

"I can call Mr. Moore for you."

Walker gripped the doorknob when he heard the name, the desperation in the doctor's voice. "You know him?"

The doorknob half-turned, the door creaked, the slower he pulled it open.

"Please close the door."

"I should go."

Walker walked past Leslie's desk toward the coat tree. He reached into his jacket pocket for his wallet as he approached the secretary's desk.

"No need to pay, Mr. Thompson."

The confused expression on his face she knew from the past. "Dr. Ernest has an arrangement with the studio," she said. "A discounted rate is deducted from your pay."

Client or patient or employee—it was all the same to Warner. After hearing Moore's name in session, he thought to ask whether Ernest considered a quote from Dante above his door. 'Abandon hope all ye who enter here.'

Chapter Twenty

After the descent in the elevator where his breakfast touched his throat, Walker's feet traversed the dark marble in the lobby. Michael Rennie and Patricia Neal could keep their elevator scene in *The Day the Earth Stood Still,* for all he cared. The fresh air outside felt refreshing.

Outside, waiting for him, was Hamilton in his long trench coat. Hamilton's time in the Yugoslavian mountains had fostered a need for warmth the way a hungry orphan kept extra food in the house as an adult. He clapped Walker's shoulder. "You're green around the gills, kid."

"The elevator."

"Say no more. I dislike the damn thing myself," Hamilton said. "It's why I take the stairs up to the headshrinker's office. Twelve floors of steel and concrete suit me fine. No amount of Scotch in my morning coffee could get me into that mousetrap on cables." Hamilton lifted his chin to indicate the front entrance. "Some young kid is at the helm until Mr. Edwards recovers. Let's walk and talk to get your coloring back. There's a Simon's near Bullock's. We'll grab some coffee there."

Walker thrust his hands into his coat and started the march with Hamilton. "Tell me about Edwards."

"Negro elevator operator. Took a conk to the head after giving a perp the lift to Ernest's office. Early-morning attempt at a smash-and-grab before the doc came in, before Leslie showed up, but it all amounted to a mess of the doctor's inner office before he realized whatever he was looking for was inside those filing cabinets. Either way, he couldn't jimmy the filing cabinets and hightailed out of there when Edwards interrupted him. Rode the whole way down with Edwards to the first floor, where Edwards went nighty-night. Pistol-whipped isn't exactly sleeping on the job."

Hamilton shortened his stride so Walker could keep time and talk.

"Any chance Edwards was in on it? He has access to the building and a good cover as the elevator man. He fakes a story and accepts a few bruises for authenticity."

"Exactly the line of thinking the LAPD is taking. A detective is on the case. Not the Hat Squad, though. Chief Parker has those boys busy keeping out-of-towners outside of his City of Angels. Edwards has a bigger headache now. His employer suspended him, job and pension are in limbo. Tenants are unhappy, so Edwards has that going for him."

They stopped to wait for the light to change. Hamilton drew a cigarette from the pack in his pocket. "Want one?"

"Gave them up."

"Good for you."

"Your take on all this?" Walker asked.

"Ernest runs a pipeline of some kind for Warner, but what exactly, I don't know. I reckon the doctor keeps Warner's people on an even keel." Hamilton scratched a flame and lit his cigarette. "Creative types lead disordered lives." Hamilton breathed out a gray plume.

"Is that why you have sessions? Your life, unstable and disordered?" Walker said.

"Naw. I keep feeding the man information to see where it lands. Like releasing a fish in a lake. See where it goes and how fast it swims. Jack's metaphor. You know how he likes to talk about fly-fishing in Montana."

"Jack has you working this, too?"

"Speaking of assignment," Hamilton said, "Bet you were surprised to see Leslie? I was. Jack figured since I infiltrated the CP in Yugoslavia and I had a recent spat with HUAC, I'm primed for more therapy. I didn't argue, and I figure it's just another role to play."

"You're a good actor, John."

"I admired the rebels during the war, but that was as far as it went. You know that, don't you? I had a job to do, and I did it. Now, I wring my hands and act all guilt-ridden because of this damn committee. The thing with them, though, is they've made an industry out of fear and guilt. Much scarier than Commies, if you ask me."

"What else did Jack tell you?" Walker asked.

"He has no use for committees. You should know that. Remember Meeks? He made life miserable for you and Jack in Vienna."

The mere mention of the man's name opened a musty book for Walker. Meeks, with his feelers everywhere, corrupting everything, proved to be the silverfish that crawled out of the pages. Pure arrogance in his demeanor, faux aristocrat with his silver tea set, Meeks contaminated Vienna. "I remember him, and he reported to another committee," Walker said.

"Difference is these jokers want us to believe Hollywood is Grand Central Station for Reds, and there's a Commie under every bed. If I had my guess, Jack's orders are to safeguard intelligence from the émigrés on this coast."

Hamilton was no historian, but he was a Company man who understood resources and the value of reliable information. The Company had a Weimar on the Pacific, with the likes of Thomas Mann, Brecht, Lang, and Lion Feuchtwanger living in Los Angeles. Along comes HUAC throwing tomatoes and accusations. If émigrés started leaving because HUAC threatened their livelihood or made life inhospitable, the Company risked a critical lifeline to Europe. Those folks had seen Hitler, and the last thing they wanted to see and hear was the American version of Stalin in a senator and his henchmen. Hamilton asked Walker for the latest on his end.

"Warner asked me to write about Dachau, and I just found out Dr. Ernest knows Warner's clearance man, Moore."

At Wilshire and Fairfax, they stopped to admire the red curve of the S in Simon's above them on a pylon that would scare a blind man's dog. The drive-in restaurant was a dramatic number in the Streamline Moderne style, encased all around in plate-glass, circular, and screaming out its presence to the street and parking lot. A blonde in a tilted hat, smart uniform, and feet in roller skates breezed past them.

Hamilton opened the door. Cool frosted air justified Hamilton's long coat.

The coldness made it impossible for Walker to smell the cigarette smoke on Hamilton. They had to choose between red leather booths or the stools and countertops. OrderMatic menus were at both locations either way. They picked the counter. They ordered coffee and watched the girl wheel away on skates and return with the hot pot and two mugs. She turned over the heavy mugs onto the counter like a magician did cards and poured their coffee.

"Ernest knows Moore, huh?" Hamilton said.

"Not sure how, but I'll assume Moore is Warner's leg man. He grilled me after Vera's party in case HUAC had questions about my personnel file at the studio."

"Don't take it personal. The moguls are a tight-fisted crowd."

"I made one comment to Warner about Dachau. Next thing I know, he's pushing me to write about the camp." Walker saw Hamilton's face twitch. "What is it?"

"Could just be family guilt. Warner is a Jew. He had to know what was going on in Europe. Even if he was born in Canada, Warner is still a Jew. Their culture and religion bind them in ways we can't understand, but what I don't get is why he named names to HUAC."

"Terry at work said Warner had union problems over some film he did at FDR's request. The way Terry explained it, Warner surrendered names to HUAC as payback. Warner has it in his head that he can do a message film with Dachau."

Hamilton blew on his coffee. He took it black. His steady breath created dark waves until he spoke again.

"A film on Dachau will do more than make people think. Telephones will ring off the hook from coast to coast. Truman won't have a minute of peace. Citizens will want to know just how much the government knew about the camps. Assume you told Ernest about this project?"

"I did, and I voiced my concerns to Warner: the public isn't ready for it, but Warner insists I write about the camp without anyone knowing it."

"I've got to hand it to you, Walker. You've accomplished what I couldn't. It'll be interesting to see where this fish goes in the pond. The doctor will pass along what you said to Moore. Let's see how fast that fish swims."

"So much for confidentiality."

"Yeah, like priests don't talk about sins they hear in confession. You'll get Moore's ear. Ride this one out, Walker. I should vamoose." Hamilton lifted his long arm up for the bill from the skating princess.

"I'll take care of it, John."

"Thanks. Give my regards to Jack."

"I will." Walker retrieved his wallet, peeled a Washington off for the girl, and told her to keep the change. That was when he found the note from Leslie in his wallet. She requested they meet. She had written down the time and place.

Chapter Twenty-One

It was fun-time. Jack Marshall Junior and his friends were out in the street in a game of freeze tag while the girls on the sidewalk with Elizabeth were drawing chalk squares for hopscotch.

The same car, the same two men were talking to the neighbors on the other side of the street. It didn't seem to bother Betty's neighbors to have a pair of men in front of them, eyes obscured by Hudson frames, one asking all the questions while the other one copied their answers into a flip pad. Betty could tell these men were inquiring about her and Jack. Now and then, one of her neighbors would look toward the house. She didn't care if they saw her or not. She watched, and they kept answering questions.

From one house to the next Betty observed them from behind the gauzy material of the curtain. The dark suits worked their way down the street, writing more notes, turning white flags over for pages while the children played. The men covered one side of the street, down the block, one neighbor to the next and to the next. Lips moving, more notes and flipped pages.

Betty had roast beef planned for dinner. Some of the husbands on her street tinkered under car hoods, and one of them was pushing a hand mower across his lawn to save himself the chore on the weekend. Jack was still at the office. Her world from behind her window was adults, children, and two strangers. No sounds except when a boy yelled Freeze! She took out pen and paper.

Turkey in the Straw could be heard playing from down the block. The slow ragtime tune meant the Good Humor truck was crawling its way up Annunciation Road. Elizabeth would rush in, beg for money, and promise that the ice cream would not ruin her or her brother's appetites for dinner.

"Mom?" Elizabeth yelled. Elizabeth rushed into the house to solicit money.

"In here, Elizabeth," Betty called out, paper and pen placed inside her sweater pocket.

"I want a toasted almond, please."

"And what about your brother?"

Betty knew the answer. Jack Junior and Senior always picked the chocolate-covered vanilla ice cream on the stick. Betty and Elizabeth were the ones who experimented with flavors and new items. Betty handed her daughter a dollar.

"And I want change, Miss Elizabeth Marshall."

Elizabeth bolted without a reply to catch the truck. The tinny music neared; the song proved irresistible to all the children. Betty could see them running into their houses for money and back out into the street for ice cream. Like ants, they swarmed where the white truck pulled to the curb. The music played. The man in the white uniform and hat and his dark bowtie moved from behind the wheel to a counter space where he would dispense refrigerated treats amidst yelps and yells, making change from his coin changer on his hip at the end of a bandolier strap.

Junior stayed with his friends, seeing his sister had his order and their mother's money. Betty walked down the few steps to the walkway. She had lost sight of the two men across the street because of the truck and the children crowded around it.

She reached into her pocket and touched the piece of paper on which she had copied down the license plate number. She had noticed earlier the two men used the same make and model car, but different plates. To her horror, Betty saw one of the two men standing next to Elizabeth, paying for her ice cream, and handing her the toasted almond bar first, then Junior's Good Humor. A dollar curled over Elizabeth's clenched fist.

Betty rushed forward, took Junior's ice cream in one hand, and grabbed Elizabeth's free hand with the other. Betty tried to locate the man's partner and, not finding him, turned around and came face to face with him. And with a bully's assurance, he reached into her sweater pocket, pulled out the small piece of paper, and tore it into confetti.

Junior charged across the street and confronted the man. "Why are you bothering my mother, Mister?"

"Let's go inside, the two of you," Betty said to her children.

The two men stood there staring at Betty, expressionless. Elizabeth started crying and dropped her toasted almond. Junior thought about rescuing the fallen ice cream, but asked his mother to give his sister the Good Humor. Elizabeth took it but didn't eat any.

Betty had a phone call to make. She remembered the license plate number.

* * *

Burbank. In time for lunchtime, Walker parked his car between the two parallel white lines under the jealous eyes of writers outside in small huddles with cigarettes in one hand, white Styrofoam cups in their other hand. No Terry in the crowd. Walker closed and locked his car door.

The midday heat bloomed early. Miss Elkins intercepted him on his way to The Pool. The sound of her heels preceded her. Like an approaching colt. Not a gallop and certainly not a canter, but soft clops announced her. Her white dress, a carnation behind her ear, and her makeup copied poster art.

"Mr. Thompson, I've been meaning to talk to you."

"It's Walter, please. If it's about my coming in late, I can explain," he said, but her face said her agenda read differently.

"Mr. Warner was insistent I show you to your new office."

"New office?"

They continued walking down the long white corridor in what felt like a quarter mile from The Pool. A new office might explain the gauntlet of stares in the parking lot. Walker was the fish relocated to better waters.

The first thing he saw in the room was a fresh Remington Super-Riter on the desk. Nice familiar Army green. Warner was no fool. He may have been upgraded to a prestigious typewriter, but the limited décor said something else. Desk and chair of sleek wood, the ream of paper, a cup full of sharpened pencils, and shiny paper clips said writing was the sole purpose of the room.

"I took the liberty of moving the contents of your desk and your things from the Pool," Miss Elkins said. "Your coffee and supplies are over there in the kitchenette."

The space was bigger than his apartment. Walker surveyed the rest of the office. Against the wall sat a womb chair and an ottoman next to a leather couch. Agents in Central Casting may have used the same furniture to woo the next Gardner or Harlow off the bus at Union Station. The Muse in all her incarnations. Miss Elkins wasn't finished with her tour.

"You have your own phone line. A small bar with amenities is in the console." She opened the display to reveal beer and hard liquor. "Mr. Warner told me to remind you lunches can be delivered, if you place your order with me by 11 a.m. Here are your keys." She placed a small ring with three keys into the palm of his hand. "One is for your desk. Lock up your work at night. This second key is to your office door."

"And the third one?"

"Your private washroom." She pointed to the door to the back of the office. "Any questions?"

"Where's the private plane?" The blank face told him the joke landed like a cantaloupe. "Thank you, Miss Elkins. I'll let Mr. Warner know what a fine job you've done."

She left. Warner wanted Dachau. A surprise awaited him on the other side of the typewriter. He rotated the champagne bottle in the Pelican cooler, running his hand around the top and touching the gold lid when he heard a knock on his door. "Come in," he said to the door.

"Seems the new guy is moving up in the world. Fancy office, new typewriter, new everything. Not bad," the man said.

It was Joe Teague.

"Didn't know you visited the office, Joe."

"I've been known to from time to time."

Teague eyed the black leather couch. "May I?"

"Go ahead."

Teague sat down, testing the leather with his fists, before turning horizontal, putting his feet up, and letting out a long exhalation. He lit a cigarette and lowered his arm to forget about the smoke for a while.

"What can I do for you, Joe?"

"Nothing. I just wanted to congratulate you. I'm not quite sure what it is you did to warrant the amenities, but it must be something good. Imagine what the other writers must be thinking." Teague's hand came up for a puff.

Walker couldn't resist. "I figured if you're stumped, then they must be at an even greater loss. Weren't you a writer?"

Teague's tight grin suggested he remembered what it was like to eat glass.

"I like that, Walter. 'Were.' But you know what?" he said, leg swung over into a seated position. "I'm just here to wish another writer the best of luck, even if it means Warner has you on some special project of his. Don't ask how I know because it's unimportant. Just understand there's nothing new under the sun out here, Walter."

"Thanks, Joe. I'll remember that. Any other advice?"

"Yeah. Don't forget Jack Warner is the Sun King; he bestows warmth and wealth wherever he strolls. The orange groves bow to his largesse, and the land flourishes when the king is pleased. You do your job, and everything is right with the monarch. Don't do your job, and you'll find the white lines in the parking lot blacked over, the lock to your office changed." Teague held his hands up in mock surrender. "Toil away, my friend. No need to tell me about the project. No need at all. Let that typewriter over there become your heartbeat. When it stops you either move on to the better life, or you've died. Do your special whatever for Warner, and I'll go and do mine."

"Thanks again, Joe. Appreciate it. Like you said, I'll do my thing, and you do yours. I didn't know you did projects for Warner, too. I thought he retired you to the Dead Letter Office."

Teague blew smoke at Walker. The tactic worked in films. The bad guy challenges the good guy with smoke in the face. In real life, the same guy would be lucky to keep his teeth in his head.

"I do special projects, too," Teague said. "Doing them for years, long before you showed up. I didn't go solo until now. Me and a guy named Charlie Loew worked together, delivering payroll to blacklisted writers. In fact, we threw some green at gray-listed writers. Oh, from the look on your face, you don't know what that means. Those are writers not quite condemned but not quite good for Public Relations. Don't look so surprised, Walter. I'm sure the professor explained it all to you. You know who I'm talking about. Terry Doyle. It was Charlie and me, but now it's just me, Joe Teague. I like working alone, and I'd prefer to keep it that way."

"I'm happy for you, Joe, but no need to mark your territory. We're not in a nightclub. Mickey Cohen taught you scare tactics well. Save the routine for someone who'd appreciate it. I heard about Charlie."

Teague took a long drag. His cigarette had burned down to his fingers. The ash held tight. Expensive cigarettes, quality tobacco. "And what's a new guy like you hear about Charlie?"

"He met with an unfortunate end."

"You heard right. Murdered. I hear things, too, Walter."

"Really? What do you hear?"

Teague leaned over and whispered, "I hear HUAC plans to call you up."

With that, Teague tapped ashes on the floor.

Chapter Twenty-Two

Walker was weekending in Malibu. He was driving down the highway to Santa Monica through easy traffic. He saw the long pier and the arch. A soft breeze, bright colors, people moved about as he searched for a parking space in some shade since the sun was baking skin and roasting wood. Santa Monica was all noise, of people and kids, gulls squawking in search of food, and the smell of salt and the thick odor of tar in the air.

A fine mist from ocean spray slapped Walker's face. He stopped short for a child running with a Tiki creature in her hand. A woman on the other side of the pier was teaching her daughter how to haggle with a fishmonger for the best bits for a bouillabaisse. A hawker yelled out, "Taffy and Taquitos."

Leslie waved, and he started walking toward her. She faced the waves and watched tykes on floaters in the water with their dads against the foam. She was wearing a yellow sundress, eyes hidden behind dark cheaters.

"How are you, Walker? It's been a long time since we talked."

"It's odd how two people can live in the same city and never cross paths, isn't it?" He pulled out his sunglasses. The glare off the water and all the open air gave him the excuse to hide his eyes behind green-tinted lenses.

"Funny how work brings people together," she said. "Vienna and now here on a sunny Saturday morning."

"Jack hadn't told me he put you inside the doctor's office."

He started from the top: his interview with Jack Warner in the hallway, Cagney's Yiddish, what Terry said about the unions and HUAC, which brought him around to his meeting with Moore after Vera's party, and meeting Joe Teague twice, first at Billy Gray's Band Box and then again in his new office, and the revelation about Teague and Loew. He finished up with Warner's request to pen a screenplay about Dachau. He mentioned how Warner could get him anything he needed to make this pet project work, including scripts. He also mentioned Hamilton out on the street, their long walk to get some coffee. He had heard about Mr. Edwards. Told her Ernest knew Moore, and Teague said HUAC would be calling on him. They started walking together. She asked him what Jack said last.

"He's having the police drill into Mr. Edwards. It buys us time."

She stopped. "A sacrifice? Mr. Edwards could get hurt. He hasn't been at work, but I assumed it was to recover from his injury."

"No. Edwards was suspended, pending the outcome of the police investigation." A seagull screamed overhead. "Don't worry, Leslie. Jack will keep Edwards out of harm's way.

"All the way from DC?"

A gaggle of kids shrieked by with popcorn spilling on the pier. The head of the pack declared which amusement he wanted to ride next, reminding the group they were wearing all-day wristbands that entitled them to unlimited rides. "How about you?" he asked.

"Not much to say, Walker." She spoke about Ernest, their drinking at the Ambassador, the restaurant in the hills above the city, more drinking, and Vera's party, the morning after, and her account of the morning she found Edwards. She said she failed to get the keys to the filing cabinet, and Ernest had a new set of filing cabinets installed, with new locks. She mentioned she had lost her small gun. She said it was sentimental to her, like Grable, his .45, was to him.

"What's special about it?" he asked.

"Red Croix de Lorraine."

"French Resistance. Any ideas who might've stolen it?"

"None. I was careless. I checked my purse, and it was gone. I'm beginning to think I'm getting too old for this."

"Don't be ridiculous. Quite the crowd there at Vera's place. Any one of them could've lifted the gun. Still can't get into the doctor's files?" She shook her head. "Thinking of maybe…trying to…"

"Use my charm?"

"A delicate way of putting it, but yes," he said. There was nothing to add, so he listened to the carnies try to entice visitors to their booths.

"I tried. The only thing Phillip Ernest has a passion for is his collection of pens."

"A shame since most of Warner's staff is in those cabinets," he said and realized he had just underscored her failure.

"You said Ernest knows Moore, right?" Walker nodded this time. "And Moore works for Warner?"

"He clears new employees for HUAC in case they make the rounds."

"You had, but Moore has to keep track of the writers. What if Moore kept files of writers who changed studios? Warner would want to keep track of them regardless of where they went. You mentioned how he could get scripts for you, regardless of the studio. Writers move around, and Warner could use Moore to track them. Warner is as competitive as he's concerned about liabilities. If Moore is on the Warner payroll, and Warner refers staff to Ernest, then Ernest is on Warner's payroll."

"A syllogism of sorts," Walker said. "Blackmail is a liability, but not if Warner has the dirt first. There's a two-for-one special. Warner anticipates HUAC through Moore, and he has leverage on his writers through Ernest. Clearance and Liability are the same thing."

Leslie and Walker stopped near the carousel to sit on a bench. They watched the all-wooden carousel turn with its painted ponies and chariots, its shiny mirrors and poles churning kids up and down to the sound of Scott Joplin. They both could relate to the one kid on the outer edge of the merry-go-round on the dark horse, trying and trying to grab the brass ring.

Chapter Twenty-Three

"Maggie, this is Vera." The voice exited the receiver calmly before it cracked into a sob like a wounded dove.

"What in the world happened?"

Through wet sounds and gasps, Vera asked, "Have you seen today's column?"

"I've told you a thousand times, Vera, you shouldn't read the gossip rags. Come on, compose yourself, and I'll see you when you come in for your appointment with Ernest today. Ten o'clock."

Another wail. Leslie closed her eyes in frustration. "Vera."

"You don't understand, Maggie. You don't understand. They ran a picture."

"The hell with them, Vera. Let them run a picture. It won't be the first time for an unflattering photograph. People will forget about it by afternoon."

"You don't understand, Maggie."

"What don't I understand, Vera? Explain it to me."

Between sniffles and sobs, waiting for Vera to be coherent, Leslie was thinking how lucky she was she didn't have children or other attachments. She had no patience for drama. The sniffling and the congested sound abated. Leslie tried a more soothing approach. "What don't I understand? Please explain it to me, Vera."

"The picture they ran..." another sob.

"They ran a picture...and?"

"It's a picture of me and you... a picture of us in bed."

* * *

Walker gave Jack a complete report at the end of the weekend. He thought often of Leslie while driving down to Burbank. He wished he had been more compassionate about her 'failure' and wished she had been warmer to him than the deep-freeze blondes he saw on the beaches from the road.

The writers still gave him dirty looks. Even the after-hours cleaning staff of coloreds and Mexicans were giving him the eye, too, as if he didn't belong in his own office while he worked on Dachau. There was no title for the screenplay yet, but he aimed for some play on words, since the name Dachau was derived from a Celtic word for water. The writing went as writing goes: contemplation, sketching out an idea or a scene, and then some momentum, tuning dialogue, and calibrating exposition in long jags at the Remington. He understood why writers smoked and drank. He preferred to pace the room, walk in the solitude of the comfortable cell Warner created for him.

Terry was the only writer after Teague to visit him in the new office.

Walker skipped on Warner's offer for lunches because Terry made it a regular ritual to show up with food from restaurants and vendors in the area. Walker's favorite was the machaca burrito, a slow-cooked Mexican dish of mystery meat, likely a cheap cut, onions, some tomatoes, and chilies. There was a cart near enemy territory, Columbia Pictures. Terry made sure Warner didn't know about his excursions. Terry preferred the carne asada and taught Walker a true burrito should not have rice. That was the vendor cheating the customer's stomach.

There was Terry's knock on the door with today's lunch of Bob's Big Boy burgers, fries, and two Cokes. Walker cleared papers aside.

"How's the writing going?" Terry asked, setting down the food. "We ought to try Bob's Pantry in Glendale next time. He has this amazing chili spaghetti."

"I'll save up on the heartburn. People in The Pool still hate me?"

"Don't let them bother you, Walter. Do whatever you need to do to get ahead. Warner is tough, but if you do right by him, he'll treat you all right."

"Joe Teague stopped by. He acted a little jealous, but I let him talk. There's something off about that guy."

"I know what you mean. He doesn't know when to stop with his gangster mannerisms. He's watched too many George Raft movies."

"But he does know gangsters, Terry."

"Walter, listen to me. The only gangster you need to worry about is Jack Warner."

They ate their burgers. Walker liked that his burger and fries were crispy. Coca-Cola was coming out with a new bottle size, but Bob's Big Boy was faithful to the hobble-skirt design, six and a half ounces in green glass.

"Teague told me HUAC is calling me up."

Terry wiped his mouth with a napkin. "Could be just trying to rile you up. Joe plays that way. Your talk with Moore was proforma for all new employees. I'm sure he has cleared you up, and you won't be hearing from HUAC. If Warner has you screwed into the chair on a project, then your priority is to deliver it. Snap, set, and kick the ball through the posts."

"What's with the sport's metaphor?"

"Half a day on some knockoff of *National Velvet* and the other half on a film about Jim Thorpe."

"Okay, one last thing about Teague, and I don't want to sound like I'm criticizing you, Terry, but you were pretty deferential to him that night at Billy Gray's."

"More like I was trying to stay away from him. Let the man treat me like a shoeshine boy. I'm okay with it. I'd rather have Joe think I'm soft in the melon and leave it to him to dirty his own shoes."

"What's that supposed to mean?"

"Joe Teague pals with gangsters. It's inevitable he'll do something they won't approve of, and one day someone will find him in the LA River or not find him at all."

"He seems to be doing well, if you ask me, Terry. Living and breathing and making payments to fronts with a pair of healthy lungs and legs."

"Course he does, Walter, so long as Teague doesn't go spending Warner's or somebody else's money. Warner may give some play money for girls and booze, but that's as long as Warner receives scripts."

"Spend somebody else's money…is that what Charlie Loew did?"

Like Olivier forgetting a line, Terry's jaw unhinged. "I wouldn't know," he said. "Rumor says Loew was free-lancing, you know, stuff on the side."

"Like a special project." Walker was enjoying the salt on the last of the fries.

"You can say that. I heard Loew was making deliveries, but he was getting greedy and…"

"And keeping some of Jack Warner's money?"

"Worse."

"Worse? What would be worse?"

Terry wiped his hands on a napkin. "Loew was making deliveries, so I heard, on the side for Columbia. And God knows there's nobody on this earth Warner hates more than Harry Cohn."

"Think Teague ratted Loew out?" Walker knew from Terry's expression he had the wrong end of the cat.

"Remember how I told you Loew knew Mickey Cohen?" Terry asked.

"Yeah, he paid protection money to Cohen after the Burbank Strike, but Teague knew Mickey, too. Teague admitted to me he worked with Loew, but he's solo now and likes it. He said it as if it was common knowledge. Is there something I'm missing?"

"What's across the street from us?" Terry raised his hand to point at the windowless wall.

Walker glanced over his shoulder. "Columbia."

"Harry Cohn's studio. Teague and Cohen were allies since the desert first had sand. Mickey Cohen and Jack Warner? Not so much. Now, this part is conjecture. I told you everybody knows everybody in this town. Harry Cohn has his own underworld friends, but they're in Chicago. I had heard that a certain individual in Chicago invested in Loew, because he was interested in the movie business. Mr. Chicago didn't like hearing Loew was also working for Warner, but he tolerated it, and Warner didn't like it that Loew did the occasional job for Harry, but he tolerated it."

"Money." Walker chewed slowly. He sipped cola. "It's all about the money."

"Until Loew throws the cash around, and people started to ask questions, as to where all that dough came from. The Outfit doesn't like attention. Mickey Cohen drew attention to himself with the IRS, and he's on his way out. Johnny Stompanato is in. Money is money, and life goes on, so long as you don't get flashy or spend someone else's cash. As for suspects, take your pick from Cohen or Stomps, or Mr. Chicago. If you ask me, if the moguls didn't short Loew's fuse, then the Outfit did."

Terry started laughing, almost choking on his Coke.

"What?"

"There's this apocryphal story I heard once. Jack Warner and Harry Cohn wanted to take out contracts on each other. These two hitmen fly in from the East Coast. Cohn and Warner haggled the poor bastards on the price for the contract, to the point the killers shot each other instead of taking the job and gave the moguls a discount on the ammunition." Terry cleaned up and cleared his side of the desk. "I ought to scram."

Chapter Twenty-Four

Water filtered through the grounds, and the smoky sweetness of fresh coffee teased his nose. The Italian grocer in Lincoln Heights promised him this roast would be worth the additional cost. The weekend proved exhausting, with Leslie in person and Jack over the phone. The morning drive didn't help. He was about to pour himself a cup when he heard the trotting sound of Miss Elkins. Heels clattered, and then she rapped urgent knocks. A dear John to his cup of Joe, Walker realized his coffee was not meant to be.

"Morning, Mr. Thompson. Please come with me. There's a meeting."

"This early? With whom?" he asked, but she was gone. She walked, and he followed. He followed her down the long, white corridor, followed her on the buffed floor, followed the beats of her heels, past the sad, solemn Negro cleaning man with the swaying mop, past the unlettered office doors, past The Pool's door, the glass still gray from the lack of light and life behind it, past more doors and down more hallway with more walls, more waxed flooring, until her clops slowed and stopped at the unknown door.

"They're waiting for you inside."

Mr. Moore and another man sat at a table with two chairs opposite them. Exposed to daylight, Moore's features aged a decade since the night after the Mulholland party. The other man was slim, in a conservative gray suit, white shirt, and black tie held in place with a tie bar. Walker noticed the pinky ring, the hooded eyelids, and immediately thought cobra and lawyer. Redundant, but this was shaping up to be Act Two, HUAC preparation, the meeting with the confessors. The walk with Miss Elkins foreshadowed the convict's death scene.

"Have a seat, Mr. Thompson. We've been waiting," Moore said.

"Would've appreciated some notice, Mr. Moore. I could've brought my morning coffee with me."

"Our apologies. My colleague and I won't take up too much of your time, but we prefer to conduct these kinds of meetings before the rest of the staff arrives. There's no need for rumors and speculation."

"What kind of meetings?" Walker asked. Still no introduction to Moore's sidekick. Walker decided on initiative. "Name is Walter Thompson, writer."

The thin man remained coiled on his chair. Walker had noticed the manicured nails before he sat down. "What can I do for the two of you?"

There was another knock, the sound of Miss Elkins's voice again, and that of Jack Warner this time, insisting he be given entrance. "Thank you, Miss Elkins, I can manage from here," he said, entering the room and closing the door behind him. Warner pulled up the chair next to Walker. Warner's suit was tailored perfection, but aggravation gave him thinker's lines on his forehead. "Why wasn't I notified? Thought you worked for me, Lenny."

"Mr. Warner, there's no need for you here."

"The hell there isn't, Lenny. You've poached one of my writers without the decency of telling me. The man at least deserves some company on this side of the table, which is why I'm here. Two against two makes fair. Let's get down to business." Warner's fist struck the table.

The small man spoke: "Your presence is not required, Mr. Warner."

Warner glared. His eyes said pipsqueak, but Warner rubbed his jaw instead. "There's a punch for you. Told what to do in my own house. The nerve these days."

"That really isn't necessary, Mr. Warner," Moore said. His eyes looked to the man next to him. "Have any idea who he is?"

"I know who he is, Lenny. I know exactly who he is. You've got chutzpah, Mister, but this is my studio, my house, and I expect respect under my roof, like a phone call or a letter." Warner slapped the table. "Now, if you two have business, then let's get on with it. Let the record show Walter Thompson is present with Jack Warner."

"This is informal, Mr. Warner, and as you can see, there's no stenographer here." Moore's sideman said, with the clinical indifference of a coroner.

"Just like your type to not want a transcript," Warner said. "Get on with it, Lenny, unless our esteemed guest has more to say."

Moore's legal pad appeared. "When we last spoke, Mr. Thompson, you provided me with details of your past. You discussed your military experience and your post-war education."

"I did."

Moore rolled over the blank first page of his canary pad, took out three pieces of loose-leaf paper, and laid them out in front of Walker and Warner. The first piece of paper, the white one, he set down in the middle, and on either side of it, he placed two other pieces of paper, one black and the other, gray.

"Truth is always white. Lies are black, and half-truths are gray. Mistakes, indiscretions, if surrendered honestly with remorse, are considered truthful. White. Ambiguous or deliberate and selective statements that lead us to inconclusive conclusions are gray," Moore said with his finger tapping the gray piece of paper.

"Do we understand each other?" the other man said.

"Yeah, it's the old shell game from Coney Island," Warner answered. He also tapped the table. "If he invokes the Fifth, it looks like he has something to hide, or he's dodging the question, and he's in the black. In deep, and the only way out is to go white."

"There's no need for me to invoke the Fifth Amendment," Walker said.

Hooded eyes and Mr. Moore sat back, excited. They both smirked as if they found easy prey. Warner whispered into Walker's ear. "Sure, you know what you're doing? I can get you a lawyer and stall them. Just say the word, Walter."

"That's kind of you, Mr. Warner, but I don't think it's necessary," Walker said. "The snake and his charmer here see me as the mongoose."

Moore swept his pieces of paper under his legal pad. "There really is no need to be adversarial. Shall we start again?"

A single nod. Walker's.

"As I said, when we last spoke, you attended a party on Mulholland."

"I did. Vera Williams's party. It was a pleasant evening," Walker said.

"You met Miss Williams and saw a few writers there, correct?"

"I met her. I saw a lot of people."

"You also met Miss Williams's companion?"

"I did?"

"Miss Margaret Gardner, who works for Dr. Ernest."

Moore produced a picture. Walker didn't remember any flashbulbs. The picture was right there. It didn't appear doctored. Leslie was in her black dress and diamond choker, and Vera was in a sequined dress, with one arm around Leslie, a glass of champagne in the other hand. Queen of the ball with her princess, and there was Walker at court as knight-errant.

"I met her, yes. Didn't meet Ernest at the party, though. I met him later. She's Vera's companion?"

"Before we move onto which writers were present, you also provided me with details of your life prior to employment with Mr. Warner," Moore said.

The small man next to Moore shot up to his feet and leaned over the table with the indictment coming out of his mouth with some spittle. "The 42nd and 45th Infantry Divisions liberated Dachau. Guess what? Your name can't be found on the rolls."

"Why would my name be there?" Walker asked, calm as crushed ice, seeing Moore coaxing the other man back into his chair.

"I don't understand. Please explain, Mr. Thompson," Moore said.

"I served in the Texas division, 36th Infantry Division. As for the concentration camp, the division took the Kaufering sub-camps on April 30th of 1945."

"Likely story," the lawyer said. His rolled onto his hip over in his chair and stared at Walker. "I have friends in the Army, Mr. Thompson, and if you're lying…if you're lying, I'll…"

"You'll what, you little runt?" Walker said and stood, making it his turn to lean over the table. "I've seen your kind before: tony education, bespoke shoes, with Daddy and Granddaddy lining up all the right schools and diplomas for you, their little prince. Mommy potty-trained you, tied your shoes, and wiped your nose. You've never served, did you? Oh, I've seen your type before…oh, I have. Ready to send men to damnation, a regular hawk about war so you can further your cause."

The smallish man smirked. "Cause, you say? We have a regular Smedley Butler here, Leonard."

"Stuff it. Don't twist my words, little man. All I'm saying is there'll come a day when one of your kind gets through OCS when Daddy and the judge, friend of the family, can't get you any more deferments. You're the man the enlisted men will kill before the enemy does."

"Calm down, Mr. Thompson." Moore's hand invaded the space between Walker and his adversary. Walker turned his attention to Moore.

"Ah, the hell with him and the hell with you, too, Mr. Moore. I'll say it because someone has to say it. This no-name Napoleon over there with his nasal voice is only good for one thing, and that's for talking French through his nose or for finding truffles."

"Better than speaking kraut," the other man said, standing up again with his fists on the table.

Warner rose, his hand on Walker's shoulder. "Some temper, you have. Please sit down."

There was a knock at the door, and Miss Elkins walked in. She appeared ill at ease, as if she walked in and saw blood and knife, victim and murderer.

"A man is here with documents for you, Mr. Moore."

She let in a marine in a green and khaki service uniform.

"I've been asked to deliver these to you personally, sir. You requested them," the marine said. He handed the sealed envelope to Moore.

"I don't remember any request for documents," Moore said as he broke the seal and read the sender's name to his companion. "Says the defense secretary."

"Couriered personally from DC, sir," the marine said. "Those were my orders. Will that be all, sir?"

Moore was busy reading when he said, "Yes, yes, that'll be all, soldier."

Moore was surprised, as was Warner when Walker stood up again. He said in a measured tone. "For all your education and arrogance, you should know you never call a marine soldier. It is marine, United States Marine."

Walker's tone was enough to make the Marine turn about-face to him and stand at attention. "Thank you, Marine. Dismissed."

The Marine snapped a salute, and Walker returned it.

"Miss Elkins?" Warner said in a low voice.

"Yes, Mr. Warner?"

"Our guest here must be tired from his journey. See to it he has breakfast and accommodations. As our guest, I'd like for him to have a tour of the studio with unlimited access. All compliments of Warner Brothers, of course."

"Thank you, sir. Thank you very much," the marine said with some excitement at the possibility of meeting movie stars. Once the uniformed man left the room, Walker and Warner sat down. Miss Elkins stood still at the door for a moment. She blushed and stole a quick look of admiration at Walker.

"What do those papers say?" Warner asked Moore.

Moore, as he was finding his chair to sit, said, "Like Walter said, the 36th. These papers convey his Army service and awards: Silver Star at Monte Cassino; Bronze Star with Valor device in Alsace along with a Purple Heart, and another Bronze Star, second valor device at the Battle of the Bulge. Participated in the Dachau liberation, it also says, April 30, 1945." Moore shuffled papers and counted them in silence. "The rest here are lengthy descriptions for all his commendations. Signatures and attestations are impressive. Patton, Marshall, and other officers."

Warner rose up from his chair. "I'm satisfied. Walter has work to do. Unless you two have something else to say or add, I believe this meeting is adjourned."

Moore's right-hand man stood up again. He snapped up the envelope from Moore's hand and said: "I'm not done with you, Thompson. You'll be hearing from me, Warner. This isn't finished. I have plans for the two of you."

"I'm sure you do," Warner answered with civility. "Mr. Moore can show you the way out. Have a good day, gentlemen."

They heard pattering heels. Miss Elkins knocked again. She rushed over and whispered something into Moore's ear. Whatever the secret message she told him, Moore's eyes bulged, his lips twisted as if his breakfast curdled in his stomach.

Walker meanwhile asked the other man, "You Jewish?"

"And what if I am?"

"I'd like to offer you a little advice, but since you don't speak German, I'll say it to you in a language you should know. It's a Yiddish expression I heard among the camp survivors."

"We really should go," Moore said to his colleague.

"So soon, Lenny?" Warner asked.

"Yeah, what is it?" the lawyer asked Walker.

"Mensch tracht, un Gott lacht," Walker said, hearing Warner chuckle as his hand directed Walker and himself to the door.

Out in the hallway, into the cool air, Walker and Warner walked down the polished floors, relieved to return to the playground of clichés, metaphors, and dialog in need of the blue- pencil. Maybe change a ribbon.

"Like what you told him back there, the Yiddish part," Warner said.

"A person plans, God laughs."

"Yeah, that. You have quite the temper, Walter."

"Can you blame me? By the way, who was that guy?"

Warner shook his head and put his hand on Walker's shoulder as they continued walking. "That guy is chief counsel to Senator Joseph McCarthy. Name is Roy Cohn. Don't you read the papers?"

Walker stopped walking. "You know I can't keep track of the names around here. There's Mickey Cohen, gangster. Harry Cohn, president of Columbia, and now this character, Roy Cohn, lawyer."

"All gangsters," Warner said. "But Harry Cohn is the biggest one of them all."

"Wonder if Roy is a relative of his?"

Amused, Warner said, "There's a thought."

Walker had two thoughts: couriered from DC and Jack.

Chapter Twenty-Five

Yet another man operated the elevator when Leslie stepped in. This replacement exhibited some expertise at the console, which was an improvement for her stomach. She thought of Mr. Edwards and of Jack in the long ascent. The new man was all plastic, start to finish, from his hello smile to monotone announcement of the destined floor. The chiming bell offered more variety.

At the twelfth floor she turned right and headed to Ernest's office. At the dark end of the hall, the door was slightly ajar. There was a shard of light across the mausoleum-gray floor. She approached the door, holding her purse. Leslie wore gauntlet gloves. She started thinking alibi, but not before she saw the scene.

The door creaked like a cliché. The anteroom was untouched. She closed the front door behind her. Her desk was as she left it—neat and orderly as an obedient child's room, with papers under the crystal paperweight and a typewriter asleep under its cover. She looked to the other door, also ajar, where sunlight made a small spotlight on the floor to mark where she should stand.

Ernest was at the desk slumped over, his hands outstretched like Dutch Schultz in death, but, unlike the gangster, Ernest left no rambling speech for the ages. There would be no rushed car ride to the operating room. His ferry across the River Styx was inside an ambulance to the morgue under a mute siren in the morning traffic, or whatever time the City Coroner collected the body.

She noted the time on her wristwatch. She undid a glove and touched his neck. Still warm. Face down, he had made his final bow to the workday when a single bullet entered the back of his head. She saw the entry. Small caliber. Exit wound was unlikely. The bullet was inside the man's head, along with his final thoughts. She put her glove on.

Ernest had known his killer. Sitting casual there at his desk, likely talking while writing the very notes she would have typed up later that morning. There was no ballpoint pen in his hand, though. No paperwork under his face. There was nothing but the open butterfly of a manila folder under his face. Leslie peeled up the edge of the manila folder. No name.

She turned. Exposed to the air on their steel rails, two filing cabinet drawers had been pulled open. She bent over the one closest to the floor, T through Z. She raked the top of the files, front to back, with her gloved finger. No THOMPSON or WILLIAMS.

There had to be a file on Walker somewhere, albeit a thin one. Her eyes confirmed again. THOMPSON and WILLIAMS files were missing. The other open filing cabinet was clients G through L. The thick file on John HAMILTON was there. She fanned the tops of the files from front to back. Another gap. This time, it was in the L section. No LOEW file, if it ever existed.

Leslie closed both cabinet drawers. She was thinking. *Closed file cabinets will force the Homicide detectives to focus on the body. The killer took the cabinet keys off Ernest. Probably still has them. Killed him, started the treasure hunt, but pressed for time flees, knowing the secretary was due in the office at any moment.*

She looked at Ernest again at his desk, back to her, slumped over, barely cold.

Now, where were those missing files?

Behind the desk again, she stopped when she saw it on the floor. Cross of Lorraine on white grip enamel. Blood on bone. There was nothing to suggest it was hers. Leslie picked it up and placed it in her clutch.

The desk. Maybe Walker's file was in the desk. Maybe Ernest hadn't had time to file it.

The desk was a monstrosity in mahogany. Four nicely picture-framed molded dovetail drawers on both sides of the desk. The doctor in the middle blocked the center drawer. Inconvenient, she thought, but there were eight chances for missing folders here. Start from the top on the left. It was time for a game of Crazy Eights.

She examined the warhorse of a desk. There were scratches and contusions in the wood. The slide-out shelf stuck but came out with some effort. The next door required a pull but produced nothing interesting. Numerous pens rolled about like sailors on rough seas. The next drawer offered up an assortment of paperwork of thank-you notes. The third drawer revealed the wolf in the man: a girlie magazine hidden under invoices too old to be relevant to the taxman in this decade. Last drawer. She half-expected the contraband bottle and solo glass. Surprised to feel weight behind the last drawer, Leslie yanked on it and fell backwards onto the floor.

In this bottom drawer, Ernest stored books. No Freud or Jung here. Leslie scanned the names on the spines. Psychologists, no doubt. She thumbed through Eugene Aserinsky's book about dreams, a draft of a journal article by Lawrence Fouraker and Sidney Siegel on the psychology of bargaining and negotiations, and a proposal by a certain Ward Edwards to study decision-making at Stanford. Wedged in the back of the drawer was a Gnome Pixie camera with 620-film.

I've got to get out of here.

It was then she noticed the extra space in the back of the drawer. There was a considerable amount of paperwork in the doctor's neat hand: ledger-style notes with dates and times. All recent, but some pages were older, dated 1947. Person or persons involved were noted with initials to the left. There were cryptic bursts of verbiage that included more initials to the right. She aligned the heavy drawer onto the runners and pushed the drawer in. Perspiration beaded on her forehead.

I must leave now. No time to find those missing folders.

Leslie ran to her desk and grabbed an oversized envelope. She grabbed a pen from her holder and scrawled out the address in fast cursive. From one of her drawers, she found stamps and affixed the postage. Airmail.

Out of the office into the hall, closing the office door behind her, she squeezed her clutch under her arm and dropped the envelope into the Cutler mail chute. Through the stairwell door, she started her descent, stopping to take her heels off after the first few stairs to move faster and make less noise. Hand on the railing, using the elbow turns to propel herself faster around corners, breathing hard, she moved down floor to floor until she startled herself and the unexpected person going the other way.

"Vera."

"Maggie? What on earth are you…"

"No time to explain, Vera. Just come with me. Why are you in the stairwell?"

"Awful string of elevator operators since Mr. Edwards, so I decided to walk up to see if I can get a walk-in appointment with…."

"Not today, you don't." Leslie crooked Vera's elbow in as an accomplice to a crime after the fact, while the Postal Service obstructed justice.

Chapter Twenty-Six

The hours evaporated before Terry decided to give Walker's door the lunchtime knock. Walker stopped his typing. He was in the mood for Mexican and could use the company and fresh air. "Can we do Mexican?" he asked Terry.

"Sure, whatever you want. Mexican is always good."

"You mentioned a vendor near Columbia. Let's go there,"

"It's where they filmed *The Three Stooges*."

"Any problem getting on the lot?"

"Not at all. I know someone. Besides, everyone loves this guy's food," Terry said, seeing the time on his watch, "We should go."

"Great. Happen to know if there's a payphone near the cart?"

"Think so, but what's wrong with the phone on your desk?" Terry asked

"I would, but after my morning with Moore, I'm a little paranoid."

"Can't blame you. Was Moore heavy-handed with the thumbscrews? Heard Warner was with you. That's a first,"

"News travels fast, doesn't it?" Walker checked for his wallet and picked up his sunglasses.

"Everyone's heard about it by now. Elkins can't keep a secret. A marine to the rescue, Moore put in his place, and RC out the door with his tail between his legs. Word's gone around you're a real war hero. I gotta ask, though, Did Moore do his three pieces of paper?" Walker nodded, and Terry laughed. Walker reached for the one sheet on the typewriter and put it in the drawer with the rest of the draft. "I've got to lock this up."

"Right, your secret project."

Terry waited in the hallway while Walker closed and locked his office door.

"RC?" Walker asked.

"RC…we always use initials. JL is Jack Warner. LM for Lenny Moore, and RC is Roy Cohn. He's a piece of work."

* * *

The file's small typescript hurt his eyes worse than headlights at night. The fluorescent rod above him needed changing. It flickered a metronomic beat like some SOS signal. The lighting in the room took on a grainy texture, and opening the Venetian blinds overtook the fluorescent lights, but the pulses remained detectable in the afternoon shadows. They made Jack irritable.

He set the file aside; he was standing on his desk to remove the annoyance overhead when the phone rang. He sank to his knees and answered the call. "Yes."

"Mr. Marshall?"

"Chief Parker?"

"I wouldn't mind if you called me Bill from time to time."

"To what do I owe the pleasure?" Jack reached down and flipped on the recording switch in the cabinet on the right side of the desk.

"A situation that concerns us both. An unfortunate one."

Jack found his chair, dragged over a pad, and picked a pencil. "Listening."

"The Negro elevator operator, Mr. Edwards. I'm sorry to say that option has exhausted itself now, and not without some consequence for Mr. Edwards. He's suspended and I believe even with a report exonerating him from my department, the damage has been done. Nobody can compel his employer to reinstate him. That, however, is not the only reason why I called. There has been another development, Mr. Marshall."

"Another development?"

"Phillip Ernest, the doctor, is dead. Murdered in his office. As for pertinent facts—there was no sign of struggle, small caliber to the back of the head, single shot, the rest of his office appeared in order, but my officers are unable to locate his secretary, a woman named Margaret Gardner. We've discussed her before. My men took a statement from her after the initial B and E. She's a murder suspect now. Thought you'd like to know all this, Mr. Marshall."

"The details you've provided suggest a professional job. No struggle. No theft. Any chance Mickey Cohen was involved?"

"I doubt it. Mr. Cohen is not known for subtlety. His work is usually grand drama. With Cohen, you expect lots of blood and lots of lead."

"Point taken, Bill. Perhaps, wrong time, wrong place for the doctor, and the perp from the initial B&E returned to the scene."

"Possible," Parker said. "There's one detail thing that bothers me about the whole affair, Mr. Marshall, and that's the way Ernest was killed."

"I'm not sure I follow."

"Ernest was found comfortable and dead at his desk, plugged in the back of the head. Ballistics says .22 caliber was used. Lethal and dainty."

Jack was hoping Parker wasn't implying a woman for a suspect.

"A .22 fits the MO of a contract killer. Up close and personal," Jack said.

"It does, but I'll be frank now, Mr. Marshall. I've directed everyone to Edwards the first time around. Then, there's the man's statement about the gun used on him. No .22 there. You can see my predicament, can't you? Not having the secretary for questioning presents a wrinkle. This homicide paints her good as either suspect or accomplice."

"Or a material witness," Jack said. "Something could've happened to her."

Jack heard Parker rustle a page, "Afraid and on the run, or kidnapped?"

"What would be your standard operating procedure?"

"Find her, question her, and investigate Ernest to find a motive for murder."

"I wouldn't presume to tell you what to do in your city, Chief Parker, but I'm inclined to think you might find Ernest much more interesting than Miss Gardner."

"Research requires time, Mr. Marshall."

"I hear you're understaffed. I'm asking a lot of you, Bill, but I have a question for you." Jack waited a beat. "When you first contacted me, you directed me to a murder scene. Security issue, you said at the time. What can you tell me about Mr. Loew?"

Jack heard Chief Parker's chair squeak.

"Loew was involved in something. An affiliate of organized crime, perhaps, but I'm not a hundred percent sure. One of my top priorities is to eradicate the Syndicate here in Los Angeles, but I don't have any dirt on Loew with the organization, but whatever Loew was into was enough to get him killed."

"Eradicating the Syndicate is quite the order, Bill. May I ask what your approach is?"

"I've established a repository of sorts for police chiefs around the country," Parker explained, "something of a resource they can use to know the whereabouts of criminals. The problem with these gangsters is they commit crimes, close up shop, and move elsewhere, like Cleveland, for instance, and that makes it harder for us to pinch them, but if Cleveland were to know the hood was in their city… you see my point."

"Get yourself a conviction in Cleveland, and you can map the Syndicate's membership."

"Think of this system I've created as a lending library among chiefs around the country, except the files on criminals are the books." Pause. "But you understand that in doing all this, I've wandered into someone else's yard, or this person thinks every police department in the country belongs in his backyard."

"I have an idea whose backyard you're talking about."

"I know it doesn't help you with the Loew case, but let what I've told you about the library sit in your ear, while you work your investigation. Is there anything you can give me?"

"I can't go into detail, but I don't think the mob is in the equation the way you thought it is, Bill. Your instinct that this is big is correct. What exactly, I don't know yet. I need time."

"Fair enough, Mr. Marshall. I'll focus on Ernest, and ease off Edwards, and try to find Miss Gardner when I get around to it."

"Thank you, and next time…"

"Next time, what, Mr. Marshall?" Parker asked.

"Call me Jack."

* * *

Terry and Walker finished two cemitas with Mission Orange Sodas. The small voyage into Harry Cohn's kingdom was not all corned beef and cabbage. The lunch crowd was large enough to fill a metropolitan square, even if it wasn't Main Street USA.

"I see a payphone," Walker said. "I need to make a call. Have a pen?"

"Sure," Terry said, unclipping a ballpoint and giving it to Walker, who placed the pen inside his shirt square. Walker walked over to the booth with a wad of napkins for note paper, dialed the number, and turned his back to the crowd and Terry. "It's me," he said into the receiver.

"It's mid-week, Walker. Everything all right?" Jack asked.

"Depends on how you define all right. I don't have much time. On a payphone here, and it's lunchtime. I've had a second run-in with Moore and the pleasure of meeting Roy Cohn. Thanks for that courier, by the way. Those documents shut Moore up. Not sure about RC, though."

"Initials, huh?"

"Seems to be the convention here."

"Have some unexpected news for you."

Walker pressed his ear into the receiver. He stayed facing the wall, so that no one would be able to read his lips. Not that he would do much talking.

"Ernest is dead. Details suggest a professional. Leslie isn't around, can't be found, and the police will start looking for her. I've bought us some time. Whatever Ernest was doing was hot. The police will investigate him first. She is second, so find her first, determine what she knows, and tell her to keep a low profile until I can bring her in."

"Understood. With RC in the picture, I'm staying in Burbank."

"Wise. You know what to do when you need to call."

Walker did know. Use a different payphone every time; they couldn't be tapped, unless the same one was used out of habit. Residential and office lines could be tapped and mined. He ended the call. Walker unclipped the pen, looked at it again. Birome ballpoint. He stuffed the unused napkin into his pocket. He walked over to Terry. "Thanks for the pen, Terry."

"Welcome. None of my business, but is everything okay?"

"Everything's fine. I needed an insurance quote. Had to jump through hoops to get an agent."

"Always angling for a better deal? Can't blame you. Hey, are you doing anything tonight? I know this place on West Sunset. Chaplin owned the building years ago. Come with me. You can use a break after this morning. Meet in the parking lot at 7?"

Walker agreed to Terry's proposal.

* * *

Lunch, the heat, the idea of siesta, the morning theatrics, or all of it combined accompanied Walker to the leather sofa in his office. He collapsed into its scent, closed his eyes, and opened them again, staring at his ceiling. He heard a knock and then saw Jack Warner in the room.

"You should relax."

"Hard to after the morning I've had, Mr. Warner. Sorry, I lost my temper with Roy Cohn."

"Moore will remind him to think twice before calling up a highly decorated veteran. That stunt can backfire in front of an audience."

Walker wasn't convinced since Cohn had John Hamilton called up before HUAC.

"Cohn will be thirsty for revenge," Walker said, aware of the cliché.

"True, but for now, relax. How's the project going?"

Walker pointed to the desk. "Well. It's locked up."

"Excellent. Go and enjoy yourself with Terry tonight." Walker rolled to his side in his chair, in obvious surprise at Warner's statement. "Relax, Walter, I told him to take you out and show you a good time. Let's just say Terry is doing a project of his own for me, too."

"Thank you, Mr. Warner."

"Don't mention it, and by the way, try out our food in the Commissary next time. I can always get Mexican brought in. I don't like the idea of my writers venturing over to Harry Cohn's picture factory."

Walker's phone rang. He lifted himself up and out of the soft leather, picked up the phone, and said, "Hello…yes. Thank you for returning my message."

He paused and listened and said, "Thank you." Walker reached for a pad and pencil but didn't write a thing.

The voice on the phone told him, "Call VW."

Warner was still standing there. "I needed an insurance quote. Thought I'd see if I can get a better rate for my car," Walker said.

Warner bought it and wished him a good night.

Chapter Twenty-Seven

"Wait," she said to Vera as they joined the crowds moving upstream on the sidewalk.

"What's the matter, Maggie?"

Holding her at the elbow, Leslie said, "You've got to call the police."

"What? Why?"

"Vera, I don't know how to say this any other way, so I'll say it plainly, but Dr. Ernest is dead. Murdered."

"Phillip is dead? You saw him?"

"I did. He was at his desk." Leslie explained the body's position and that Ernest had died from a single shot to the back of the head. "The police will see the schedule and want to talk to patients."

"But you're his secretary, and they'll…" Vera said.

"I know, but when I last spoke to the police, all they knew about me was that I was on temporary assignment. That'll delay them some, because they'll have to call the agency first."

"But didn't the elevator operator see you this morning? The police will know you'd gone up to the office."

"You're right, but they might assume I'm also a victim. A kidnapping, perhaps. The detectives may conclude the stairs were used, and they'll be scouring twelve flights for clues."

"I don't know about this, Maggie. The elevator man didn't see me. You didn't kill him, did you?"

"Of course not. Please, just do this for me and talk to the police, Vera. All you have to say is you came in for an appointment; there he was at his desk, slumped over dead. Tell them you experienced an awful fright and needed time to collect your nerves. Play up the hysteria and the drama."

"And what will you do? I mean, the police must know where you live, and they'll come looking for you."

Leslie worked a hangnail with desperation. "They will, but I'm thinking…"

"Do that, and here are my keys," Vera said, giving her a ring of keys. Leslie expressed surprise. Vera was the calm one. "My car is two blocks north of here. You can't miss it; it's a white Chrysler, a Saratoga Club Coupe. You remember the way to the house on Mulholland?"

"I do. I don't know what to say, Vera."

"The other keys are for the front door and the main door. I'll take a cab."

Leslie hugged her. "Thanks."

"Time for me to act," Vera said.

Vera returned the other way down the pavement to another high-rise building, the home of the LAPD, to play the distressed and dismayed damsel while Leslie put on sunglasses and pulled on a kerchief until she found herself the fast car.

Once in the car Leslie tested the limits of the racer. Two extra cylinders for additional horsepower and Hydraguide steering allowed her to jab the Chrysler into the vein of LA highway to Mulholland. She passed the moving trucks and the downward stares of the men in their cabs. With the bright glare of southern Californian sunlight all around her and the candid hills up ahead of her there was speed and blown hair, a white car, her sunglasses pulled down like a visor on her quest to Vera's house.

Leslie settled in. The phone rang.

"Vera," she almost purred into the phone.

"No. It's me. We need to meet."

Walker named the place and time.

* * *

"I'm sorry, but I have to work late. Something has come up," Jack said into the phone. Again, he heard Betty's rote and patient "I understand." She didn't bother to mention the children, the missed dinner, or their bedtime ritual. A knock on his office door, Jack waved in the analyst in, the unbent envelope clasped to his chest said Urgent Report in tall red letters. "I should go," Jack said, hanging up the phone on Betty in mid-sentence.

"I'm sorry to interrupt, Mr. Marshall, but this is critical."

"Please sit," Jack said, pointing to the chair in front of his desk.

"How much do you know about the Custodial Detention List?"

Jack shrugged.

"How about the Security Index?"

Jack shifted in his chair, and his face twisted into uncertain suspicion. "I've heard of it, vaguely. Supposedly, Hoover kept a list of foreign nationals and recently naturalized citizens he wanted to keep an eye on. Why?"

"Hoover wanted more than that, sir. He devised a list, like you said, but he had plans for interring those he considered sympathetic or susceptible to Communist propaganda." The analyst pulled out a perfectly unwrinkled piece of paper out of his protected parcel.

"Internment?" Jack asked.

"Executive Order 9066 allowed for the incarceration of Californian and Hawaiian Japanese in 1942. Hoover's list, starting from 1939, consists of German, Italian, and other Americans, coast to coast. Attorney General Biddle ordered Hoover to abolish the CDL, which Hoover did, but he kept and maintained the list, which he renamed as either the Security Index or Administrative Index, or SI and AI, respectively."

Jack scanned the list. "Hoover has a predilection for initials, doesn't he?"

"He does, but that's not the worst of it," the analyst said.

"It's not?"

"No. While FDR condoned detention camps for the Japanese, Hoover made plans for concentration camps."

"Concentration camps? That couldn't be possible these days," Jack said, placing the paper on his desk.

"I'm sorry to say it is possible, sir, with Congress approving The Internal Security Act of 1950, which allows for such camps in the event of national emergencies. Those who are suspected to be members of the Communist

Party since January 1, 1949, can be detained in these camps without trial. That brings me to the list you gave me."

"The list from Charles Loew?"

"There was staining. Moisture and ink, but we were able to identify and match numerous initials after we cross-referenced them with Hoover's list from 1939 through 1942. Hoover supposedly surrendered his list to Biddle and the Justice Department in 1943. Loew's list provides more initials, sir."

"Initials are rather vague…doesn't prove much," Jack said, absorbing the revelation.

"We thought the same. Initials can mean anything. The initials from Hoover's past list, however, did yield names. It took time, but many of those names provided intelligence abroad. Since Loew has been implicated in delivering payroll to blacklisted writers, we started correlating the newer initials between Hoover and Loew's list.

"Conclusion?"

"Blacklisted writers at Columbia, MGM, Paramount, Poverty Row, RKO, and Warner Brothers."

"This list of his…is it in Loew's writing?"

"No. We have determined, however, that the page was torn from another source, possibly a notebook of some sort. Different ink and penmanship, consistent, but not belonging to Loew."

"I see," Jack said.

The interdepartmental mailman arrived and placed items on Jack's desk. The analyst talked while Jack sorted his mail. "I can draft quick profiles of the studio writers we think correspond to the initials, if you like, Mr. Marshall."

Jack shifted again in his chair, this time forward and concerned when he saw the airmail envelope. He turned it over and examined the handwriting. He opened a drawer, took out a pair of gloves, and unsealed the envelope with a letter-opener. He pulled papers out of the envelope. The analyst reached into a side pocket for a pair of white librarian gloves.

"That won't be necessary, I'm afraid. There is another priority, I'd rather you consider these initials from the files of a Dr. Phillip Ernest. This paperwork has dates. See for yourself," Jack said, handing over the paperwork.

"I will, sir."

"And…wait one moment, please," Jack said, pulling up a small pad of paper. He scribbled and tore the page off. "I suggest you use these initials as a possible key in your research."

"Most of these make sense: TD for Terrence Doyle, VW for Vera Williams, but JL for Jack Warner?"

"John Leonard."

Chapter Twenty-Eight

A current of excitement and restlessness coursed through Leslie. A feeling not unlike the thrum and throb of too much caffeine in the veins after the accidental adventure at the office, she paced the room, enigmatic grin on her face, like a Mona Lisa, except she was ready to jump out of the picture frame. "Let's go out tonight, Vera."

"Are you crazy? I just gave the performance of my life to the police a few days ago. This is my first murder, darling, and you're supposed to be laying low." Vera worked the ice bucket with tongs, doling out cubes into a highball glass.

"But we could have fun."

"Where did you have in mind?"

Vera came Leslie's way, her drink in hand but not quite there to her lips. Leslie named the place. Vera's expression looked as if the Sphinx received the answer to the riddle. "You'll have to persuade me, dear," Vera answered.

"I can do that."Walker turned the roll on the typewriter to read the latest line.

***

His Dachau story from memory had turned down roads, careened around corners, some unexpected and sharp. Characters had conversations in his head. He described settings using spare and stark details. His Dachau was the real Dachau with no weepy string-music ending. People died. More people would die, but he wanted the audience to understand Dachau was a place of death, of extremity, where the soot and smoke left a metallic taste on your tongue.

And that smell.

Walker remembered and excised stereotypes. The old joke amongst the infantrymen was you knew when the Germans were nearby because you could smell sauerkraut and cabbage in the air, as if our cousins in language and the enemy across the field sweated differently than us. Walker removed other horrid clichés, such as the perfumed French, their worm cheese and awful accordion music; the Italians and garlic; the condescending British; that every Russian was named Comrade Boris or Ivan, or everyone believed every American had endless cigarettes whenever they met friends on the road, or Field Ration D bars, chocolate, for children in liberated towns and villages.

Walker read the last typed line.

His character had vomited. The bodies weren't shown but implied. Walker employed symbolism. He described two pillars of smoke, the results of aerial bombardment and tank assaults. This last image and line occurred after opening the door to the crematorium. He relayed what he had witnessed years ago that April. Factual and bare as the bones among the ashes, he hoped his dialogue didn't sound like a conversation with a mathematician.

Walker saw Terry before he knocked.

Terry clapped his hands together. "I know that look; it's the look of a writer who has just finished a story. How many pages, sport?"

"Ninety."

"JL will want a hundred and twenty. Two hours of screen time. No, aim for a hundred-fifty minutes, knowing it'll get chopped some," Terry said while Walker locked the drawer. He rubbed his hands together. "Anyway, I stopped to ask if we're still on for tonight?"

"Don't see why not, although I'd like to change my shirt and tie first. Parking lot at seven." Walker wanted to say 1900 hours out of habit. "Remind me again, where are we headed?"

"Chaplin's old place on the Strip. You'll like it. Food is good, and you'll love their hobo steak and signature dessert, a snowball." An enthusiastic

Terry, like a kid who read the dessert menu first, explained away. "It's vanilla ice cream encrusted with shredded coconut. The drinks are good, and the women there are so beautiful they hurt your eyes. All that should distract you from Joe Teague."

"Teague? Joe Teague will be there?" Walker said, somewhat surprised.

"Sorry to spring it on you at the last minute, but remember when we talked about fronts and scripts?"

"I do…and paying off listed writers."

"Joe Teague has a new partner."

"Who decided Teague needed a partner?" Walker asked.

"Who do you think? JL, of course. There's a glitch, though."

"Let me guess: you're the one who has to break the news to Teague."

"Aw, c'mon, Walter, don't be like that. Teague knew JL would pair him up with someone. One person can't do all the work."

"Yeah…it'd be a shame for all that money to sit in one pocket. How do you think Joe will take the news?"

"That's why you're with me, Walter. Safety in numbers."

"Geez, thanks, Terry. Ever cross your mind if Teague sees me with you, he might start thinking down the road, I might be your next partner? Forget what happened to Charlie Loew? Teague could run nervous."

"But, JL and Teague both need each other."

"Symbiotic, is that it?"

"Dip into the thesaurus much?" Terry dismissed the dig with a wave of his hand. "Fine, make fun of me, but JL follows Machiavelli's advice about keeping enemies closer. Anyway, I'm one of the more pleasant faces around MGM, RKO, and other studios, including JL's beloved across the way, Columbia. Relax, you worry too much, Walter. There's a natural logic to it all." Terry walked to the door. "See you at seven?"

"Will do. How about lunch?" Walker checked the drawer. Locked.

"Care to celebrate with a cigarette outside instead?" Terry said. "I know you don't smoke, but indulge a hopeless writer. Lungs instead of liver."

"Sure."

They walked toward the doors, on a long concourse of polished flooring that reminded Walker of bowling balls. Sparkles and speckles. Terry maintained a discipline of sorts; he kept his cigarette in check, unlit. They approached the Writers' Pool and heard a commotion. Elkins was in the hallway. The door to the room, thrown open.

"Miss Elkins, is there something wrong," Walker asked.

"Nothing, Mr. Thompson. Mr. Moore has the matter sorted."

Walker heard the familiar 'come with us' from the night of Vera's party.

Two men emerged into the hallway with Irving Hackett, who struggled and writhed like a worm on the hook. No other description sufficed. "There's nothing wrong with the papers in my desk. I didn't do anything wrong!"

"Others may beg to differ," one of the men answered.

Walker watched Hackett being dragged away, knees bent and feet scraping the floor. He screamed and protested the whole way. Walker realized that he had never heard the man's voice before, thought of him as nothing more than a desk. An inanimate object, a silent voice at Vera's party.

"I didn't do anything wrong," echoed down the hallway, under the bright light and off the clean floors.

Walker asked the secretary, "What papers was he talking about?"

"It seems that Mr. Hackett was trying to unionize writers here in the studio, and Mr. Warner frowns upon it."

"Man was the quietest thing. I never heard a word from him," Walker said. "Terry?"

"Don't look at me. I only work here."

* * *

Vera tied the knot to her robe and splayed her wardrobe closet open. None of the dresses were meant for a woman in her forties. Leslie heard the screech of hangers and caught a whiff of the scent from the dry cleaner's. Baking soda in a sock could get rid of it, she thought.

"I think I'll wear this," Vera said. She held up a red and black mermaid dress.

"Is there something that won't upstage you?"

165

Vera sorted through hangars. "How do you feel about green?"

"Color of jealousy," Leslie answered as she sat up in bed and yawned.

"Here, try this one," Vera said, a choice selection in her hand. "This one is from MGM. It's long, and it'll make you appear taller. You have more legs than bust."

"I don't want to look like an Amazon, Vera."

"Unapproachable is more like it. Try it on. Adrian designed this number. There's a man who knew how to mask a woman's imperfections. Give it a try."

Leslie disrobed and slipped into the dress, pulling it up. Vera pushed the wardrobe doors back into place so the mirrors could do their job. The Adrian dress was an emerald green of pure sheer and slink.

"Zip me up, please," Leslie said.

Vera pulled up the zipper slowly and Leslie could feel the warm breath on the side of her neck, Vera's eyes peering over her shoulder as they both checked the image in the mirror.

"Vera?"

"Yes."

"Do you have a wig? I'm thinking, blonde."

* * *

Chaplin's former property on Sunset in West Hollywood was ideal for secrets, clandestine affairs, and meetings. Wood paneling, tables, and plush leather booths under lighting that became more intimate the farther guests ventured into the establishment.

The hatcheck girl was chewing gum to pass the time before she had to retrieve the next ticketed item in her perfumed lair of fur stoles. Walker never understood the idea of wrapping a dead animal around your neck in a city that never went below fifty-five degrees. Filled with dollar bills, her tip jar was large enough for a fat goldfish.

"Cohen had a business hand in the place," Terry said. "There's Joe at the leather booth. Don't know the man next to him."

"Looks like he's from out of town," Walker whispered. "Maybe Joe believes in safety in numbers, too. Could be his idea of a partner."

The man seated next to Joe was wearing clothes fresh from the display window. Solid six feet, clean cut, trim frame, and a face as boring as mayonnaise. The Syndicate avoided ethnic types wherever possible. No Irish brogues or Dago speech, or verbs out of order.

This man fit that casting call with his white dress shirt and limp dark tie, the conservative gray flannel jacket, and starched pocket square. Nice and predictable, except for the slight bulge under his armpit. No chance he was an insurance agent in the field or an accountant with his adding machine.

"Hiya, Joe. You remember Walter Thompson."

"I do. This is a surprise," Joe said flat-faced and monotone.

"Introduce us to your friend here?" Terry pulled up a chair opposite the leather crescent.

"In due time," Teague said.

Joe's friend's eyes cased the restaurant. He looked as if he could detect a mouse in the darkest cornfield. A waiter waltzed up. Teague ordered a double scotch and Terry a martini. "How about you, Walter?" he asked.

"Water, ice cold."

"And you, sir?" the waiter asked Joe's friend.

"Tap, ice cold."

The waiter returned with the waters for Walker and the mystery guest across from him. Teague and Terry waited. Walker took a cautious sip, eyes up at the man across from him. Teague let out a breathy whistle. "Check out the number that just walked in. Johnny Stomps will be all over her like a dog on a fresh bone."

Both Terry and Walker glanced up, in the walled mirror they recognized Vera Williams in red and black lure, a siren gone strapless, breasts forward and buoyant. On Vera's arm was a statuesque ice blonde in heels with smoked eyes, no blush, and pale pink lipstick. She squeezed Vera tight to her and guided her to the leather booth near them.

"And here comes Johnny Stomps," Terry said. "A blonde shows up, and he's a Navaho missile locked on a target. This should be fun, boys."

Johnny Stompanato didn't have to muscle his way through the floor. People parted. Walker could tell Leslie had spotted the approach. Johnny Stomps was a barrel-chested brute and didn't have the intellect to survive a game of Chinese checkers with her, but she might like him. Leslie preferred the rough type. Passionate when not on the juice, and not at all intellectual. Whittaker fit the bill like a poster plastered to the front door of a theater.

The reflection in the mirror showed Stomps trying his best. He lightly touched her wrist. Leslie pulled in Vera closer. Vera said something. Stomp tried again, but Leslie started moving again. Walker saw her walk away, and Stomp attempted to catch her shoulder. Walker heard the dreaded voice-over in his head.

Don't. Stick with starlets. She'll kill you with your eyes open.

They stood up when Vera and Leslie came to the table.

"Evening, gentlemen," Vera said. "I thought I recognized you, Mr. Doyle. If I recall, it's Mr. Teague, correct?" Teague nodded. And in Walker's direction, "And you are Walter Thompson; we met briefly at my party."

"You have an excellent memory, Miss Williams. Thank you."

"This is my friend, Miss Margaret Gardner."

"Evening," Leslie said. "Vera and I decided to enjoy a night on the town. May we join you for a drink?"

Teague, taken by surprise, remembered his manners. He signaled for a waiter, but two arrived, ready with chairs. "Leather for the ladies. My friend and I will give you our seats."

"Champagne cocktail, please," Leslie told one of the waiters. Vera asked for a Pink Squirrel. Teague's nameless friend hadn't said a word. He took his water with him.

Walker sat in a chair next to Leslie while Vera sat next to her. Leslie put her small purse to her left and lightly squeezed Walker's thigh under the table. She undid the clasp and pushed her purse toward him. As chitchat crossed the table, her eyes glanced down at the purse. Walker saw the grip of the small gun. There was more talk, more of the dead stare from Teague's friend until his eyes moved and caught Walker's attention. Johnny Stomps was headed their way. Walker pocketed the gun into his jacket pocket.

"Ladies, allow me a round of drinks as an apology for my behavior earlier," the gangster said. "I insist." It was an impressive sentence from a man not known for his elocution or fashion sense. Stomps was wearing dark slacks, silver buckle, and a casual shirt open high and wide.

"That's nice of you," Teague said. "The ladies have placed their orders, Johnny."

Even if they had Mickey Cohen in common, Teague didn't appreciate Stomps' audacity to muscle in on his guests. Walker felt Leslie's hand on his thigh again.

"C'mon, one round, Joe. It's not like any of us are stopping at just one drink tonight."

"We're good, Johnny," Teague said.

"Don't be like that, Joey, old pal. Just trying to make good here. You know me. Beautiful ladies, and I can't resist. I wanna see them have a good time. Let me take care of the entire table. What do you say? For old-time's sake, in Mickey's place. He'd like that."

"Thing is, Mickey's not around, Johnny. Him and Chief Parker and the IRS are doing a formal dance before he takes the stretch in the slammer."

"You know Mickey. He'll beat it."

"I don't think so. Now, scram."

"Hey, I was being polite," Stomps said. He stepped toward Teague, when Teague's friend from back east, or Chicago, or from wherever, stood up and unbuttoned his suit jacket. He spoke his first words of the evening after he ordered his water. "Didn't you hear the man? Go away and let everyone enjoy the evening."

"Who's this, Joe?" Stomps asked before he threw a punch that connected with nothing. Teague's friend delivered a solid left hook to Stomp's midsection and aired him out. He whispered into the man's ear, "And just think, I'm right-handed. Time for you to go before I turn you into squash."

Stomps backed off to recover. Not so much as a weak grin or goodbye.

"I think it's time to leave," Teague said. "My apologies, ladies."

Vera reached for Leslie's arm. "There's some sound advice," she said. "I certainly don't need to be reading about this in the morning papers."

"Impressive left hook you have there," Leslie said to Teague's friend.

"Former welterweight."

"If that's the case, you've managed to keep your face in one piece," Walker said.

"Didn't lose much, only when I was told to," Teague's man answered. The remark might've explained the Cohen connection, Walker thought, while the ladies left, and half the room watched the green dress leave.

Teague offered Terry a business card. "We need to talk business soon. There's my number. Call me, and next time, don't bring the Boy Scout here. No offense, Walter."

"None taken," Walker said, with money in one pocket, a gun in the other, and a stomach interested in its next meal. Felt like the infantry again.

Chapter Twenty-Nine

Jack Junior walked the floorboards with caution, seeing that his father was reading. Jack smiled, pretending to continue reading, but holding the line of text with his thumb. He let the boy approach in his pajamas and padded feet. He remembered doing the same thing with his own father, remembered what it was like to approach his old man, afraid, respectful, and in awe. Decades later he realized his father was an ordinary man, taciturn and proud. The man remained that way to the day his father gave him a firm handshake before he died. He placed the book, face down at his desk, to keep his page. "I can hear you behind me," he said.

"Sorry to disturb you, sir."

"You're not disturbing me."

"But you were reading."

"Oh, that…it's nothing serious," Jack said.

"What's it about?"

"A detective. He's a loner. You know what loner means, right?" The boy nodded. "Anyway, he tries to do the right thing while doing his job, but he has this code, though, like a knight, and he has to make difficult decisions."

"Does he get the bad guy?"

"Sometimes he does the right way, other times he goes outside of the law."

"Not sure I understand, sir."

"Not sure I understand either."

Jack could see his old friend's face in the young boy's features. Jack and Betty married when he returned to the States. He thought how, as a younger man, he pined for Betty, but, like the knight, he quashed his feelings because she belonged to another. Jack's friend died in the war, and never learned Betty had given birth to fraternal twins.

"Can I ask you something? It's about school," Jack Junior asked.

"A problem with one of your subjects?"

The boy denied it with a shake of his head.

"A classmate?"

The boy nodded.

"This classmate a friend of yours?"

"Sort of?"

"Tell me a little more," Jack invited the boy to take the chair near his desk.

"He did a bad thing. I'd rather not say what it was," the boy said, small for the big chair.

"You saw him do this bad thing?" Jack asked.

The boy nodded.

"I see. And do you know if your friend knows you saw him do it?"

"I don't think so, but if I say something, he'll know it was me. If I tell, then I'm a snitch. I don't know what to do because what he did was wrong. You ever have something like that happen to you?"

Jack half-grinned. "I have. It's not easy. Not easy at all. It was a little different, my situation. I had a friend who I thought did something terrible, but I couldn't ask him, which made it worse. I couldn't ask him if it was true or not. In your case, you saw your friend with your own eyes, right?" His son agreed. "See, I didn't see for myself, so I acted on faith and trusted our friendship."

"What did you do?" The boy dangled his legs and made small circles with them.

"I tried to find out on my own what'd happened."

"Like the detective in your book?" Jack smiled and agreed. Junior asked, "Did you find out if your friend did it?"

"I did, and he had."

"Did you tell on him?"

"No. It was a lot more complicated than simply telling someone else. Friends have something—a bond—that can defy right or wrong. What I'm saying is you can be wrong and still be right and be right and completely wrong. I know it's confusing."

"I think I understand. Thanks." The boy jumped out of the chair. "Hi, Mom," he said as he ran past Betty in the doorframe. "What did I tell you about running in this house?" she yelled out. The boy yelled back, 'Sorry,' and his voice faded away. Jack worried about the day when Jack Junior and Elizabeth would learn he was not their biological father.

Her face pale, he asked her, "What is it, Betty?"

Her fingers played with a button on her dress. "A man who says he's your boss is downstairs. He says his name is Mr. Smith."

Jack stood up and pushed in his chair. Betty had not moved out of the way; she remained inside the doorframe. "Is his name really Smith?"

* * *

Downstairs in the hallway entrance, Mr. Smith waited for Jack.

Walter Smith was another Army man, middle-aged and fit, lean, too thin for his age, not because he adhered to the military standards for fitness as daily habit, but rather an acute ulcer prompted the removal of most of his stomach, and malnutrition did the rest. Tall and long-limbed, the man had a long face, high temples, and a widow's peak that came to a point, from which he combed back his graying hair. He turned the band of his hat slowly around on his hand like a rosary, finding comfort in the feel of the fabric against his fingertips while he waited for Jack.

"Jack," he extended his hand out for the shake.

"Beetle," Jack responded, using the man's Army nickname, which came from Smith's piercing eyes and an affectionate pun on his middle name, Bedell.

"Shall we go for a walk?" Smith motioned with his hat to the door. Seeing Betty descending the stairs, the man said, "May I borrow your husband for a few minutes, Mrs. Marshall?"

"You may, and please call me Betty."

"Thank you. I'm sorry to have disturbed you, Betty," he said, while Jack put on his coat and opened the door. Betty disappeared down the hallway into the kitchen.

Outside on the small porch, Mr. Smith buttoned his sports coat as Jack closed the door. The parked car across the street and the two men in dark suits were still there.

"Let's stand here for a moment, Jack. I want to make sure those two get a good description of us for their report." Jack buttoned his own jacket, glanced around as if he was surveying the weather for a cloud in the darkening sky.

"I never did like Edgar's methods," Jack's boss said. "Not my way of doing things. I prefer the subtle forms of surveillance and none of this nonsense with opened mail or terrorizing a man's wife and children. There are more effective methods. Let's take a walk, shall we? Take a right on the sidewalk ahead so we have our backs to them."

Smith's maneuver would force the agents across the street to either turn their car around or follow them on foot.

"I read the preliminary report," Mr. Smith said.

"On the paper Loew had on his person?"

"That and Leslie's parcel. Interesting use of initials," Smith said, hands behind his back. Jack had not received the report on Leslie's envelope.

"I assumed they were code from within the studio system, since Loew was a payoff man."

Smith stopped. Those eyes of his would have withered most men. His lips twisted into a half-grin. "Scripts on the QT for the studios. Blacklisted writers. Loew's list, however, was no simple ledger for transactions. Analysis reported a connection between Loew's note to a detention list—a continuation of a list Hoover was supposed to have destroyed long ago. He hadn't, and that's no surprise, knowing Edgar. For reasons we'll never know, Loew's killer had been sloppy and hadn't found it."

Jack understood his boss was repeating a portion of the analyst's report on Loew, but he wanted to hear the part about Leslie's envelope from Ernest's office. Smith glanced up at the trees, admiring the play of light through the leaves. Jack lifted his hand as a hello to the neighbor who opened her front door to call in her children from play while his boss talked.

"Analysis finished the forensics on the item from Leslie. Initials are indeed the recurring theme. There is some correlation between the initials on Loew's and Ernest's lists, but the doctor's list is more extensive since it provided dates," Smith said, hands still behind his back.

Jack asked, "Do any of the dates from Loew's list correspond with the doc's, or do they differ?"

"They differ. Initials on Ernest's list were shorthand for other therapists seeing actors and writers in the studio system. The dates represented appointments. Of course, we expected to see some overlap in initials for studio employees between the two lists, but the dates tipped us off. We double-checked and they didn't match the initials in Ernest's schedule."

"They matched appointments made with other therapists."

"We researched Ernest's circle of acquaintances for therapists. Their initials matched to dates of appointments with people in the studios. Seems Doctor Ernest was the nerve center for a network of shrinks collecting intelligence."

"The hub of a wheel," Jack said.

"And each of his colleagues was a spoke."

Smith stopped to suggest they sit on the park bench. In his Army days, Beetle liked to drape his right leg over the left one when he sat down to talk in close quarters. This habit, Jack learned, signaled subtext; it was the time for Jack to listen.

"We may have a problem now the wheel has stopped moving with Ernest's death. Loew was on Hoover's list, and his use of therapists to gather intelligence. I'm certain Loew was killed over it. The question is, why shut down the nerve center of a successful operation by killing Ernest? He and his colleagues have patients who name names and keep Hoover's Red List growing. We both know Edgar is pragmatic with any information he obtains, either for hunting Communists or for whatever usefulness it may serve him, now or later. Your thoughts, Jack?"

Jack winced, troubled. "I buy that Ernest was the spider in Hoover's web of informants, but Leslie's note said files were missing. She couldn't confirm for certain if there was ever a file on Loew. Why take two or three patient files when so much more was available?"

"I don't have an answer for you, my friend."

They sat silent, staring ahead at the occasional passing-by of cars in the street. Dusk was setting in, and the trees swayed. The street reflected the occasional glitter of glass shards in the asphalt. Smith folded his hands over in his lap.

"The problem is Hoover and what he does with information. This is a domestic issue, and we were restricted to international situations; that was the understanding between the Company and his FBI, but Hoover isn't one for boundaries."

Jack turned sideways on the bench to face his boss. He now repeated a portion of his conversation with Chief William Parker, the part about his wish to create a nationwide system to manage the interstate movement of criminals and their activities. "When Parker called me, he said it was a matter of national security."

"As far as he's concerned, it is for Chief Parker because J. Edgar Hoover wants his so-called system to control all domestic law enforcement. Set aside the obvious tyranny, we both know Parker and Hoover dislike each other. Hoover doesn't approve of Parker's methods, and Parker dislikes Hoover's incessant interference. Both men are alike, and yet differ on how they implement their ideas. The sticky wick, as I see it now, is Hoover's actions has the Company on a collision course with his Bureau."

"Parker said he'd buy me time for Leslie."

"That's fine, but we have to tie this up somehow and soon. I suggest you resolve this without having me or Hoover in Truman's office. If things don't go well for Leslie and Walker, then Hoover has his ammunition against us. This could be the end of us all and everything we've worked to create. Hoover is an isolationist, and that's not an attitude in keeping with the real world. You know that."

"I know, Beetle. I know."

The two men stood up, shook hands, and walked away in opposite directions from each other.

Chapter Thirty

Vera insisted on the place in West Hollywood. While they changed clothes, she enticed and assured Leslie with, "You'll just love this place in WeHo."

The Yellow Canary lived on a block with little traffic, but when night came there were bright lights, music, and people. Quiet by day it became omnivorous at night, which is to say something for William Mulholland's idea of a fountain in the desert.

Vera had chosen an evening gown that took the narrative from the floor up to her shoulders in silver satin, and the V-neck invited eyes to appreciate her cleavage. Leslie selected the Chiparus number from Vera's wardrobe, a gold dress with fabric arranged in grooves as solar rays. Vera said the torso of a statue of Queen Nefertiti in Tut's tomb had inspired it.

When they arrived at the Canary, Vera's arm threaded through the open space in Leslie's arm at her elbow. Vera glided with Leslie into the establishment. A chanteuse was singing a torch song over the piano's slow and saddest keys. Vera received nods and smiles as she paraded Leslie to her reserved booth, a curved leather seat behind a table with a view of the room.

Leslie thought the place's décor confused, caught somewhere between an airport's Art Moderne and some expatriate bar on the Left Bank. The restaurant's logo of a yellow canary inside a cage with an open door hung high on the back wall. There was a dance square in the middle of the floor in front of their table and plenty of other tables around it with stark white tablecloths and spotless crystal. The bar gathered souls in want of a table and liquid sustenance.

The waitress arrived, perky and prompt, with a pad and pencil. Vera ordered a pair of champagne cocktails.

"I'm so glad you're with me, Maggie. I adore the blonde hair. You could pass for Lizabeth Scott if I saw you on the street." Vera's compliment came out like a cat's purr. Leslie would've thanked her and basked in the adulation, but she saw someone and warned Vera.

"Don't look now, but someone is coming towards our table."

Like a battleship that had spotted the enemy, the woman steamed across the parquet floor. Leslie recognized her as one of Hollywood's leading ladies, famous on both stage and screen and most recently for helping Harry Truman get elected.

"Ah, yes. The bitch is forever on the prowl," Vera said under her breath.

"Darling, you didn't say hello," said a husky voice with a Southern twang in a tailored linen suit. For all the glamour and aristocratic pretense, the woman eyed Leslie as if she were a gallery girl at a brothel. "And who's this morning glory with you, Vera? I must know."

"This is Margaret Gardner."

"Charmed, Maggie," their unwanted guest said, gauging Vera's response to her use of Maggie. Vera's hand squeezed Leslie's thigh under the table. For strength or restraint, Leslie wondered. The regal one wasn't finished with Leslie. "I don't think Vera cares for me since she hasn't had the decency to tell you my name." The statement came with a flutter of eyelashes. "I'm—"

"Don't you have an understudy to corrupt and exploit," Vera said.

"All in good time, Vera. Corrupt and exploit I shall, but I do allow my victims a breather before the pounce. As for you," she said, eyeing Leslie's face and then her bosom, "Any time, Dahling," before she slinked away to find other prey.

"Still the shark at a crowded beach in July."

"Do relax, Vera. Let's enjoy our dinner, and you shouldn't let her bother you. A person like her may seem attractive, but nobody would stay with her. Too much work."

"Do you think she's attractive?" Vera's insecurities crept in. "I hate to admit it," she said. "I was like her once." Vera searched for their waitress and drinks. "I apologize for being petty, and you're right that I shouldn't let that drugstore wench ruin our evening, but, I confess, there was a time when I possessed looks, and I was as ruthless and confident as her."

"All a state of mind, Vera, and you are beautiful."

"You're awfully sweet, Maggie, but looks are everything. Never mind. You're right…we should enjoy our dinner. We didn't have much of an evening last night, with that awful scene with Stompanato and that prizefighter."

"Men like them are usually good for only one thing. Otherwise, they're quite limited."

"You mean limited to intimidation. You do know Johnny works for Mickey Cohen?"

"So, I've heard," Leslie said as their waitress placed two flutes on their table. When Vera's fingertips touched the glass, the young server's hand touched hers. "Compliments of the house because of the delay."

The waitress walked away and glanced over her shoulder to see whether Vera tracked her. Leslie nudged Vera's shoulders. "See, you still have it; she has eyes for you." Vera blushed.

"You were saying something about Stompanato and Cohen," Leslie said.

"He runs the white-slave trade racket for Mickey. I've seen his girls; they come to LA with stars in their eyes and end up with VD, hooked on pills, or both. You said you were more impressed with the brawler than with Johnny Stompanato."

"Maybe I was. I admire a man who can take care of himself. Perhaps physical prowess is what I covet most…but it doesn't mean I'd settle for it."

Vera enjoyed a sip from her champagne cocktail. She watched Leslie's lips touch the crystal and imbibe a small peck of bubbly. "I see…you're the love and leav'em type," Vera said.

"Could be. It also could be a case of I don't know what I want." Leslie offered Vera a wry smile.

"Tell me, Maggie. Did you notice Walter looking at you? That's twice now."

"The writer fellow?" Leslie took a longer dip from her champagne.

"Forever coy, aren't you? Mr. Thompson looks like a man with an appetite."

"He may have been hungry, Vera. We were in a restaurant, remember?"

"He was clever, how he was looking at you. I'll give him points for being discreet. The quiet ones are usually imps and satyrs in disguise."

Leslie giggled and hiccupped. Bubbles from the champagne tickled her nose and sizzled in her throat. "Most men are brutes, most of the time," she said. "A woman prefers a man who takes his time. Walter is the reliable kind, the type for the long, slow burn when a girl is good and ready."

Vera sipped. "Are you ready for the long, slow burn?"

"I wouldn't be here if I were, Vera."

"But you do like him?" Leslie detected the sad drop in Vera's voice.

"Let's just say I admire him, and let's agree this is neither the time nor place for schoolgirl jealousy, Vera." Leslie placed her hand on Vera's thigh, surprised but not shocked to find Vera's legs parting ever so slightly.

"I wish I'd met you years ago."

Flute of champagne near her lips, Leslie said, "But would you have appreciated me?"

"I'd try," Vera said into her own champagne.

The waitress returned to take their order. They decided on seafood because it was light fare and left more room for drinks. They ordered dessert ahead to give the kitchen time to prepare it. The chanteuse at the piano left, and an ensemble replaced her at the stand. They played clear and bright jazz that sparkled against all the crystal in the room.

"Has this place made the gossip sheets?" Leslie asked over dinner.

"The muckrakers know of it, but they haven't bothered with it yet. Safe for now, I suppose."

"Are you still upset about the picture they ran in the scandal sheet?" Leslie asked.

The champagne tickled her nose again, but the bubbly didn't burn this time. They finished their shrimp, and the waitress swept it away and told them dessert was on its way. Across the room, another server approached their table, a large platter balanced on her shoulder. They waited until the dessert was served and apologized to the waitress for not ordering their after-dinner drinks. Leslie wanted a brandy and Vera, nothing. She still had her champagne.

"I was…I am…I don't know, Maggie. At least nobody will recognize you, but it's a headache all the same for me. It's not what I need in my life right now."

"We both know when the picture was snapped, but any idea who might've taken it?"

"Oh, I have an idea," Vera said over the dessert, a marble of vanilla ice cream streaked with chocolate. Next to it was a zigzag streak of ganache, crowned with a fleshy strawberry suggestively halved. "I'm certain it was Phillip."

"Dr. Ernest?"

"Doctor? Please, like the man needs a license to be a bastard."

"How can you be certain it was him?" Leslie asked.

"Phillip always carried this dinky little camera on him when he came to my parties. He always belabored the point with guests, saying he was an amateur photographer, which they believed, but I think it was all a pretense for him to keep score on who attended my soirées. When I saw our picture in that rag, I knew it was him because I'd recognize his handiwork anywhere."

"His camera or style of taking photographs?" Vera asked.

"Camera," Vera said. "It was some small job made in Wales. I didn't even know the Welsh made cameras. Anyway, Phillip claimed this camera of his was focus-free. Point and shoot. No instant camera has that clarity of image. You saw the picture in the paper. Phillip carried the damn thing either in his pocket or hung it from his wrist. He'd snap pictures on the sly, particularly of writers at my parties. Actors are shutterbugs, but writers are private types and a little resistant. Hence, the need for speed and stealth."

"But he took a picture of us sleeping," Leslie said.

"He did, didn't he? I suspect it was out of spite and a little jealousy."

"Jealousy?" Leslie sat back with a small brandy the waitress dropped off.

"Oh please, Maggie, don't be so innocent. You're endearing, but don't overplay the part."

"Vera, I have no idea what you're talking about."

"Ernest saw me arm in arm with you all evening. He's a rather insecure man."

"Jealous of me?"

"He was, and he wasn't the only one," Vera said.

"What do you mean?"

"Need I spell it out for you, Miss Margaret?"

"Now, you're the one being fresh, Vera."

"I saw Walter and the way his eyes ransacked you. Like a kid in a candy store before dinner. Phillip couldn't have been blind to that either. And why wouldn't Phillip be upset? You slept with him earlier that night."

"Vera!"

"Spare me the theatrics and denials, Maggie. I couldn't care less. I know from experience what a few drinks will do to Phillip; he starts thinking he's Popeye with a can of spinach when he's actually Swee' Pea in need of a nap. God, men are so predictable."

Leslie's cheeks flushed. "Seeing us together explains jealousy, but spite?"

"Ernest sold the picture to the tabloid, didn't he? There's your spite."

The bandleader asked for a quick break. Around the room, polite applause lifted, and the light dimmed for intimacy and quiet conversations. Their waitress lit a candle inside a netted holder and pushed it to the center of their table. Vera declined another offer of an after-dinner drink. Leslie ordered another brandy and waited for its arrival before she talked to Vera.

"Enough spite to kill him for it?" Leslie asked.

Vera shifted uncomfortably on the leather like a witness on the stand.

"What if I said maybe," Vera said.

Leslie sipped brandy. "The police need to establish a motive. The picture is a powerful motive."

"You forget I talked to the police. I came clean about seeing the photograph, so unless the skunk at the tabloid who bought it fesses up to paying Ernest for it, or the police are able to prove Phillip snapped the photo, I'm in the clear."

Vera stared ahead. The fingers on one hand tapped the beat to the jazz number on the tablecloth. Leslie watched Vera's breathing. Calm and steady as a butcher on the killing floor.

"Devil's advocate here, but what if he kept a negative?" she asked.

Vera took a sip of leftover champagne and answered, eyes focused ahead on the bandleader. "He probably sold that with the picture. I said he could be a bastard."

"I'm not inclined to think he sold it, Vera, because Ernest is the type to keep copies and records. You know, obsessive. I'm thinking, keep the negative for blackmail. Perhaps Phillip has done this before with you, with others. A good detective can find the money trail." Leslie lifted the snifter of brandy nearer to her lips while she waited for Vera's response.

"Blackmail doesn't always involve money," Vera said.

"If he took pictures at parties, he probably stored other kinds of information."

"And what if he did?"

"Pictures or secrets?" Leslie asked.

"Secrets."

"What secrets?"

"What do you think?" Vera said, holding her empty champagne flute with a welder's grip. "Phillip asked me to host parties. Not reefer or sex parties, but honest social events. It started out that way. Invite old friends and acquaintances, he said, and it'll help drum up my practice. Since I worked at several studios over the years and given my family history, I've come to know many people in the studio system. Like I said, Phillip zeroed in on actors and then writers. He took some on as clients. Next thing I know, Phillip is starting a franchise."

"A franchise? I don't understand, Vera."

"Phillip recruited colleagues and acquired more clients. He'd take a percentage for the referral, I guess. Once, during our brief affair, I saw Phillip making notes, but I never could understand them; but I do know he built himself a nice nest, feathered with enough secrets to blackmail half of Hollywood. The studio bosses would pay handsomely for it. Jack Warner's hatchet man, Lenny Moore, got wind of it, and the next thing you know, Phillip is the studio shrink."

"What about Charles Loew?"

The flash of shock across Vera's face was worth an Academy Award.

"What about Charlie? How do you know him?"

"Ernest mentioned his name once," Leslie said.

"Charlie was a sweetheart. A little eccentric and flashy with his money, but a gem. Charlie didn't mix with Phillip at my parties. He'd stick close to the other writers."

"You don't think Charlie could've been into blackmail?" Leslie asked.

"Charlie? No, not Charlie. If anything, Phillip blackmailed Charlie." Vera made puppy eyes at Leslie's brandy. Leslie eased the snifter over. "What makes you so sure, Vera? That Charlie and Phillip didn't work together."

"Because Charlie had his own secret. Look around, Maggie. Other than the jazz band, do you see any men here?"

The place was full of pretty canaries, aware they were inside gilded cages with an open door but knew they couldn't fly through it to freedom. Just like the real world.

"So, Charlie was being blackmailed because he was…" Leslie said, stunned.

"And so was I. There you have it," Vera rapped the table like a hanging judge. "For all the decadence in Babylon, certain things remain outré. Did you know Johnny Stomps runs a service for baritone babes?" Vera closed her eyes; the lids moved in recollections of past deeds. Vera opened her eyes, her face dreamy. "I sank deeper into the mud with Dr. Phillip Ernest. He worked friends from my parties into his office to an enterprise that lined his pockets, and he had to have the last word on everything."

"Incredible that Phillip would jeopardize all that over jealousy and spite. If he had done to me what he did to you, I know I would've shot him."

"Phillip was arrogant and knew he'd get away with it. Somebody had to stop him."

"That day you were coming up the stairs, I was coming down them."

"I took the stairs to avoid the elevator man," Vera said.

"You knew I'd find the body. You took the gun from my purse."

"That I can explain, Maggie."

"Please do."

"I turned back up the stairs because I heard the sound of heels at first. I knew it had to be you. I felt horrible at the thought I might be implicating you. I would've explained it to you, but I didn't think you'd understand. As for the gun…I saw it in your purse. Forgive me for prying, but I wanted to see if there was proof of you and Walter."

"Walter?" Leslie asked, failing to hide her surprise.

"I thought he'd given you his telephone number. He hadn't, but then I saw the gun. So attractive with that lovely cross on it. I figured with so many people at the party you'd think it was somebody else who nicked it. I'm sorry. I'm really sorry, Maggie."

"And what made you pull the trigger?"

"I went to confront Phillip, to scare him. I was tired of him being my pimp, him using me for my friends. He was so smug there at the desk, scribbling away. I was behind him when I brought up that horrid picture. And you know what? The bastard laughed at me. Just laughed, as if it was nothing. I don't know what came over me, but I took the gun out of my purse. I've never used a pistol in my life, Maggie, but I pretended like I was a murderess in a B-film. I pointed it behind his ear and…"

"Squeezed the trigger. For someone who has never used a gun, you did quite well."

Leslie recalled her first kill. A German. Not one iota of hesitation on her part. She shot him in the chest first. He glanced down in shock to see the small wound start to bloom, and as she stepped forward, their eyes met before she placed the muzzle under his chin, and he tasted the bullet after she pulled the trigger.

Vera's eyes were shiny, about to unleash tears. "The gun frightened me, and I panicked and dropped it."

"Don't cry, Vera. Now tell me, did you take anything from the office?"

"Files. I took my folder and a thin one on Walter. Call it curiosity, but I wanted to know more about him."

"What about Charlie? Was there a folder on him?"

"Yes. I took it. Charlie was an old friend. I wanted to protect him. Protect his memory. Charlie didn't deserve what happened to him."

"Did you think Phillip had a part in his death?"

"Not that I could tell."

"You said Phillip was scribbling something at his desk when you confronted him. What was it?"

"Some ledger with initials and dates. Lots of dates and initials," Vera said, staring off. "A lot of JT and LM."

Leslie realized someone else had made good time because there was nothing under the doctor's face, nothing but a manila folder. A thief, possibly the same burglar from before, may have been hiding in the hallway, tucked inside another office, when she dropped the letter to Jack down the chute.

The starlet from earlier was approaching the table. Leslie saw the calculated wobble in linen on its way to their table.

"Hello again, ladies," she said with an alcoholic slur. Emboldened, she eyed Leslie. "You know if you get tired of this sewing circle, you could come to my table."

"No, thank you. I enjoy the company I'm keeping," Leslie said.

The famous actress huffed and left. Leslie took the strawberry and placed it into her mouth. She let the initial tartness give way to sweetness. Vera was surprised to find her dinner date pulling her in closer. Leslie placed a soft kiss against Vera's lips.

"You always taste sweet," Vera said in a subdued whisper.

Chapter Thirty-One

The typewriter's bell, a heavyweight's victory, lingered in the air. Dachau was on paper. Complete. Finished. Two hundred and forty pages: an extra forty minutes of screen time. Twenty-four hundred seconds of margin for the editor. Terry rapped on the open door.

"I finished it, Terry."

"Excellent. Warner might move you back in with us common folk."

"Or he could put my desk out in the parking lot and change all the locks."

"JL has been known to do that. I'm here to ask a favor. Teague called. He named the place, and I'd like to have you with me for moral support."

"You don't have a good feeling, do you?"

"That guy with Joe last time sucker-punched Johnny Stomps, and he walked away from it. No guy does that without his obituary in the newspaper the next morning. I've asked around, and he checks out as a fighter, all right, but nothing else. He boxed in and around Philly, which explains the Chestnut Street look, but no word if he's Syndicate."

Walker pulled the last piece of paper off the roller, put it in the drawer, and locked it. "So, the guy is hired muscle. Doesn't make him Murder, Incorporated. Where does Teague want to meet?"

"Near an old steel plant over on Main Street. The place is storage for chemicals for the brewery."

"Think I've seen it; the place with the big tower?" Terry said yes. "What time?"

"He didn't say, but Moore said eight tonight."

"Moore?"

"Don't go cockeyed on me, Walter. Lenny Moore is the social director around here. How else would Teague know who to deliver the payroll to?"

The studio system, their moviemaking, their mix of fantasy and reality moved to the puppet strings in the hands of outsized and ruthless personalities such as Sam Goldwyn, Louie B. Mayer, Jack Warner, and the lesser-known Lew Wasserman. Leonard Moore danced when Jack Warner's fingers moved.

"Think JL wants you as Joe's new partner?" Walker asked.

"Far as I know, yeah."

"And you think Joe has other ideas because he might bring muscle?"

"Safety in numbers. Why not? Are you in or not?"

Terry had a case of the nerves. Walker could tell. Terry looked like one of the last two kids in PE class, behind the line and waiting to be picked for a team. "I'm in. I'll meet you in the parking lot around seven, and we'll take your car."

"You're swell," Terry said. "Appreciate it. Want some lunch?"

"I can't. Need to run an errand, and let JL know I finished the project."

Walker surprised himself; he had enjoyed writing Warner's project. There were edits and revisions ahead, but the draft in the drawer was an accomplishment. He never would've imagined he had what it took to complete the task. Warner would be tougher than any Boston or New York literary agent. JL would shape the experience for the silver screen. No bluestocking in worsted wool suit or pair of rimless glasses could write that script for Jack Warner. Walker had seen the death camp, not them. He had delivered. Those few weeks in the Iowa cornfields had paid off, even if it was a front for recruiting men for the Company.

Outside in the parking lot the valley air swept in cool enough to make the eyes water and remind the living that life was a gift. In his vehicle, Walker enjoyed the faintest whiff of gasoline and pride as he turned the ignition over. He left word for Warner with Miss Elkins. He had finished the project and planned to take the afternoon off.

Walker eased the car out of the parallel lines and pointed the nose of the car due north to Malibu. He wanted to pick up Grable and visit John Hamilton on the return drive. Terry recruited him for reinforcement, but Walker wanted his own.

* * *

"It's me, Jack," he said into a phone.

"Long time since I heard your voice, Mr. Marshall. What can I do for you?"

"I need to collect on a favor. Grab pen and paper."

Jack gave an address. This meet required travel for the recipient of the call. Jack believed in sufficient notification.

"DC?" the man asked,

"The job is there. The address is a restaurant. How soon can we meet?"

"Lunchtime tomorrow, at this address," the voice answered.

"Excellent. See you then." Jack hung up the phone.

He hadn't bothered to record the conversation.

* * *

At Ebbitt's, a downtown grill and steps away from the White House, Jack confirmed mid-day on his watch. With its Beaux-Arts façade, the place was not Auden's poem on human suffering and Dutch Masters, although there was plenty of cigar smoke, plenty of sorrows tipped back along with the famous oysters. The mahogany décor, the velvet booths, and the dim glow from all the brass fixtures around the beveled glass had hosted Presidents, lesser politicians, and the theater crowd for nearly a century.

Jack requested a booth facing the door. The waiter stopped by and recited the menu. Jack chose steamed mussels over linguine with Wallonian white ale. The waiter complimented him on his selection.

His guest arrived. Always punctual, always well-dressed, wearing a midnight-blue suit with shadow stripes, single-breasted jacket over a pearl-blue dress shirt, and diamond-patterned tie, the man approached Jack. Jack stood up.

"Hello, Sheldon. Please have a seat."

"I came as soon as I could."

"Much appreciated," Jack said, summoning the waiter for Sheldon to place his own order, pastrami with robust mustard and sauerkraut. Sheldon chose Duvel beer. The waiter returned with the Belgian ale in a tulip glass.

Jack slid a sealed envelope across the table. "The assignment," he said. "Before you open it, there are caveats. This is a delicate situation. Time-sensitive. The target is very dangerous, and I chose you because—how do I say this with tact? You have access to a world neither I nor the men who report to me could infiltrate on short notice. What I need is something incontrovertible and failsafe for blackmail."

"Still in the assurance business, I see. Reminds me of when we first met in Vienna." Sheldon rested his hand on the envelope.

"Insurance and liability," Jack said.

Sheldon pulled the sealed envelope toward him.

"I do owe you a favor. You said dangerous?"

"Very. He's autocratic and vindictive. He also has fixed ideas about certain things, which means he could be careless," Jack said.

"A creature of habit, predictable but careful."

"Favor or not, I'd understand if you turned this down," Jack said. "If something were to happen, I wouldn't be able to help you. I want you to understand the risk."

Sheldon opened the envelope. His eyebrows arched when he saw the picture. "You weren't kidding, but nobody can't say Jack Marshall doesn't have chutzpah," a word Sheldon pronounced with a throaty sound. Knowing Jack didn't know the word, he said, "It means boldness."

"You'll do it then?"

"I will."

"Good," Jack said and turned his attention elsewhere. "Our lunch is arriving."

Chapter Thirty-Two

Terry waited in the parking lot like an anxious teenager, hands in his pockets and sullen. John Hamilton sat in the back seat of Walker's car as it floated across the WB parking lot. Not quite dusk, the scent of magnolias was in the air, and there was a sloppy pink smudge in the sky. Everything in the air revived Walker's Army instincts. Hamilton in his rearview mirror, Walker squinted. Hamilton was thinking the same thing. Ambush.

"You sure about this, Walker?" Hamilton asked. "I can smell the fear on him from here."

"Just remember I'm Walter Thompson."

"And I'm nobody."

John Hamilton appeared taller in the back seat, bigger without a drink in his hand. No trace of cigarette smoke on him to betray his presence in the dark. John wore dark slacks, comfortable loafers, and a blue shirt that would turn darker with the evening. Walker could count on Hamilton squaring off with Teague's fighter. John sported height and reach.

The car stopped, and Terry stepped in. Walker drove fast out of the parking lot for the highway to Los Angeles. Terry saw Hamilton in the backseat but said nothing at first. He extended his hand. "Hey, don't I know you? You're the actor—"

"You don't know me, kid."

Terry turned in his seat, taken aback by Hamilton's boorish behavior. He glanced at Walker for an explanation. There was none. Terry resigned himself to the long silence, quiet of miles between desert and civilization.

"He's a friend," Walker said after some time passed. "I'm your support, and he's mine."

"What do I call him?" Terry asked.

"Mr. Smith will do fine," Hamilton answered. Walker glanced in the rearview again.

Walker's hand pointed. "Open up the glove compartment, Terry."

Inside the glove compartment, Terry found a .22 caliber pistol with its stock and trigger taped. Terry blinked and waited for an explanation. "Safety is on, and it's loaded," Walker said. "Take it out, nose down, and get your grip familiar with the stock."

"You're full of surprises, Walter."

Terry gripped the gun, kept it nose down for obvious reasons. His lips pursed, as if he questioned the strength of the weapon in his hand.

"Ever shoot one?" Walker asked.

"A few times when I was a kid."

"Great," Hamilton said. "Tonto becomes a brave."

"Listen to me, Terry. Ignore the size of it. If the time comes, line up your sights, squeeze the trigger, and shoot."

"Don't you think they might frisk us?" Terry said.

"If they see two of us, they'll think twice. There'll be two of them."

"Two of us? What about Mr. Smith here?" Terry asked.

"I'm dropping him off before we pull into the lot."

"What's this?" Terry reached over and touched Walker's jacket. "You're carrying, too. Isn't this a little over the top?"

"You tell me, Terry. You're the one who said safety in numbers." Walker touched his side. "It's a .45. I kept it after I left the Army. And no, this isn't over the top. Think about it. Teague invites you to a secluded area. You know he doesn't want a partner. You saw his friend in action with Johnny Stomps. Add it all up, Terry. It's night and the meet is inside a brewery with railroad tracks nearby. Put two and two together."

Hamilton leaned forward. "It doesn't add up to five, Tonto."

"But Moore arranged it."

"What if he did? Doesn't mean he knows Teague's plan. If he does, we can take it up with him in the morning. For now, you need to survive the night." Walker said.

The car stopped to let Hamilton out. The car door closed without a sound.

The tower reminded Walker of the crematorium tower at Dachau, except this one was taller. Dachau's tower was shorter and connected to a bunker, two ovens, and gallows. Here, malt and yeast breathed together to make beer.

* * *

Terry received specific directions from Teague: second floor of the building closest to the tower. Climbing the stairs reminded Walker of paratrooper training at Fort Benning, of another tower, but one with a mass-exit door to mimic the door on a plane. The lateral drift apparatus for parachute landings simulated open air and sky before feet met earth. The steel-grid stairs at the brewery could tell the untold stories of thousands who climbed them. There was a door. Terry gave two hard knocks. The heavy iron door yawned up with Teague on the other side.

"We're here, Joe, like you asked. On the dot, I might add," Terry said.

"I wasn't expecting your better half."

"I see you brought Rocky Marciano with you," Walker said. Teague's fighter friend stepped out from the rows of brown bottles of chemicals behind Teague.

Terry went in first, and Walker followed. Teague touched Walker, but he threw his hand away from him. There was no chance he'd let Teague find Grable tucked under his arm. The room had some natural lighting but it was diminishing with the hour. The place smelled like the supply room of a mad scientist's laboratory. Rows and racks of amber bottles are held in place with slats of wood. Nothing here was labeled, not even with the chemist's secret code of letters or numbers.

Teague spared no formalities. "Lenny Moore said JL wants me to have a new partner. That's you, Terry. Lenny allowed me this one opportunity to talk with you and see if we'd get along together."

"Like the way you and Charlie Loew got on?" Walker asked. The former boxer advanced towards him. Teague held out his hand as if it would keep his dog at bay.

"What did I ever do to you, brother?" Teague asked Walker.

"It's what you might do to Terry that concerns me. You've already lost one partner."

"You saying I have bad luck?"

"You don't have bad luck. Only your partner."

Teague's pugilist inched closer as if he hadn't heard the referee. While Teague talked, the air on the back of Walker's neck said someone else was in the room.

"Hold on, fellows," Terry said, hands up to negotiate peace.

"It's all right, Bill," Teague to his boxer.

"It's Bill, is it?" Walker said. "It's nice to finally have a name. Terry? Say hello to Bill."

"Calm down, Walter."

"You calm down," Bill said and pulled out a gun from his pocket.

"Why don't all of you calm down?" said a third voice from way back in the darkness.

"And who might you be?" Walker yelled out.

"Yeah, Joe, who might that be?" Bill asked, his gun pointed at Teague. "Start talking."

"I can explain," Teague said. His hands fanned the air to calm the gunmen. "We do the payouts like I said, Bill. That's honest. We keep a cut, like I promised." Teague aimed his thumb at the invisible man behind him, "He gets a copy of the list."

"Shut your trap or else," the hidden voice behind Teague said.

"Or you'll end up Charlie…is that it?" Walker said.

"That was all a misunderstanding," Teague said. "Charlie got a hold of the list. I was trying to get it back from him. I don't know how…"

"I said shut up for the last time," the man in the dark said.

"Go on," Walker said to Teague.

"Charlie and I argued. He said he didn't have it, but I knew he was lying."

Teague pointed again to the character behind him. "Charlie wouldn't listen. He started saying crazy things. We argued. I had a gun. Charlie came at me, and I…"

A shot went off. Teague stumbled forward, a bullet in his back.

A perfect silhouette on the wall and a wisp of gunpowder drifted. There was a creak, and something fell. Hamilton came crashing down and landed on the shooter. Bill turned his gun toward the commotion when Terry charged him. It was a freshman attempt at a tackle but good enough to distract Bill and take him to the ground. Walker lost sight of Bill's gun.

He drew Grable. Bill hammered Terry with his fist. Hamilton and the mystery man were exchanging blows. Walker had it all wrong. Hamilton was supposed to pair off with the boxer, Teague was his man, and Terry, the wild card. Walker reached for Bill's shoulder when another shot cracked the air.

Terry managed to discharge the .22, Leslie's gun, into Bill's chest. Bill toppled over. Teague was still breathing. Hamilton played Sugar Ray against LaMotta with his man. Tight against each other, jabs and body blows didn't give Walker a clear shot. Hamilton unleashed a hook and vicious uppercut that sent his opponent to the wooden floorboard. Dust went up, and little pieces of glass crinkled. Walker rushed over to Teague. Terry joined him. Walker examined the wound. No exit. The bullet was still inside Teague, and he was bleeding out fast.

"It ain't good, is it?"

"No, it isn't. Sorry, Joe."

"Bastard shot me in the back."

"Who is he?" Terry asked.

"FBI," Teague said, his breathing labored and his face pale. "Special Agent… who…wanted writers… Charlie had the list…I didn't mean to kill Charlie." Teague's breathing, short and staccato.

"It's okay, Joe. Try and relax," Walker said, but Teague grabbed hold of Walker's cuff. "Agent took elevator…went to see the…" and Teague ended in mid-sentence, eyes wide open. Walker closed them as he had done numerous times before.

"What elevator?" Terry asked.

"I'll explain later."

Hamilton's shadow fell over them. Walker saw the tall man standing there, bleeding, swollen, and battered, with a smile that would've scared Tommy Udo in *Kiss of Death*. "I could use a drink," he said.

"We should call Moore," Terry said. They heard Hamilton's laugh, and he might've called them idiots while he headed for the stairs. "Moore does damage control," Terry said, looking panicked at Walker.

Hamilton surprised them; he returned with a bottle of beer in his hand. "This stuff ain't bad." Halls of Montezuma, shores of Tripoli, Hamilton the marine had himself a drink.

"What do we do with Mr. FBI?" Terry asked.

"I have an idea," Walker said. "But, we better move quick." He pointed outside to the railroad tracks. "I checked. The next train stops in fifteen minutes. He'll sleep it off in his travels."

Hamilton walked past Bill, laid his hand on Terry's shoulder, and said, "Good shooting, Tonto."

"Aren't you going to help us move him?" Terry asked Hamilton before Walker could.

"Hell no. I've done my part. You two carry him. I'll meet you in the car, where I'll enjoy this fine beverage."

Chapter Thirty-Three

Oversized envelope. Postmark: Boston. No handwriting. PERSONAL AND CONFIDENTIAL was typed on the front and a tag to the plastic bag from Analysis cleared the specimen on Jack's desk for fingerprints. There were none other than those belonging to postal employees who handled the document.

Jack turned on the desk lamp. He pulled open a drawer and took out a pair of gloves and his letter opener. He pierced the edge and let the blade create the sleeve through which he could extract the contents.

A document. Six photographs, all black-and-white, slid out. The photographs interested Jack. Their subject, clear as a flare in the night sky. Excellent composition. Items were discernible: a clock betrayed the time, and the linen, the hotel. The faces—and it was the same two in every picture—were not blurry or subject to speculation. He jiggled the envelope once more. Out popped the negative strips.

Jack's ears moved when he smiled.

* * *

He closed the taxi door behind him, in his hand a fresh envelope with the photographs from Sheldon inside it. Jack gazed up at the concrete building. The architectural style matched that of the man he was visiting.

Jack signed his name into the visitor's log, showed his identification, and moved to the elevators, knowing the man at the front desk would make a phone call upstairs before he arrived.

The ride up was soothing and quiet. He looked over to the elevator operator, a Negro. How ironic, Jack thought. Chimes, the car stopped to accept and discharge passengers until Jack was alone again on his way to the destination. Only very important people visited this floor.

The door opened, and another man was waiting for him. "May I help you?" he asked Jack.

"Mr. Hoover, please."

"And you are?" The young man was doing his duty, wearing the regulation starched shirt, black tie, and flattop. Another marine, first job out of the Corps.

"You know who I am, Marine. The call came up from downstairs long before those elevator doors opened."

"This way, Mr. Marshall."

Jack followed. In the main area, they passed the Dillinger exhibit. Jack asked for a moment to write something for the suggestion box next to the infamous bank robber. Jack picked up the pen and scribbled: Chief William Parker loves what you've done with the office.

He resumed his journey with the young man to his destination. J. Edgar Hoover's office was neat and orderly. Not a crumb on the carpet or a mote of dust in the air. Jack sat in the leather chair in front of the massive desk without being asked.

"Good morning. I assume you're recording this."

"Please make your point, Mr. Marshall. I'm a busy man with a schedule to keep."

"I'm sure you are. Do your old friends still call you Speedy? Did you have your two soft-boiled eggs this morning with soft butter and coffee, black and in porcelain? I want to make sure I haven't disrupted your routine." Jack glanced over his shoulder. "You've slowed down the elevator considerably. I'm familiar with the model and its speed. Never mind, as nothing is beyond your reach."

"Do not exhaust my patience, Jack."

"Glad we've returned to a first-name basis since we last talked. I was getting tired of hearing you refer to me as Donovan's son of a bitch. I'll get to the point."

"Please do."

"I have two agents in the field. I need for them to come in and I want them unharmed." Hoover watched Jack the way a snake watched a cricket.

"They've stumbled on something I want," Hoover said.

"Fair enough. I have what you've lost in this envelope," Jack touched his breast pocket. "Loew's list. I have it and kept a copy for myself. Need I explain?"

"No, you don't. What do you want in exchange?"

"Safe passage for my two people and your word to hold harmless from any reprisals, Miss Vera Williams, Mr. Terry Doyle, and Mr. George Edwards. When I say reprisals, I mean just that: none by you, ordered by you, or done freelance by one of your zealous agents."

"Quite the breakfast order, even from you, Jack. You want me to step all the way across the street on this one for a dyke with Communist sympathizers for friends, a leftist scriptwriter, and a Negro elevator operator."

"Mr. Edwards was doing his job, Edgar, like the man who runs your elevator in this building. The rest of them have done no harm. Didn't you twist her arm once before?"

"Miss Williams supplied my office with critical names."

"She might have, but it's all tainted by the threat of blackmail. As to your quaint aspersion, we shouldn't cast stones about what people do in the bedroom. You, of all people, Edgar. I am curious, though, as to how long Phillip Ernest was on your payroll?"

"Since '47, and does it matter now that the man is dead? Vera Williams killed Ernest."

"I think a convincing argument can also be made that some two-bit boxer and his buddy, Joe Teague, did it. The boxer was found shot with the same gun that killed Ernest. Ballistics can verify the gun if it's found, and I do believe in sudden miracles. Problem is how do you explain the bullet in Teague's back. I'll bet the change in my pocket, the slug can be traced to a .38 revolver, specifically to a Smith and Wesson produced for the Bureau. You do keep records on all your weapons, don't you? Oh, one more thing:

one of your agents traveled on a freight train, and his weapon is missing."

"And your point is?" Hoover asked, eyes indifferent but jaw tensed.

"The point is he's alive because nobody wants the blood of a federal employee on his or her hands. He should be questioned. Leonard Moore should be questioned since he's been feeding names to you and Roy Cohn. What do you say, Edgar?"

"Leave my agent out of this, Jack. He's been through enough. It seems Chief Parker's Hat Squad had a talk with him before he resumed his train ride. Let's just say that Parker's men weren't as courteous as Pullman porters. My agent's assignment was to work Hollywood for Reds for me. I'm satisfied with his service. What do you propose?"

"Teague and Irish Bill got into a fight and killed each other. Teague killed Ernest for greed, for holding out, and he killed Loew for a bigger piece of the pie. Knock yourself out and say Mickey Cohen ordered it. Teague was connected to Cohen. How you handle the details matters little to me. Jack Warner, for all I care, could produce a film that proves Harry Cohn did it all. All I ask is that you let the people I named walk."

"Why should I? It's a domestic affair, remember? Your office handles international. Two different worlds, Jack."

"I counted on you to say that, and you're never been one to disappoint, Edgar." Jack stood up, pulled out the envelope from his jacket, and placed it on the desk. He buttoned his top button. He tapped his index finger on the envelope, "Your answer to why you should is inside this envelope. And Edgar, keep your Cub Scouts away from my house and my family."

Hoover reeled in the envelope and extricated its contents. Before Jack reached the door, he heard Hoover say, "Where did you get these?"

Jack faced Hoover to answer him. "International, like you said, not domestic, and by the way, I have the negatives if you renege on your word. Say hello to Clyde for me."

"Jack?"

"Yes, Edgar."

"You're still a son of a bitch."

"Happy to hear you've lost that stutter of yours."

Chapter Thirty-Four

Walker waited for Jack on the tarmac at Lockheed Air Terminal. Jack stopped at the top of the stairs, took in the paradise of palm trees and healthy sun before he descended the ramp. They shook hands, and Jack picked up his luggage.

The car engine barely had time to get hot in the short drive to Warner Brothers in Burbank. Jack ignored the stares. Miss Elkins saw Walker first, and her face shifted to neutral when she spotted Jack. Terry asked about lunch, but Walker declined while in motion. Alone in the hallway, Jack teased Walker. "Seems like you've made friends here. Do I have to worry about you returning to the Company?"

"No worries, Jack. Here's my office, by the way. I need to grab something first." Walker stripped the office of any personal effects. He left the Chemex, a handful of filters, and his last batch of coffee for his successor on Special Projects. Walker unlocked the drawer on his desk. "I don't believe it," he said. Jack turned but didn't ask. Walker said, "My manuscript is gone. This is unbelievable. Follow me, Jack. We're off to see the wizard."

Jack followed his friend's lead down the white hallways until they arrived at Warner's office. Jack and Walker waited, while a short man, back turned to them, argued with Warner.

"I can't do it. Don't you understand it's not a good time," Warner said.

"I gave him my word I'd help him find a job, JL. All the man wants to do is act and support his family."

"I understand that. I can empathize, but HUAC is calling him up, and it's in the wind he'll be listed. I can't touch him; it's politics," Warner replied, a hand on the shorter man's shoulder. "Please understand my situation."

"Everything is political, JL, including a promise to a friend."

"Tell you what. Does he know how to write?" Warner asked.

"How the hell do I know? He's an actor. Do you know how to paint houses?"

"I'd learn if I had to. I'll send someone over to talk to him. I'll arrange a quick apprenticeship for him—a crash course, if you will," Warner said.

"Does it pay?"

"It'll pay. The money might not be what your friend is accustomed to, but he won't starve," Warner responded as he escorted the diminutive man to the door of his office.

"Swell. I appreciate it, JL," the man said, putting on his hat. He saw Walker and Jack waiting in the hallway, but Warner had not. "Pardon me, gentlemen."

Jack took off his hat. "Good day to you, Mr. Bogart."

Warner yelled from inside his office, "Next! I don't have time to turn straw into gold."

Walker walked in with Jack at his side. "Who's the friend, Walter?"

"A friend from back East and my former boss."

"I see." Warner tapped a stack of papers. "I've read your manuscript. A fine draft, Walter. It needs work and some tightening, but you've impressed me. As you know, I'm not inclined to give compliments. You've done good quality work. Wish I could say the same for my other writers. You'll see my appreciation in your next check."

"Thank you, Mr. Warner."

"Unfortunately, your initial assessment was correct. The public isn't ready for this subject matter. Life in a concentration camp cuts close to the vein and blood of what's happening in this country. I remembered your word for it, Walter. You said allegorical. I should've listened, but that's not to say I won't re-examine the script when the political climate is more hospitable."

"If the time is ever right, Mr. Warner," Jack said. "Name is Jack Marshall."

Warner shook Jack's hand. "My pleasure. What can I do for you, gentlemen?"

Walker extended his hand out. "I need to go, Mr. Warner. It's been a pleasure."

"You're leaving?"

"Afraid so."

"Would you consider contract work?" Warner asked.

"You mean, like Teague and his partner, Charlie Loew. No thanks."

"That's studio politics, Walter. Terry and Moore can make those wheels turn 'round. You enjoy writing, Walter, and I wish to encourage it. Strictly writing."

"I'll consider it."

"I've admired your studio for some time," Jack said. "Didn't you have an actress by the name of Vera Williams? She was my favorite."

"Heard of her? I just got off the horn with a director back east asking for her. First thing this morning, too. It had to be six a.m. there."

"Really?" Jack said.

"I almost hung up on him until he told about a strong rumor he heard among his friends in DC that an actor I've been wanting for some time is about to be cleared by HUAC."

"All politics, like you said, Mr. Warner," Jack said.

"Indeed. If I can only find where the man docks his boat, I'd get a contract and a case of Scotch out to him," Warner said without much satisfaction. "Walter?"

"Sir?"

"Just because you're leaving me doesn't mean you can walk through Cohn's catastrophe of a lot for lunch. Please, keep in touch, and think about my offer. Strictly writing."

* * *

Leslie joined Walker and Jack for the visit to Mr. Edwards. Neighborhood eyes noticed the Kaiser from their windows. Walker parked out in front of the single-story Craftsman near Jefferson Boulevard. They exited the car together. Jack retrieved the small valise he placed on the floor in front of his seat. Jack could see from the way the curtains in the Edwards home moved someone had seen them. Leslie behind him, Walker to his side, Jack was about to knock on the screen door when the main door opened.

"Mrs. Edwards, I presume."

"Are you two gentlemen law and order?"

"More order than law, ma'am. We'd like to speak to your husband," Jack said.

"Etta?" a male voice yelled from somewhere behind her. "Who's at the door?"

"Folks who say they ain't police and want a word with you," she hollered over her shoulder. She pronounced police with two equal syllables.

"Let them on in then."

She opened the door. The house was modest, dignified. George Edwards had his discharge papers in a frame on the wall. A small upright piano braced the wall, topped with photographs of family members, sharecroppers from the overalls and field hats they were wearing that day. Younger versions of Edwards appeared in several more frames; his ageless face made an estimate of his years impossible. A wedding picture of the happy couple captured in an oval looked out over their living room. Edwards sat in his chair waiting. He stood up when he saw Leslie.

"Miss Maggie? What a surprise seeing you. I heard about Dr. Ernest. My condolences."

"Heard about Dr. Ernest is right," his wife rushed to his side. "Police came here to ask my husband about that, too. The man gets attacked on the job and then has the wherewithal to kill a doctor. The gall of those detectives."

"Hush, Etta," Mr. Edwards said.

"Don't you hush me. I saw with my own eyes what those people put you through. You were the victim one day, criminal the next, as if they couldn't make up their minds, so they made you both. Lose both your job and your pension."

"You lost your pension?" Leslie asked.

"Not technically, Miss Maggie. Suspended from the job and told my case was under review. I believe the company wants to hire me back, but they're afraid, with the robbery and homicide and all the attention from the police."

"Suspended my husband says. You'll have to excuse my negative mind, but my husband believes in the good in everyone, whereas I can't from experience. Could explain why we married. Opposites attract, they say."

"That's why I'm here," Jack said. "May I sit?"

"A white man asking a black man if he can sit. I might faint," Etta said.

"It's your house, Mrs. Edwards," Jack said.

"It is until the bank forecloses," Mrs. Edwards responded. "We thought we'd own our home one day, but with him losing his job, nobody wants to hire an old man. It's been hard. Anyhow, I'll leave you be with my husband and fetch something from the kitchen."

"I'll help." Leslie, her eyes wet, followed Mrs. Edwards.

Jack placed a briefcase in front of the man. "Mr. Edwards, I want you to take this."

"What's that?"

"Something to make up for what's happened to you. There's enough there for you and your wife to live comfortably for quite some time," Jack opened up the valise for Edwards to peer inside.

"I pay my mortgage with that, then I'll have myself a real problem with men from the IRS," Mr. Edwards said.

Jack handed Mr. Edwards a folded document. "Not true. Here."

"What's this?"

"The deed to your home and property. You're relieved of your debt."

"My mortgage is paid? I don't understand. Who are you?"

"Someone who remembers what it is to be discharged, Mr. Edwards."

"Why are you doing this?"

"We should leave now, Mr. Edwards."

Jack offered his hand, and Mr. Edwards shook it. Walker did the same.

Mr. Edwards walked them to the door. His wife returned with a plate of biscuits, but realized her guests were headed for the front door. Leslie joined Jack and Walker and stopped with Mr. Edwards holding the door open.

"Thank you, Miss Maggie," he said and held his hand out for the handshake. She brushed aside his hand and gave him a peck on the check. "Take care of yourself, Mr. Edwards."

* * *

"Is anyone hungry?" Walker asked when they stepped outside.

"I am," Jack walked around the front of the car, telling Walker he wanted to drive. He also asked because he saw there was a note under the wiper blade. Walker closed the passenger door. Leslie said, "Wherever we go, I'd like to make a call first because there's someone I want to invite to lunch."

Jack unfolded the note and read it. "Chief William Parker loves whatever you did at the office."

Looking down the street, he saw and heard an LAPD squad car turn over its engine. A dress-white sleeve stuck out the window and waved.

Acknowledgements

I'm grateful to my publisher, Level Best Books, for their continued faith in my work. Thank you, Dames of Detection.

Hugs and friendship for Shawn Reilly Simmons, my editor.

I'm thankful for the generosity and feedback from my proofreaders Dean Hunt and Joseph McMahon, and continuity editor Deb Well.

I'd like to thank Dave King, who read the novel and offered suggestions and encouragement.

As always, nothing but gratitude to my fellow Level Best authors, and to friends of the pen and keyboard in crime fiction, the best and most supportive community around for a writer.

About the Author

Gabriel Valjan is a member of ITW, MWA, and a lifetime member of Sisters in Crime. He is the author of *The Company Files* and the *Shane Cleary Mysteries with Level Best Books*. His work has been nominated for the Agatha, Anthony, and the Silver Falchion awards. Gabriel received the 2021 Macavity Award for Best Short Story and the Shamus Award for Best Original PI Paperback Novel in 2024. He is a regular contributor to the blog *Criminal Minds* and an active supporter of writers on social media. Gabriel lives in Boston, and answers to a tuxedo cat named Munchkin.

AUTHOR WEBSITE:
  https://gabrielvaljan.com/

SOCIAL MEDIA HANDLES:
  https://x.com/GValjan
  https://www.instagram.com/gabrielvaljan/
  https://bsky.app/profile/gvaljan.bsky.social

Also by Gabriel Valjan

Shane Cleary Mystery Series
  Liar's Dice
  Hush Hush
  Symphony Road
  Dirty Old Town
  The Big Lie

Company Files Series
  The Devil's Music
  The Naming Game
  The Good Man